Sisters In Love

by

Gloria Jo Russell

Gloria Jo Russell

Paperback

ISBN: 978-1-918039-16-0

Published by: Good Reach Publishing

Dedication

To my first born: Antony Russell and his first born Tashon Russell

Acknowledgment

To all the dedicated persons who gave of their time to make the
publication of Sisters in Love possible

Table of Contents

About the Author

Gloria Russell has lived in both England and Jamaica, cherishes travel, and is fascinated by how people react. Those experiences inspired the creation of Sisters. While the narrative is largely fictional, it incorporates real elements that are not identifiable as any living individual

Chapter One

What do you do when everything you had grown up to believe in comes and smacks you upside your head?

I tried counting sheep without the slightest success. I tuned the radio to a softer-playing music station, but that did not help either. The room became humid while I tossed and turned, but I decided on not opening the windows for fear of mosquitos, but equally, I was never comfortable with using the electric fan. (My thinking was that all the fan did was to circulate the dust and hot air around the room instead of giving real fresh air.) A cold shower brought the perfect release to my tired and aching body, but not to my troubled mind.

I remained confused and unsure on how to solve, repair and move forward with all that had taken place in less than twenty-four hours, which was more than half the sum total of the years of my life, yet with all life's ups and downs, heartaches and disappointments, I was never prepared for this. I took a cold Red Stripe beer from the fridge and stepped out on the back veranda, clad in light cotton shorts and a vest. The darkness was interrupted by a few twinkling stars, but it was cool, and the rhythm of the waves splashing at intervals on the rocks made sweet music. It was Dad's favoured place to relax, being fully grilled and meshed to keep out the pesky bugs and flies. I sat in the chair opposite the one he would have sat on. I imagined he smiled at me and advised. (Relax, pet, and take a deep breath; just close your eyes and relax.) It had always worked. I took a long drink from the bottle of cold beer, said cheers to my imaginary dad, and then commented aloud.

"One thing for sure, life will not be the same after tonight, eh, Dad?" I fell asleep seated at the spot until summoned awake by the crowing of a rooster in the distant countryside.

Day one

My first thought was, what really led to my dad having a heart attack? I stretched and relaxed my body in the warmth of the early morning sun while my mind roamed. One moment we were enjoying the sun, sea and fresh food and fruits, not to mention some warm conversation between a father and a beloved and loving daughter; then the next moment I was rushing him in a wheelchair down the corridor of our local hospital to the emergency room.

Memories of the previous day rolled around in my head, while I tried to put all that had happened in understandable bites. At the hospital, I waited for what seemed like a lifetime until the doctor called my name. When he took my hands in his, I feared the worst, then he smiled at me.

"Your dad will be fine. He is sedated at the moment, but you can sit by his bed until he is able to speak. We will have to keep him for the night while we monitor his progress, but for now he is out of danger." The doctor kept hold of my hand as we walked to the bedside of my dad. He summoned a porter to find a chair for me to sit on before hurrying off to attend to another emergency. Relieved, but still very anxious as I sat at Dad's bedside waiting for the drugs to release his mind. His body jerked a few times, then went back to being motionless. I brought his hand to my lips, kissed it and whispered. "Dad. Dad, are you awake? Dad!" His eyelids twitch a few moments before sliding open. Then they moved to and fro, surveying the room before resting on me with a smile.

"There you are, my pet." He said. Trying to wet his lips as he spoke. I rose from the chair to hug and kiss him on the forehead. "It's ok, Dad, we are at the hospital. The doctor said you are going to be alright; just relax. No need to talk; just relax." But his voice was strong as he remarked. "Sorry to scare you, pet; it must have been that last piece of pork skin I could not refuse." We both laughed.

More like the extra glass of whisky, Dad. I have always noticed you stopping at one, but I do remember you were on your third drink before you held your chest."

He gave a rumbling laugh and held on to his chest while doing so.

"Oh well, something has to take me home, may as well be something I love."

He laughed again, but his face showed he was in pain.

"The doctor said you suffered a heart attack, dad, so take it easy, OK. He wants to keep you in overnight, just to allow the drugs to do their work."

After a deep sigh, my dad replied:

"Under one condition."

"And what would that be?" I asked.

"That you will stay the night with me. We have to talk."

"You need to rest, dad, but I will stay with you."

Dad immediately started to remind me of things he remembered about me as a child. After an hour or so, the doctor returned to check dad's blood pressure and listen to his heartbeat. Then he remarked that all seemed to be progressing well. He offered to send me a more comfortable chair via the porter to enable me to have a more restful night.

We had left the house in a rush but not in panic. I had locked and secured all the doors and windows, and my own car was locked up and parked in the carport. We had driven in dad's jeep to the hospital while he instructed me on the location of the entrance to the hospital, and continued to describe the parking and waiting areas, in a whispered shallow voice, stopping every so often to catch a breath.

Earlier, we had been enjoying the last of our Sunday evening dinner when suddenly, dad held a hand over his chest following a strong bout of laughter as we reminisced on the antics of one of my siblings. He sent me to fetch a bottle of tablets from his bedside table and hurriedly took a couple of the pills, followed by a few swallows of carrot juice. I waited until he relaxed back into his chair before I asked:

"Dad, are you OK? What are the tablets for?"

He swallowed hard before he answered me:

"My doctor thought I needed to take them, my pet, but he also said I should get to the hospital if the pain gets severe, which I fear is what might be happening now. So I think that we should be making our way there if you don't mind driving."

When he held on to his chest with both hands I did not hesitate.

"I will get to the jeep while you fetch your handbag, my love."

He was quite calm and collected, so I had no reason to panic; I simply followed instructions. But later, I had no choice but to panic. On reaching the hospital we were told to wait in a crowded waiting room where dad took another two tablets, then collapsed to the floor. I screamed! A woman sitting on a nearby bench rushed to assist me in getting him back in the chair. I feared the worst, so I did not hesitate. Grabbing hold of the wheelchair, I turned it towards the door I had taken notice of when we first arrived. It was situated nearer to the entrance hall, before we were ushered towards the waiting room. Without knocking, I burst into the doctor's office screaming:

"You have to help my dad, something is wrong, he isn't well, please take a look at him."

The doctor, thank God, realised that it was a heart attack and attended to him immediately.

My dad had been my hero and role model. He stood strong and tall (reminding me of Sidney Poitier), he had that demure charm, and always with a composed smile on his face, sophisticated, and even without a jacket and tie he would appear immaculately dressed for any occasion. He was a ladies' man with the manners of an old-fashioned English gentleman. He never let the attention of any woman go to his head by flirting with them. He always showed equal attention and affection to all his children, and for that he had my respect. This kept me closer to his side, equalled only by my younger sister Rose.

"I am feeling a little thirsty, pet," Dad whispered.

I had dozed off while reminiscing. I shook my head vigorously from side to side, releasing me from my own daydreams.

"I still have some of the coconut water in the cooler, Dad. I have been sipping on it, but I am sure there is enough left."

I left the chair to retrieve my oversized handbag. There was no cup in the small cubicle we were in, so I held the spout of the cooler to his lips, allowing him to sip until he was satisfied. Then he laughed and smacked his lips.

"Thanks pet.my stomach still unsettled but I guess that's because I made such a pig of myself, with the extra piece of pork skin, sweet potato pudding and ice cream. I must say it tasted real good though."

I gave him a hug.

"Well, we had not been able to enjoy Sunday dinner together for a while, but next time I will make sure you eat smaller portions. Don't ever want you giving me such a scare again."

I laughed, trying to keep my nerves calm, before replacing the cooler on a nearby bedside cupboard, then drew the chair closer to his bedside and took hold of his hand to reassure him I was close.

His hands were warm and soft. I kissed them lightly, reminding me as I did of my five-year-old, when he had to be admitted to hospital for tonsillitis.

"You know, Beth…"

Dad's voice was low but very clear as he cleared his throat and started again.

"You shouldn't worry too much about your kids, I have a strong feeling that you will be hearing from your husband soon. You just have faith my love, you know, you should also try and read the Bible sometime my pet, I quite like Psalm thirty one myself; if only because my grandmother use to have me read it to her night after night until I could say it without opening the book"

He then recited the psalm word for word. I was impressed. I had never seen Dad take up a Bible in the house, but for as long as I can remember, he did have one on his bedside table. In the past couple of years, whenever he was invited to church, he would also make sure I went along with him, insisting that God would not bless him if he were to leave me at home. Even then he never travelled to church with a Bible or hymn book, but he never failed to sing lustily to the hymns. The one I most remembered was *Roll Jordan Roll*, which blended in with his rich bass voice. It brought a smile to my face whenever the song was played on any religious programme on the radio, because he would hum along, wait until the chorus, and then join in with a lusty "Rooool Jordon Roooool.

Dad's memory was as clear as crystal that Sunday night while we were at the hospital. He started telling me stories from his early childhood in the countryside where he grew up with his brother and grandmother (most of which I had heard before), but his early years in England were stories he had never told, and it was a lot to take in. Some statements I questioned in my mind, but I allowed him to talk without interruption, while I tried, as it's my nature to do, to figure things out in my mind while he spoke.

He was able to describe the birth of each of my sisters to the last detail, remembering also the first time each of us spoke or took our first step. He spoke proudly of our accomplishments as we got older and was saddened by all our disappointments. When I thought that he was talked out, he counselled me on my own life, advising me of the way forward and how I should approach my husband and my future.

Finally, when I felt my own eyes closing, he squeezed my hand, waking me with a rendition of *Roll Jordan Roll*.

"Beth, my dearest, I am so happy to have you by my side. I love you, and you have my blessing in whatever decisions you take. God bless you, my pet."

Drugged by sleep, I whispered, "Love you too, Dad."

Chapter Two

I woke up almost shouting… "Yes, Dad, I am coming."

I was quite embarrassed when I stood up and was face-to-face with the doctor.

"Oh dear, I must have been dreaming," I muttered, then sat down quickly, realising that I was still at the hospital at my dad's bedside. His eyes were closed, and he had the most handsome smile on his lips, which brought a smile to my own face, and I reached out to hold his hands, which was so cold that I started to rub it between my palms.

A nurse entered the cubicle.

"Doctor, it's past nine-thirty. I should have been gone from eight."

She emphasised the eight as she stood in the open doorway looking directly at the doctor, not even acknowledging that I was in the room.

"Just give us another ten minutes, please, nurse. I will drive you home myself."

I turned my wrist to glance quickly at my watch.

"Nine-thirty? Oh my gosh, I am so sorry, but Dad had me up all night talking. I had no idea I had overslept. Do you want me to leave while you get on with what you need to do, doctor?"

I let go of Dad's hand, and it fell back on the bed so awkwardly that I was shocked and took notice. The doctor was by my side before I hit the floor.

"Mrs Kworari, I am so sorry. Your father passed on at approximately six forty-five, but I asked the nurse not to disturb you and to allow you to wake naturally. I looked in when I heard him singing *Roll Jordan Roll*. Your father took his last breath shortly after you fell asleep."

For a moment, my own heart stopped. I felt a movement coming from deep down in the pit of my belly, then it evolved into a scream. When I was all cried out, I kissed Dad's cheeks before the doctor pulled up the sheet to cover his face. The porter was summoned, and I was given a pile of papers to sign, which I did without reading. My eyes were locked on the grey coat of the porter as he wheeled away the covered and lifeless body which was once my warm and loving father.

"Will you be able to drive, Mrs Kworari? If you are not able to, I could call a taxi to take you home. But my nurse has to be back on duty tonight, so I really need to drive her home."

I shook my head from left to right, then quickly changed to up and down.

"No, doctor, I don't need a taxi. I will be able to drive home, thank you. And thank you for helping my dad. Do you think I could have your phone number? I am not sure what I am supposed to do now. I have had close family members pass away, but it was never left to me to make any decisions."

The last few words brought tears back to my eyes, and he hugged me firmly.

"Take a deep breath, Beth. Try and relax; there is no rush. Drive carefully home, take a long shower, then call your family and those you need to inform. The important thing is not to panic, and please, try and have a family member or friend stay with you tonight."

I wanted to stay in his arms forever. But he rocked my body free from his chest (as my dad always did). I turned my face away, feeling guilty for my thoughts. He held me firmly on both shoulders.

"I know it's not the best advice, but be comforted that your dad loved you and is depending on you to be strong. Call me anytime."

He took a business card from his breast pocket and placed it in the palm of my hand, then gently closed my fingers around it. We were interrupted by a stern call from the nurse he had promised to drive home.

I sat in Dad's jeep on the passenger seat for a while, as if I were waiting for him to come and drive us home. My mobile phone rang, and I hurriedly rummaged through my bag. The chirpy voice of Ms Mac rang out on the other end.

"Miss Beth, were you held up in the traffic, miss? "I heard an accident on the road. Are you alright, miss?" Without waiting for an answer, she continued:

"I know you drive well, but you have to watch out for those mad taxi men; one nearly ran me and my husband off the road this morning. The office is open, and everything is alright; you take your time. Anything you want me to do until you come, miss?"

She had spoken long enough to allow me to collect my thoughts.

"No, Ms Mac, but I won't be in until lunch; I just have a few things to take care of."

"Not a problem, Miss Beth, I will have lunch ready for you. See you soon, bye."

The phone call allowed my mind and body to shift into gear. I climbed over onto the driver's seat and headed towards the office. On a normal Monday morning I would be needed in the office, where, for the past three years, I had been working as manager, taking charge of the day-to-day running of a business which was started and is now fully owned by my dad. I, being the manager, allowed him the luxury of much-needed free time.

We had fallen into a work routine which saw Ms Mac opening the office at nine. Then, if my dad or I had not yet taken a client to the airport or collected one from the airport, I would arrive an hour later. My father would present himself round about two-thirty, but never later than three o'clock. He would first have his main meal of the day, prepared for him by Ms Mac. After that, he would check and balance the books and deal with any new business before closing up shop at six o'clock. Of course, more often than not, our days were spent on the road with our clients, but on my ideal days, my car, following Dad's jeep or him keeping up behind me, would head home on at least three evenings of the seven days.

A mobile phone rang out. It was Dad's. I reached for it with my left hand, extracting it from the clear plastic bag given to me at the hospital containing his watch, bracelet, rings, a heavy gold chain and the lower plate of his dentures, along with a heavy brown leather wallet and a large bunch of assorted keys held together by a wooden shape of Africa. His clothes and shoes were in a green plastic string bag on the floor of the jeep.

"Good morning, and how may I assist you?" was my well-rehearsed greeting.

"May I speak to Mr Creary?"

Asked the caller. I stammered that he was not available.

"Oh, that's too bad; we are about to board, but I wanted to thank him for giving us such a splendid holiday. My wife and I thoroughly enjoyed our holiday thanks to him, and we will be booking again for next year. I wanted to let him know from now, but no matter, I will be sure to call again when we have settled in back home. But do tell him thanks a bunch, from both of us. And oh, please let him know; that would be Mike and Mary. Thank you so much, bye!"

"You are welcome," I replied.

But the caller hung up as if in a hurry. I realised then that I had turned into the driveway of our office complex. I replaced the phone in the bag on the passenger seat. Ms Mac was already running towards the jeep.

"Oh, it's you, Miss Beth. I was running because I thought it was Mr Creary, and see, even John is coming."

(John was our driver, messenger, handyman and boy Friday.) Ms Mac shouted over her shoulder to tell John that it wasn't the boss driving the jeep. It was John who pulled the door of the jeep open.

"Miss Beth, do you have anything for me to carry? I have a bag of jelly and some orange for the boss, but I will wipe down the jeep before I pack them in. Are you ok, miss? You look like you want to cry!"

Ms Mac gave him a shove with her hip.

"Shut you mouth, John. How are you so fass?"

Then she turned towards me, resting her hand on my shoulder, concerned.

"All the same, Miss Beth, you are not looking too good. Come inside; the water in the kettle is still hot. I can make you a cup of that coffee you like."

She led me by the hand and sat me down behind my desk. John had taken up my handbag from the jeep along with the plastic bag from the passenger seat containing Dad's possessions.

He placed them on the desk and then commented,

"But don't – this is Mr Creary's lucky chain!"

He stopped as Ms Mac placed my cup down in front of me on the desk, the hot steam hitting the back of my hands, which were covering my face.

"I've seen this kind of bag before. This is hospital business. Mr Creary at the hospital, Miss Beth?" John asked, concerned.

I could see through my fingers that Ms Mac was again moving him out of the way, bouncing him to one side with her large hip.

"How can he be at the hospital when he is not sick?"

The last three words from Ms Mac were said in a whisper, then she hugged me, or rather shook me by my shoulders as I burst into loud bawling, letting the words out.

"Daddy's dead; my dad is dead!"

She shook me by the shoulders again.

"How is he dead and he didn't tell me? He called me Sunday evening and begged me to buy three big lobsters and bring them in this morning."

Ms Mac cried out, "Lawd, oh good Lawd, is he dead for true, Miss Beth? How is he dead?"

I told her through my sobs and cried, "He had a heart attack!"

Both Ms Mac and John cried in unison, "Good Lawd!"

"That was the same thing the doctor told him after he had that stroke," said John, as he sat heavily in a nearby chair, cupping his head in both hands.

"My father had a stroke, John?" I asked, surprised. "When?"

"That was from before you came to live with him, miss, but lucky I was in charge of the driving that day. And he was lucky too, because we had just picked up a doctor man at Norman Manley Airport. And it was that doctor who took charge when he told me to drive to the University Hospital.

I buss every speed limit and drive up there fast, fast. I was so worried and frightened for the boss I called Ms Mac at the same time toask her what to do. Since then I always remind him that he should take things easy. The doctor even gave him some pills and told him to get a check-up at his own doctor.

I know he visits a doctor down at the hospital, because I took him there myself a few times. But this morning when he never turned up for our regular swim, and when he didn't answer my phone call, I just feel that maybe he had to collect someone and he had no time to let me know."

John sat down, holding his head in his hands and rocking his whole body from side to side, as he wept like a baby. Ms Mac marched up and down in the office space with one hand on her head and the other clutching her belly.

"Oh Father God, oh Lawd Jesus, what a trial, what a cross. How could you take away Mr Creary? Lawd have mercy, what are we going to do?"

As much as she was lamenting, she was very much in charge of the situation.

"Miss Beth, you are not in any condition to be at the office; you need to go home and call your family. You can't go through this; it's too much."

Then she again placed her hand on her head and cried out.

"Precious Lawd, take my hand. Lawd, cover me, and cover Miss Beth. Lawd, I'm begging you to take charge of the situation. It's rough, Lawd, it's rough."

She stooped to the ground and then rose, shaking her body as if shaking a coat from her shoulders, but soon collected her thoughts.

"Miss Beth, do you need me to call a taxi, Miss? You know, maybe John should drive you home. Miss Beth, you know that I and John are your family; we can take care of the office. You need to go home and do what you need to do. If we get a call that we can't manage, I will call you and let you know. But you have to go home, Miss Beth. And later I will send John with a nice dinner for you, but go home, Miss Beth."

She gathered up my handbag and keys. I took up the plastic bag with Dad's precious things as she marched me from the office back to the jeep.

"Take your time, drive home, miss. Take your time. God go with you."

But I still had to assure her that I was able to drive myself home safely, while she still insisted that John should take me home. I hugged and kissed them both and assured her that I would be fine.

The main road was heavy with traffic, forcing me to drive slowly. Dad's mobile phone rang out again, giving me a jolt. I quickly got hold of it and turned the phone off, my body trembling like a leaf. My mind started to play tricks with me, a little voice telling me I should turn around and go back to the hospital, that my dad was waiting for me. I imagined him calling my phone, wondering what was taking me so long. Then I recalled the scene at the hospital. I found myself hitting the brakes of the jeep to avoid running into a coaster bus ahead of me. Without a second thought, I turned off the main road onto a roadway recently used as a bypass road. They had diverted the traffic from the main road while repairs and new pipes were being laid.

The old diversion signs were still lying along the side of the road, some painted, others just showing large arrows along garden walls. The roads in the estate were now returned to normal traffic and thankfully still in good condition. I drove through the estate and wandered off the beaten track, as my dad and I often did on most evenings while I drove behind his jeep.

The 'For Sale' sign was still swinging in the wind, making its own music as it rocked to and fro.

I remembered that first time we took notice of the sign, or in my case the garden. I blew on my car horn to alert Dad to stop. We stood for a while looking over and through the fence. I remembered Dad saying the garden was enough to sell the house, but he also commented:

"You will have to build a garage on the side and put up some gri on that veranda. It's quite nice without grilles, but it may not be safe."

After that, we had always slowed down as we passed. Dad's comments each time were, "The sign is still up, Beth."

My thoughts at that moment, as I sat admiring the garden from the window of Dad's jeep: (now or never). I reached for my mobile phone, and instantly it rang in my hand. I took a deep breath before saying hello. A cheerful stranger on the other end of the line answered."

"Good afternoon, may I speak to Mrs Kworori?"

"Good afternoon, this is Mrs Kworori. How can I assist you?"

"Oh Mrs, we have been trying to call your father; please hold on."

18

A lump came to my throat as I heard the young woman call someone to the phone.

"Good afternoon, Mrs Kworori, and congratulations."

A male voice sang out on the other end of the phone line. I placed the phone closer to my ear and asked, "Excuse me?"

"I am the manager and agent for the Horse Shoe. I forgot to take the sign down over the weekend, but your father and I looked over the property. No light, but water is still there, but of course you will need to visit the respective utility office and have those transferred in your name. Please apologise to your father for me; I should have been handing over the keys as we speak. He is late in coming to the office, but I wanted to tell him I have all the paperwork in order and would not mind dropping it off for him on my way home this evening, if that is ok with him."

The caller realised that I was silent, and for a moment there was no response or comment. So he questioned, "Mrs Kworori?"

I was looking for the 'For Sale' sign, which I could have sworn was over the gate when I stopped. It was not there. But an elderly man now stood behind the gate and began waving the sign at me, beckoning me to get closer.

I addressed the man on the other end of my phone.

"Yes, sir. I am still here; that will be fine. I should be home at four. Thank you."

I replaced the mobile phone in my bag as I walked towards the gentleman standing by the gate.

He was sporting a wide grin, as wide as his moustache, as he held out his right hand towards me with the sign still in his left hand.

"Pleasant afternoon to you, Ms Creary. I was expecting your father. But congratulations to you are in order. I expect that you want to have a look around; come on in. You are such a fortunate young lady to have such a caring father."

His words stopped me in my tracks; only the flood of water down my cheeks was moving. The man moved quickly towards me and placed his hand around my shoulders.

"Oh, I am so sorry; I did not mean to upset you, my dear. I am just an old fool sounding off. I have no children of my own, you know, so I do admire you and your father. My wife and I often see you both when you stop to peep through the fence, so I was not in the least bit surprised when the agent brought him along last week and he agreed on the final price. And we had a chance to talk after the agent left. My wife and I were so delighted to learn that he wanted to surprise you for your birthday. So I know this must leave you quite emotional – two big celebrations. I am so happy for you, my dear."

He had dropped the sign and was patting my shoulders with both hands, while I was searching in my bag to find something other than the sleeve of my blouse to dry the tears on my face and stop my nose from running.

"Allow me to offer you a cool drink; you can come and sit with us for a while. It's a lot to take in, but you have so much to give thanks for."

I allowed him to lead me through his own front gate, where his wife was busy arranging the veranda chairs. She stopped and wiped her hand on the hem of her apron as he introduced her.

"This is my dear wife, Mrs Budd, and of course—

He laughed. "I would be Mr Budd."

I blew my nose and dried my tears before shaking both their hands and introducing myself as Beth.

"We are delighted to meet you, Beth, but I am sorry your father is not with you. We had such a good talk with him last Wednesday, didn't we, Budd?"

She nudged her husband with her elbow, encouraging him to agree with her, and at the same time beckoned me to sit. I had found a small white hand towel in my bag and was using it to stop my running nose, then drying the tears from my eyes. Mrs Budd offered me a glass of iced tea. It would have been the first thing to touch my lips all day. At the office I did not get a chance to drink the coffee Ms Mac had made for me. The glass went to my head and did not come down until the last drop. When I opened my eyes and replaced the glass on the coffee table, they were both looking at me with intense anticipation, so I explained:

"I am sorry; I have not put a thing to my mouth since leaving the hospital."

The obvious question they both asked came in unison.

"Hospital?"

I stammered and mumbled before audible words left my lips, informing them of my father's demise. They both sat in silence, as if wondering what to do next. Mrs Budd remarked that she was so looking forward to having another chat with him. Her husband stated, in a very typical English accent:

"Good Lawd, this is most unfortunate. We were just getting acquainted. How awful for you, my dear; this is a dreadful thing to have happened."

I was still in need of more liquid.

"Mrs Budd, would you mind giving me another glass of that iced tea?"

My glass was refilled, and I deliberately drank slowly while I observed the elderly couple who sat facing me. They seemed to have aged in seconds. Sorrow and pain took over their faces. Mrs Budd sat rocking herself back and forth, although she was not seated in a rocking chair. Mr Budd reached for my shoulder and patted it in time with his wife's rocking.

"My dear, please accept our deepest condolences. We are grieved, even though we had but a short conversation, and my wife and I were so looking forward to knowing him better," Mrs Budd muttered.

"This is very sad. Please let your mother know that she has our deepest sympathy, and anything we can do to assist her—and yourself, of course—please feel free to ask."

At the mention of the word 'mother', I was on my feet. I explained to them that I had not informed my mother or any other family member of my dad's death.

"I am so sorry; I really need to go. I really should be making a few calls."

They both stood up simultaneously.

"Of course, we understand. I will hold on to the keys for you, if you do not mind." He quickly added, "To look after the garden until you are ready. And, my dear—"

He went over to the side table and wrote on the back of a card, then handed it to me as I let myself out. And I could have sworn I saw misty eyes as he waved and said, "Please, feel free to call us anytime."

"I drove as fast as the traffic would allow me. What would I say to Mum? How would she take this news? I felt the need to take a long shower while I thought of ways to announce Dad's untimely death. I collected all the phone numbers of the family members together on one sheet of paper, but I had not eaten all day, so I made myself two large sandwiches and was about to sit when I was alerted by a loud knock at our gate. A man in a brown suit, complete with tie and a pocket handkerchief, was making his way in before I could reach for the grill keys.

"I hope that you don't mind that I am a little early. I am Mr Grey from the estate agent. My business in town went a lot quicker than expected, and would you believe that there was no traffic on the road?"

He shook my hand through the veranda grill.

"No need to let me in, but I am pleased to meet you and to offer my congratulations personally. I believe today is also your birthday?"

I took the large brown envelope from his hand.

"Thank you, but my birthday will not be until Wednesday. Do I need to sign for anything?"

His eyes lit up as he smiled. He shook his head from one side to the other.

"Not at the moment. Mr Creary has done all of the important paperwork. Your lawyer will inform you of all other requirements. Your father has also sent in the cheque to close the sale."

He turned to leave but stopped, as if he had forgotten something important, then he faced me again.

"Oh, and please give Mr Creary my regards, and tell him I will have some business for him in a couple of weeks."

The sound which escaped my lips took him back to my side, asking if I were okay. I had to wait for the lump in my throat to melt before explaining what had happened to my dad.

The young man could only mutter, "Oh my goodness."

As he held on to the grill gate for support, John came through the street gates, swinging the carrier bag which no doubt contained my evening meal. He and Mr Grey started up a conversation while I returned to the sitting room to get the key for the veranda grill. I took the bag from John and walked both men back to the street gate. I felt at that moment that I really wanted to be alone, but as I waved them goodbye, a dark blue Jaguar sports car drove up and parked in front of the gate. Out came a tall and dark stranger clad in a full light blue linen suit, dark glasses and a sporty straw hat, walking towards me. First he took off the hat and then the dark glasses before I realised who it was.

"Doctor?"

"Hi Beth, you don't mind me calling you Beth. Your surname makes you sound so foreign." We both laughed.

"Beth will do, thanks. I must confess I did not recognise you in your street clothes."

He explained, "Oh, I try not to be on duty twenty-four seven. It can be so boring when people expect to see you in a white coat everywhere you go."

"So you like to be incognito?" I remarked.

I had already led him through the gate, and we were about to enter the veranda."

"I was about to have a sandwich, or if you would prefer a cooked meal, our driver just brought dinner from our cook at the office, but I would have to open it to see what she has sent me."

"Those sandwiches look tempting enough, I would love one with a coffee, if that's ok by you."

"Not a problem at all, please sit while I get another cup, the teapot is full. Both my dad and I love coffee so I have gotten used to making a full pot."

He placed his hat, keys and glasses on a nearby low table, then asked,

"How has your day been so far?"

I felt it was necessary to tell him chapter and verse from the moment I left him at the hospital.

"So you have not gotten in touch with any of your family members yet? Will you be ok being on your own tonight?" the doctor asked, quite concerned.

"I will be fine, thank you, and it will probably be the best time to call my mother and sisters, keeping in mind the time difference. It was so kind of you to stop by, I really do appreciate it. Right now I feel like a fish out of water with all of this. I have been to a couple of funerals but not for anyone close. Now for my own father! I have no idea what I should be doing next."

My phone rang and I had to leave the veranda to answer it.

"Yes Ms Mac, he brought it, thank you. No, I have not had a chance to open it. Oh I will, it's just that I had made myself a sandwich. Yes I do have a friend staying, no need for you to come really. Yes I will get an early night. Thank you Ms Mac, have a good evening."

When I returned to the veranda the doctor was on his feet and reading a message on his pager.

"Beth, I am so sorry, there is an emergency, and I have to report to the hospital in Port Maria, but I will be off duty for two days after tonight. If you like I could come by about this time tomorrow and assist you to sort out what you need to do, would that be ok with you?"

26

"Could you really? Thank you so much, it's fine with me, I really do need your help, trust me."

He shook my hand then gathered his hat and keys.

"If you're staying home alone please lock this grill, and if I get a break tonight I will call. On second thoughts I wouldn't want to wake you. Just keep safe until tomorrow, ok."

"Ok, doctor. I plan to do just that; you keep safe yourself."

I watched him walk away, thinking, 'That was how I remembered my father looking in his younger days.'

I had my sandwich and coffee before I cleaned up the veranda, switching off the lights and replacing them with the yard light, which shone all the way to the street gate. Next came the kitchen.

Ms Mac cooked up curried lobster, which was in one dish, white yam and sweet potatoes in another, and the third had large slices of tomatoes, cucumbers and lettuce. But I had no appetite to eat, so I placed it all in the fridge. Then I remembered the coconut and other fruits John had placed in the back of the jeep. I felt they could keep it, so I made no attempt to return outside.

In the sitting room, Dad's diary and his briefcase were still where he had left them on the Sunday evening. My mind went into a business mood. What if one of our customers was left stranded? I leafed through Dad's diary quickly.

Sunday: dinner date with Beth. (Appointment kept, I thought)

Monday: Meeting with Mr Grey and my new friends, the Budd's.

Tuesday: renew insurance, pay taxes.

Wednesday: Service to Beth's car and lunch date.

Thursday: free.

Friday: Delivery; tickets and airport drop for the Spencers.

I then checked with my own diary. Except for Thursday I had no other appointments.

"Thank God," I whispered.

The previous weeks were filled with back-to-back pickups and deliveries for both Dad and me.

My dad had been operating and managing a small travel agency, which had evolved into a tour guide and taxi service for visitors. But before I joined him, he also arranged for his customers to collect and deliver visas and birth certificates from the relevant offices in Kingston. His business was then operated from his front room. He would collect and deliver and often had a lot of cash in his jeep or at the house. He was held up and robbed of some cash a short time before he requested that I should be his partner in the company and live with him at the house. But the unpleasant experience also made him seek out a business premise and computerise his accounts, allowing the customers to deposit monies in the company's bank account directly. He had mentioned the incident only once and never wanted to elaborate on it, saying it was not worth speaking about.

But that robbery may have been why he had that first stroke.

A few months back he told me to sit with him while he did the accounts, pointing out all our debtors and creditors, showing me how to update the company's email account on the computer. These were all new terms I was not eager to know, but Dad was always keen on electronics and new technology and was the first to try out new things.

And he sent for the computer all the way from America. Then he spent days, if not weeks, setting it up at the office and the house. I showed scant interest, and only because he was so keen on showing me his own, along with the company's bank accounts, his lawyers and all other details he thought were relevant for me to know. I had thought to myself then that he would have wanted to keep them private. Not only that, but he gave me a spare key to the small chest safe he had installed in his bedroom closet.

He had also given me a list of names and numbers he thought would be of importance to me. I had folded the paper with the list of names and placed it in my dresser drawer without a glance. Also, not being as comfortable as I would have liked with using the computer, I paid very little attention to his instructions, telling myself that I would never have to deal with it.

I returned to Dad's mobile phone and checked his messages and missed calls, returning them with an apology. The phone numbers of my mother and my six siblings were listed on his phone. I made myself comfortable on the settee. What will I say to Ma? How will she react? Nervously I dialled her number. The phone rang until I was about to hang up. I wondered if Dad had the correct number; I had not spoken to her for a couple of years, not even remembering her last birthday or Christmas.

"Hello, hello, may I speak…"

"Hello," came a strong English voice, followed by a flat Trinidadian.

"Oh, it's you, Beth." I could hear the disappointment in her voice.

"I thought it may have been Pat or Pru. I so need to get to New York or Miami. These rags I am wearing are so shabby, not to mention my wigs; they are all in need of replacing, and you should see the state I am in."

She would have gone on talking in similar fashion for another hour had I let her. I shouted over her voice.

"Ma, Mother, I have some bad news!"

"Beth, you are always so melodramatic. What could possibly be bad news except that maybe that father of yours kicked the bucket!"

I almost dropped the phone. Had she been close enough to touch, I surely would have wrapped something around her neck. I sobbed aloud.

"Yes, Ma. Dad is dead."

Then, as calm as you please, she continued,

"Well, don't upset yourself so much, my dear; these things happen. But I need you to keep your head. Don't move anything until I get there, you hear me, Elizabeth? Do not move a thing. I will call your sisters; you just do as I say and wait until we get there."

I was flabbergasted. I could not believe my ears. I replaced the house phone on the hook with such force that it was a wonder it did not break. How could she be so cold and uncaring? What could Dad have possibly done to her to make her so mean? It took me a while to calm down; I could not move from the settee. An hour or so later the phone rang, and I was afraid to pick it up. I should have left her for last, I told myself.

"Hello, Beth? Is that you, Beth? It's Patricia, my love. Mother called to tell me the news, and of course I called Pauline. You know she works at the airport and was able to get us flights arriving in Jamaica next week, but we are not too sure which day because she has to ask for time off from her work.

Of course, she will also book us into a hotel in Montego Bay. It would be much more comfortable, don't you think? Anyway, Mother wants me to remind you to lock up Dad's apartment until we arrive. Will you do that, Beth?"

"You know she needs to sort out paperwork and the will and so on; she wants to be able to do the right thing."

I did not, and could not, answer Patricia. I allowed her to repeat herself until finally she said, "All right, Beth, I know that you may be quite upset, which is why I think you should allow Mum to handle things. I will give you a call on Monday as soon as we are sure, okay, my dear?"

I sat paralysed; not even my brain was able to function until my mobile phone rang out, and I jumped and sprang from the chair to answer it, saying hello in a whisper.

31

"Beth, sweetheart, are you okay? It's Prudence. I just received a phone message from Mum, not quite understanding the message, but I am about to board for Amsterdam. Take care, my love; I will call you as soon as I get to our hotel."

I said goodbye to Prudence and pressed the red button. My mobile phone vibrated in my hand, and I again said hello.

"Hi Beth, it's my day off today, but Mum sent me an urgent message to call her about Dad. Do you have any idea what it's about?" Instantly I cheered up.

"Hi, baby girl. How are you?"

We spoke for a few moments and caught up. Rosemarie was the last of seven and the one who looked the most like Dad. She inherited his dark, cool skin tone and the straight black Indian hair. Dad always told her she was his grandmother reincarnated.

"So where is Dad?" she asked. I told her straight up,

"Our dad died between Sunday night and Monday morning at the hospital."

We both cried for ten minutes or more before she could ask,

"How did Dad die? Was it in a car accident?"

She also went on to confess that Dad had spoken to her about his heart condition the very week before. She did not think that it was that serious.

I explained what had happened from the time Dad and I had lunch until he died. We spoke for a further twenty minutes or more, and she promised to get back in touch later that morning. But being able to speak to Rosemarie made all the difference; we had such a close connection. And I felt bad at not calling her first.

As a child, Rosemarie kept very close to Dad, so much so that we nicknamed her Ghost. She never played much with our other sisters; if I were not around, she kept to herself, yet she knew everything they got up to. She would pop up where she was least expected without saying a word. She observed every detail with dark and mysterious eyes but never commented. And I loved that Patricia and Pauline were ever fearful of her presence and would never attempt to harm her as they did Sophia.

Dear Sophia. The complete opposite of Rosemarie. Sophia inherited her mother's side of our family. She had golden hair, smooth peachy skin, blue eyes and a figure to die for. She would have won any Miss World contest hands down. Rosemarie had always stayed in touch with Sophia and had promised to call her to relay the news about Dad.

Having calmed my mind after speaking with Rose, I dialed Jacky's number. Her phone rang unanswered, but with Jacky that was not unusual. She was the last to be called and the first on my list for the first thing next day.

But I needed to clear my head. Even after talking to Rosemarie, I was still so disturbed about Ma's comments that they kept me up and made me restless. So I got a cold Red Stripe and stepped out on the back veranda."

Chapter Three

Just Faith

I opened my eyes the following morning and imagined seeing Dad sitting across from me. He smiled and held up his cup towards me.

"Here's to you, my pet; have faith."

I turned to stretch the sleep and pains from my body. When I looked again, he was gone. "Good morning to you too, Dad," I spoke aloud.

The plates and leftover food were still on the table from our Sunday afternoon meal. It was Tuesday morning, and I had completely forgotten to clear them the evening before. The ice cream had melted and was looking like something in a science lab.

I cleaned up and had a shower before Ms Mac called.

"How are you feeling this morning, Miss Beth? We never got any new bookings yesterday, but John has gone to MoBay with the van since morning to collect a family, and then he is to take them to Negril. I never want to be in the office alone, so I asked my husband to stay here with me. You don't mind, Miss?"

"Morning, Ms Mac. No, I don't mind. I have no appointment for myself, and Dad's diary is also clear, so I will remain at home today, but call me if anything comes up."

"For sure, Miss, and my husband and I will bring your dinner for you on our way home."

"Thank you, Ms Mac, but you will be driving out of your way."

"You don't worry yourself, Miss; my husband doesn't mind. Have a good day, Miss Beth."

Dad's phone was already going off with messages. I addressed them before informing his callers that he had passed, and at the same time assuring them I was capable of maintaining their bookings and seeing to their requests. Everyone was sympathetic, offering condolences, and also wanting to be informed of his funeral. I then dealt with my own messages in similar fashion before trying to contact Jacky, still with no success.

I gathered up both mobile phones and went into Dad's bedroom. One thing I would always joke with him about was that he never opened the drapes at his windows; instead, he would always leave the room light on. A remnant from England. Day or night, the weather was often so bad that you had no reason to open the drapes. I did not turn on the lights or pull the drapes, just threw myself on his bed, rolling to and fro across the king-sized space, emptying myself of tears I was to shed for some time. Finally I lay on my back looking up at a large portrait of a handsome young man smiling down at me and remembered our last hours together at the hospital.

Then my mind wandered back to London and that cold Sunday afternoon, only weeks following my unexpected return.

Standing at the doorstep to the house where I grew up as a child, my body was shaking; one, because I was feeling so ashamed, and two, because I was not wearing a winter coat. I felt so broken and disappointed with myself when I entered the taxi after finally getting the

35

courage I needed. I gave the driver my father's address. Carol wanted to travel with me and to stay a few weeks while I settled back in, but I needed to be alone when I faced my father and the family. As I stood on my father's front porch with a single suitcase, I felt like the prodigal child that I was, returning to the only place I knew I would not get rejection.

My dad took me up to my old room and plugged in an electric heater. Then he gave me a tight hug and kissed me on the forehead. The following morning my sister Rosemarie brought me a cup of coffee in bed and left me one of her warm overcoats, just in case I wanted to go outside.

A few weeks later I was sitting at the dining table on a similar Sunday evening, making circles around job advertisements which I thought suited my qualifications and/or interests. Dad sat in his favourite armchair in the far corner of the large space which was our kitchen, dining, and sitting room. He had a small radio held up to one ear and a pen and paper at the ready on the coffee table. I tilted my head to listen to what it was that he was so interested in hearing.

"Dad, when did you get so interested in Jamaica and reggae music?" I asked.

He waved his hand at me and placed the pencil to his lips, indicating that I should be silent.

"I think that our dad is getting homesick," said Rosemarie in a whisper, also giggling.

"Hush, both of you!" Dad replied, stomping his feet angrily.

"You two keep quiet; they are about to ask the final question."

Rose came and stood by my side as we looked down on our dad, who was never one for displaying such irrational behaviour. He looked up at us with an expression like 'duh!' on his face, then went on to explain in a whisper.

"They are giving a trip for two to Jamaica to the winner."

Shooing us away again with the pencil at his lips, he placed the radio on top of the coffee table and turned up the volume. We heard the last line in the song by Jimmy Cliff, *'Many Rivers to Crosses'*. The music stopped, and the D.J. announcer shouted:

"Only one river left for the lucky winner to cross. Answer the last question correctly and you will be on your way to sunny Jamaica. Here we go, question: where in Jamaica, that is, in which parish of Jamaica, would you find Mocho?"

Dad jumped up from his chair.

"Clarendon! Clarendon!"

He scribbled his answer down on the paper, then placed it into an already stamped envelope, and reached for his coat while he told us excitedly:

"I am sure I got the first nine, and this one was the easiest."

Then he was out the door. Of course, Rosemarie and I just burst out laughing. Ma came down the stairway. As cold as it was, she was wearing only a cotton baby-doll nightdress.

"You two have a right to laugh, the old fool. He really thinks he will win no contest. Mocho? "What kind of question is that?" She sucked on her teeth.

"Ma, please don't call Dad an old fool; you sound so unkind."

She sucked even longer on her teeth the second time around before announcing:

"No worry, by this time next month, I won't have to call him anything."

Rosemarie's eyes and mine met; it was clear she knew what Ma meant, but she made a hasty retreat up the stairway ahead of Ma. I stood puzzled as Dad made his way back inside the house, shaking his body as he replaced his coat on the rack.

"Nippy outside, pet; you best wrap up warm tomorrow. Not the best weather for job hunting."

"I will be fine, Dad. Fancy a cup? And just for the record, who is Mocho?"

"No, my pet, it's not 'who is Mocho', it's 'where is Mocho'! Mocho is a town in Clarendon, Jamaica, and the town where I was born. And I am hoping now to win this competition to get the chance to see my old town again."

Rosemarie came back down the stairway in time to switch off the whistling kettle.

"For what it's worth, Dad, I really hope that yours will be the winning ticket. You deserve a holiday, and it will be good for you. If not, we can always plan our own holiday to Jamaica for next year," she remarked cheerfully as she handed him his cup of coffee.

I pulled my chair closer to Dad's armchair.

"Tell us about where you were born, Dad. You have never really spoken much about Jamaica the country, only about your brother and Grandma."

Then I asked a question I was never brave enough to ask before.

"Dad, how come you got married to a Trinidadian and not a Jamaican?"

Rosemarie giggled, and Dad muttered:

"Just fate, my pet, just fate."

Rosemarie made herself comfortable on the arm of the chair beside him. Dad took a long sip of his coffee before bursting into a wide grin.

"It's true. It's been a long, long time since I have given a second thought about my homeland. I found this pirate radio station last month, and for the first time in a long time, I was hearing so much old Jamaican music. They just brought back so many memories."

He took another large swallow of his coffee and relaxed in the chair, closing his eyes.

"I can see it all now, as clear as if it were yesterday. Back then, when we left Jamaica, the farthest thing from my mind was to get married. And I would not have found myself in this position had it not been for Pauli. (Pauli was our uncle, Father's brother.) I don't think that I had ever told you girls that Pauli and I did not share the same mother."

"That's not surprising, Dad. From the photos I see, you are like chalk and cheese, almost like Sophia and myself," remarked Rosemarie.

Dad laughed.

"You are so right, my love, but the funny thing is that we were almost twins—we were born only a week apart. My father did not accept that I was his child at all. But my mother, in order to prove him wrong, waited until my little body was strong enough to journey to his home, taking me as proof to confront him. But while she was trying to convince my grandmother—which didn't take much because, as we say in Jamaica, I was the dead stamp."

(Dad explained that being the dead stamp meant he was the exact image of his father.)

He continued:

"Pauli was only a month old and was already given to be cared for by our grandmother by his mother, who was about to set sail for England. She, being a privileged brown-skinned young woman from a well-to-do family, was given the chance to travel and study to become a nurse. My grandmother later told me that when my mother heard the crying baby and was told who the baby belonged to, she stormed out of the house, leaving me in my grandmother's arms. So poor Tata had two young babies to care for, the produce of her one and only male child. She had no choice but to care for us the best way she could. So neither of us knew our birth mothers. Our father would always come to visit his mother, so we got to know him.

40

It still did not help me, because he only recognised and accepted Pauli as his son."

Dad shook his head, still in disbelief. Rosemarie hugged and rocked him in his chair.

"Really, Dad; that is so sad. Why is it that men continue to say things like that? It's so unfair."

I agreed with Rosemarie and asked Dad.

"Even when you were the one who was the mirror image? Dad, that is so sad."

He continued after giving us a haughty chuckle.

"No problem, I never knew about it at the time. Tata found all kinds of reasons to keep it from me and never allowed me to feel left out or unwanted. She would even send me on errands when she knew he was coming or save my punishment for that day, so I would be upset with her for sending me out and making me miss going out with my dad and brother.

But whenever Pauli received any money or clothes from our father, she would always share it evenly between us. Our Tata was mother and father to both of us. Even so, Pauli was in charge; I just tagged along. Each time he would return from spending time with our father, he talked endlessly about his own mother from the stories Father told him and made sure he reminded me that his father would be taking him to England to live with her as soon as her studies were over.

Not much else happened in our lives except church and school; we could not miss a day from either one. Then at fourteen years old we had to leave school and were sent to Bog Walk to work as pickers on an orange farm. Because of the distance between the farm and home, we only returned to Tata at the end of every month to get some home-cooked food and to hand over our pay. She opened our pay envelopes and would then give us pocket money, enough for our fare to return to the farm.

During that time we did not see our father, and Tata would just tell us stories she heard from his friends about him.

One day Pauli came up with a plan for us to make extra money. We would collect up the rejected oranges, and on Fridays, after picking was over, we got on a truck to Coronation Market in downtown Kingston to sell. After some time we included other things like cane, bananas, and coconuts in our stock. The money we earned never got spent, but every penny was saved towards our fare to England.

We were constantly in the company of older and wiser men, some of whom had gone to work on the Panama Canal and some of whom had gone to Cuba, telling stories after stories of their adventures. A few even left to fight in the war for England. Those who left did not return but sent letters, declaring that they had seen gold on the pavements, big houses and a good life even in the cold and snow.

So we went along with the crowd and signed up to travel to England. We were told that because we were still young, we could get work as cabin boys on the boat to pay our passage.

Pauli made me swear never to let on that we had money of our own. We gave half of that money to Tata after we told her in detail how we came to have it in the first place. She used that money to buy us long pants and long-sleeved shirts, jackets, and matching black and white shoes. Also a grip (a small brown suitcase) with our names written on the outside, and she filled it with potato and cornmeal pudding, bluedraws, roast fish, breadfruit and mangoes. Needless to say, Pauli sold most of it, so even before we got to Southampton, it was all gone.

The morning we were leaving Jamaica, four of us got a ride on the back of a truck taking bananas and oranges to Montego Bay. We got to Lucea harbour in the night and were taken down to the engine room of a banana boat. The white men didn't speak English and only showed us what we needed to do.

Apart from all of us being sick to the stomach, I remembered little else of the journey. When we arrived at Southampton, we were told to wait on the boat until someone came to fetch us. The four of us young boys who worked in the engine room came up from the hot belly of the boat to freezing cold and black skies. We were bundled into the back of a van with bags of mail and were then driven off at high speed, rocking and rolling with the mailbags.

"Here you are, boys; welcome to the motherland. Good old England. A bit nippy today, but you boys will be all right. Get a move on; I am running late already. Go on, off you get."

The driver pulled us out of the back of the van and pointed us in a direction up a small alleyway behind a row of houses. We stood, each of us trying to get our bearings, then came."

"Hurry up and get your black arses inside. What are you waiting for, the rooster to crow?"

The voice was familiar; it was clearly Jamaican, so we rushed towards the open door and were greeted by a half dozen or so young men like ourselves, who wrapped themselves in big coats and woollen scarves shortly after. They let themselves out through the front door while we were being shown where to sleep, in a room just large enough to accommodate the two small beds. Two to a bed and still in our jackets.

As soon as I got comfortable and was able to sleep:

"Alright, this is not Jamaica. Man has to pay rent. I put money in the geyser, wash up and follow Berty to look for some work, boys."

Dad started laughing, shaking his head from side to side as he confronted his memories.

The phone was ringing, and Mother rushed down the stairs to pick it up before any of us could move. Once Mother got on that phone on a Sunday evening, the house became engulfed in her loud voice and laughter. It was impossible for Dad to continue his story. He got up and retired to his bedroom. Rosy started setting up her hair for work the following morning. I went back to the dining table to hunt out and circle the suitable job advertisements in the hope of securing work on the following day.

I snapped back to reality as the house phone rang. I reached over to Dad's bedside table to retrieve it as I wiped away tears still staining my cheeks. It was the Budds wanting to know if I had been able to get a family member to stay with me and whether I was able to rest. They still expressed that they were on hand to help in any way possible. I glanced over to the clock radio; it was already past midday. I thanked them and excused myself as my mobile phone went off.

"Beth, my darling. How is Jamaica? I didn't recognise your number, or I would have called back before now. How are you, my darling?"

"I am okay, Jacky. I upgraded my phone and had to change my number. But you are sounding so upbeat; I can hear it in your voice."

"Beth, my darling, I could not be better, but let me have a quick word with Dad. Is he close by you?"

I quickly grabbed the pillow to muffle my voice.

"Beth? Beth?"

"I am here, Jacky. "Sorry." My voice broke.

"Sweetheart, I am so sorry. Are you okay? What's going on?"

"I am so sorry, Jacky, but I have bad news."

"Is Dad not well?" she asked.

"Jacky… Dad died yesterday."

"What! But I spoke to him on Saturday evening and was to call him back. Jack and I will be flying in on Friday. Beth, what happened? Did he have a car accident?"

I explained to my sister what had taken place and my call to Mother and her reaction.

"Oh Beth, this is so sad. I certainly would not have expected this. He was so happy when we spoke to him on Saturday. I told him then that I would call to inform him of our flight time. This is so sad—now Jack won't ever meet our dad."

She was silent for a moment, and I had to ask. This wasn't like Jacky; she was ever a loner, insisting that she would never ever get married.

"Is Jack a boyfriend?"

"Beth, I wanted to surprise you, but I am so happy that Jack was able to speak a few times with Dad. He wanted to do the old-fashioned thing, you know, asking for my hand and all that. The wedding is pending a couple of weeks from today. We had planned to stay with Dad until we got a final date. And we are also booked to arrive in Kingston, Norman Manley, on Friday at six p.m."

Jacky sighed so heavily it was almost as if I could feel her weight. We both cried on either side of the phone line.

"Jacky, please don't cancel. I will come and collect you on Friday; is that alright with you?"

"Ok, my darling, we will be looking out for you. Please take care of yourself, and please collect all of Dad's important documents together and put them under your bed if necessary, but don't let that woman get her hands on anything of importance, you hear me? Love you, Beth."

"Love you too, Jacky; see you on Friday."

I lay for a while on Dad's bed, thinking of the change in Jacky, and crying out aloud when I realised that Dad would not be here to walk her down the aisle. It was a double tragedy for them both.

The doctor's voice echoed through the quiet of the apartment. I ran to open the grill.

"I am sorry to turn up unannounced, but your phone has been busy for some time. Are you ok? Did you sleep well?"

He was dressed in blue jeans and a white polo shirt, a white Jockey cap to match, and a shopping bag in each hand.

"Hi Doc, How are you? I see you have been shopping; please give me a minute to find the keys."

The keys to the grill were in my hand, but my face was wet with tears, and I was still wearing the light T-shirt I had slept in, with no bra. I had large breasts, but after two children they were unattractive without support. Putting on a bra at that moment would have been too much stress, so I replaced the T-shirt with a loose-fitting floral blouse, splashing my face with cold water and grabbing a small towel on my way back to the grill.

"I did manage to get hold of all my sisters and was on the phone to the last on the list just before you got here. And yes, as a matter of fact, I did get some sleep."

I unlocked the grill, allowing him onto the veranda as I dried my face.

"Can I help you with those? Are they for me, or have you just done your weekly shopping before coming here?" I asked.

"Let's say that they are for us. I took the liberty of buying us lunch at my favourite restaurant — they cook an excellent curry goat. I hope you will enjoy it. I also have a box of milk for myself and an orange juice for you."

"Well, follow me to the kitchen, kind sir; let's get some plates. The aroma alone is reminding me that I have not eaten a solid meal since Sunday."

We sat around the dining table; the meal was enjoyable and filling.

Doc insisted on washing up the dishes, which he did while I engaged in a long conversation with Ms Mac, her husband, and John on speakerphone.

She insisted on bringing me a cooked meal, and John wanted to know if I would accommodate Dad's friends coming to the house to play dominoes.

Doc was waving and whispering no. So I quickly said no, because I was still trying to get hold of members of my family, and I may have to leave the house to meet up with family members, but maybe the weekend would be more appropriate when the rest of the family got there. They agreed.

I replaced the receiver and asked,

"Ok, Doctor, so what is this setup and domino playing all about?"

He went on to explain the practice of setup and nine nights for the deceased and what it all meant.

"Well, I can't say that I am looking forward to any of it; Dad was not a person who ever played dominoes, and he never had friends coming around the house and was never too keen on a crowd except at church."

We left the warmth of the kitchen to relax on the veranda, Doc sitting in Dad's chair as he further explained the nuances of dealing with, and the planning of, a funeral service for a loved one. We started to select the songs which would be appropriate for the service. The doctor then took hold of my hands and sighed deeply.

"You know, when I heard your father belting out *Roll Jordon Roll,* I would never have believed that he was saying goodbye; his voice was so strong. Driving here this morning, I was remembering the extraordinary story he told me about winning a ticket back to Jamaica."

I was surprised that the doctor would have known that much about my father, but I joined in as we both sang out the chorus, with him trying to sound like my dad.

"You know, Doc, I remember that song for so many reasons. To start with, I did not know that my father could sing. And then with him having to sing it at every occasion as a promotion for the radio station, after winning that contest, it's engraved on my mind."

I closed my eyes for a brief moment as the memories flooded my mind, then told him my version of the story.

"And do you know that Dad was the only one of the contestants to get that number five question right? They had asked—"

"What did Jamaicans ask Jordon to do?"

And Dad got it: *Roll Jordon Roll.* He waited for weeks, sitting by the radio every Sunday evening, tuning in to the station and listening to the programme from start to finish. My sister and I were ready to give up, thinking that nothing would come out of it. And I felt sorry that Dad was so caught up and still felt he would win for sure, no matter what we told him. Then came that Sunday evening when the phone rang in the middle of his programme. I ran for the phone to prevent it from disturbing him and was so angry I was ready to tell off my sisters, thinking they were the ones calling for Mother.

Instead, I heard a man's chirpy voice on the phone saying,

"Mr Creary, please turn off your radio."

For a moment I stood holding the phone, wondering what was happening. It was my sister who switched off the radio and took the phone from my hand, giving it to Dad. After a few yes, no, yes, nos, he replaced the receiver and said without emotion,

"They want to present me with the ticket on Wednesday."

"Just like that. That was Dad for you; he never seemed to get excited."

"Why did you decide to come home with him?"

Doc asked, as he leaned across closer to my chair, running his fingers over my hands. I was taken by surprise at his question and didn't think that I knew him long enough to go that deeply into my personal life. I went back to speaking about the evening Dad won the prize, which changed both our lives.

"You know, Doc, that evening was something else for Rosemary and myself. We were screaming, shouting and jumping all over the place with excitement. Later, when the phone rang for Mum's usual

50

Sunday chat, I picked up the phone and announced the good news to my older sisters. I could not believe that it made Mum meaner than ever. She remarked aloud:

'The old fool, how did he manage that?'

I reacted instantly and flashed back at her.

'You are a spoilsport, Mum. Please stop treating Dad in this way; it is so distasteful and uncalled for.'

She looked me up and down with a look so bad, I pulled at my clothes, thinking I was naked.

'Out of you all two, I am not sure which one is worse, but you don't mind me; next week this time I'll be out of you all's hair. I have had enough of the lot of you.'

That was the last time we spoke until last night when I called her. Needless to say, she has not changed, still as mean, if not worse."

Just then the house phone rang. I was happy to leave Doc and get a chance to wash my face again. John came by with my evening meal and found that the coconuts were still in the back of Dad's jeep, so while he and Doc chopped and poured out the water, I scooped out the jelly. Hard or soft, I love to mix it with sugar and enjoy it as a dessert after my meals.

John and the doctor seemed to have known each other. They chatted like old friends while John tried to convince us that Saturday would be the best evening to call friends over for dominoes and a drink of rum to pay respect to Dad. I finally agreed and said that Saturday would be okay.

"You won't have to do anything, Ms Beth; I and my friends will arrange everything. We have the outside pipe we can use; we can set up the cooking right under the breadfruit tree. And the outside bathroom is round the back so you can even keep the veranda grill locked; the yard is big enough for everybody."

"Well, John, now that you have your wish and you plan to take charge, it's time we leave Ms Beth to get some rest. I will drop you off to collect the van on my way home."

They both waited until I closed all the front windows and padlocked the grill before wishing me goodnight. I waved them both goodbye, thinking to myself how pleasant my evening had been. Conversation with the doctor was pleasant and relaxing. Left alone with my thoughts, I spoke his full name out loud: Lloyd Patrick Cain, affectionately called LP. It turned out that he had met Dad shortly after Dad suffered the stroke and had been seeing him as a patient every month. So I wasn't surprised when he asked about my children, because I knew my dad had their photos in his wallet and showed them off at every opportunity.

I relaxed on the sofa after turning on the TV. Dad and I would watch the evening news first on one station, then the other, before we got into a debate on the style of delivery and approach of each presenter. Then we would turn to the radio for the BBC overseas broadcast. Then, over late tea, we would discuss the day's work and plan for the following day. My tendency now is to speak out loud as if Dad were present.

"It's been a good day, Dad. You were right. Sorry I was not paying attention to the computer or the accounts, but I will collect the books tomorrow and pick up where you left off. I am not going to let you down, no matter what. I will make sure your company will keep going as smoothly as you like it."

Dad had partitioned the sitting room with a double-sided bookcase and had his office space neatly arranged in one corner, which enhanced the room rather than taking away from it. I sat myself down in his chair and carefully went through his business contacts and all paperwork— nothing that I was not already familiar with. Dad never allowed himself to have any outstanding bills; at the best of times he paid up before the due date. He had given me the password to the computer and showed me how to access the emails on the computer, but I knew that I would have to prepare my mind to tackle that hurdle. His briefcase held important papers, and it seemed to me that he had been tidying up his affairs. I placed the briefcase and its contents in the safe that he had installed in his bedroom.

I checked his mobile phone and made sure that all his contacts were sent a scripted message which also referred them to my own phone number. I then closed the phone down and placed it also in the safe.

Being still in a business mood, when my phone rang, I answered in like manner. "Good evening, how may I assist you?"

I was pleasantly surprised at the remark from the caller:

"I would love for you to assist me with a goodnight kiss. We parted company a little unexpectedly, and I wasn't expecting that interception by John. But I must tell you that I spent the most relaxing and pleasant evening and am now reflecting on our conversations. I felt the need to call you and let you know I am looking forward to our day tomorrow."

His statement brought a giggle to my throat.

"Can I confess that I also had a pleasant day, and my expectation for tomorrow is now hastened? So I thank you, and I would gladly assist you with that goodnight kiss."

I puckered up and sent a smack down the phone.

"Goodnight, my fair lady, have a restful night." And the kiss was returned.

I lay face down on my dad's bed, not needing anything else to put me to sleep.

My phone rang; the light was still on in the room. My eyes found the clock, which registered two a.m. I had drifted off to sleep before locking up, so all the house lights were still on.

"Beth, my darling, Are you okay?"

The sweet, sophisticated (posh) voice, as only the English can sound.

"Sophia, how are you? We have not spoken in such a long time. How are the twins, and how are you doing?"

"The twins are fine, and they are so looking forward to meeting you. I know it's not an ideal situation, my darling, but one cannot question these things. Beth, my love, we are presently boarding a bus to London. Mouse booked us for Montego Bay, Jamaica, arriving on Sunday. We wanted to get there on Friday, but they had only two seats on that flight. I wanted to call ahead because of the twins. Would you have room for us at your place? They are prepared to share a room with me, and I really would find it more comfortable if we could stay with you."

"Not a problem, Sophia, my love. I have lots of bed space, and I will be at the airport to collect you."

"Darling, bless you. I know that Mouse will call to confirm, but I am feeling so much better now that I have spoken to you. Stay strong, my sweet."

"Bye, Sophia."

I got up to switch off the lights and TV, which were still on. The phone rang again in my hand. A whispered voice on the other end of the line replied,

"Hi sis, I just got on a flight back to New York. I just wanted you to know that I will be in Jamaica sometime towards the end of next week. My husband's grandmother will be celebrating her hundredth birthday, so we were booked for that. Can't give you any definite date; she has done all the planning. But as soon as we are settled, I will call you. Sis, are you hearing me okay?"

"Yes, Prudence, and thanks for calling. See you soon. Love you."

I returned to my own bedroom and relaxed in the easy chair while I sipped on the hot drink of Milo, remembering what was probably Dad's confession and last will and testimony on Sunday night. Our Ms Mac was always heard repeating,

"Seven brothers, seven minds."

I now understood what she meant, thinking that in our case it could not be a truer statement. Dad had always told us stories about his life in Jamaica, but not much of his early days in England. I had always wondered and had asked how he met our mother, and he would only smile and sometimes shake his head as if he was trying to understand it himself. When I made myself comfortable beside his bed in the hospital room, his death was the furthest thing from my mind, because dad was never ever sick—no cold in the winter, no headache in the summer heat. I remember seeing his face relaxed, and his body shifting on the bed as the drug worked on his body.

"Beth, Beth."

"Yes, dad, I am right here."

"Come sweetheart, come sit close. I just had a dream about Liza."

He smiled sweetly; it was a joy to see my dad's face at that moment, so I didn't even think of asking why he used mum's given name, Liza. We have been so used to everyone using her pet name, Jenny.

"Beth, my dear child, there has been so much left unsaid."

He opened his eyes, looked across at me and smiled as he took hold of my hand in his, then started his story.

"You know, when Pauli came back to fetch me from the safe house where we were staying with all the other men who we had travelled with to England, all he said was come, and I didn't hesitate or ask where to; I just followed him. Even when he had been away for almost two years, getting his letters from an army base, I was comforted knowing he was well. It was about midday when we got to our new destination, which

56

was to be his girlfriend's house. It was wet and dark; we actually passed the house and doubled back, and then he pushed me behind some hedges at the back of an alleyway. I sat on my grip and waited in the cold until it was night. He pulled me through the dark hallway into the kitchen at the back of the house. The white woman jumped from her chair and let out a scream as her hands went up to hold the cross she was wearing on a chain around her neck.

'Oh my gosh!'

She placed a hand to her chest.

'I thought you said he was your brother?'

Pauli laughed.

"This is my brother Paul, and Paul, this is Mary. She's going to look after you for me until I get back next week."

The woman was still holding her chest and looking scared. She blurted out,

"But he is Black; how come he is your brother?"

"We have the same father but different mothers," my brother explained.

"We grew up together since we were babies, so I am sure that he is my brother. He won't bite; hold his hand." Pauli placed her hand in mine.

"Blimey, poor thing, you are freezing. Come sit by the fire, poor love. How long have you been left out there?" she asked.

Pauli shouted back at her, "Well, I didn't want your neighbours to see me, let alone him, and it took me all day to find you, love, so you are to blame; but I need a few hours' sleep so I can get back to camp on time in the morning."

He turned and ran up the stairs. The woman turned towards me then with a bright smile.

"Don't mind me, love; I just expected you to look more like your brother. You must be starving; I could do beans on toast for you and a cup of tea, alright, love?"

She was the first white woman I had stood that close to, and apart from Pauli, I was the first Black man she was meeting. So I did not escape the stare and the touch of my skin and hair. I had to remain in the house for a full week so as not to cause any problems for her by letting her neighbours see me at her house, which would have given her a bad reputation back in those days.

She was a single woman living on her own; having a man coming and going wasn't the thing to do during those times, let alone having a Black man coming and going. Pauli returned the following weekend and was able to stay for two days. But by the Saturday evening he had a plan.

Mary was working at the local pub for a couple of hours in the evenings.

Pauli got dressed up in my suit, and I got dressed up in his army uniform.

Pauli was like Sophie; not only did he look white, but he was also a charmer. He had everyone eating out of his hand before the two hours were up. He came up with a story that he worked for the army and it was his job to find lodgings for the fellows who came from the West Indies to help the motherland fight the war. He was to commend Mary and be thankful that she was willing to be of service to her country by renting this poor shell-shocked soldier (me) a room at her home, allowing me to recuperate before returning to the West Indies.

They bought the story, and I was able to go to the corner shop during the days and to the pub with Mary in the evenings, with everyone giving me a salute as they passed me by, yet no one spoke to me. I wrote everything I needed to buy on a notepad, so they just took it and handed me whatever was requested. Even when they gave me the wrong change or said something ridiculous, I said nothing, just smiled.

It was six months before Pauli returned.

This time he was home for a full week. Still acting out his part, he took me to a factory not far away from the house and persuaded them to give me a job. The best they could do for me was to allow me to sweep up and clean toilets, but I got paid, so I was happy to know I could work while Pauli was gone.

During this time Mary was pregnant. Soon after Pauli left for camp, she told everyone about her surprise wedding to cover herself and explained the pregnancy. Shortly after that, her mother took ill and later went to the hospital, where she died. Her mother had been living in her own house in Finsbury Park in London. So after the burial, Mary, being an only child, was now the owner of her mother's house, so we were able to move into the old lady's house before the baby came along.

I had to give up my cleaning job because the journey was too far from the new address. But Mary didn't have to pay rent, so we managed. I also knew that she received money from the army. She also insisted on keeping her evening work at the new pub, while I babysat and took care of Patricia.

After that, Mary suggested that when I write to Pauli, I should give her my letters to post.

I found out later that he never got any of my letters. By the time he returned, the baby was standing up and walking around. He was surprised, and commented constantly that the baby had brown hair like her mother and that she had the complexion of her mother and didn't have anything of him, but Mary convinced him, and soon enough he accepted and became a proud father. I loved the baby but felt awkward when we went out shopping together.

With Pauli gone, Mary was again pregnant. Then she told me that Pauli was in Africa and was not able to receive letters where he was. So I stopped writing. Then came Prudence; her hair was red, she had blue eyes and was even lighter in complexion than Pauline. I later found work on the night shift at a factory just walking distance from the house, making nuts and bolts.

Months later, Pauli was taken home in a Red Cross ambulance with his right hand bandaged from the shoulder, held up with a sling, and his left leg in a white plaster covered with ink marks. I later realised the ink marks were the names of his friends, as it was the custom to wish him well by writing their names on the plaster. Within a couple of weeks, he and Mary were officially married at the local register office, attended by just the three of us, but it became a big thing when we arrived at the pub where she worked and they insisted that we had drinks to celebrate. I sat on the outside with the girls in their pram. By the end of the evening, Pauli got so drunk that the milkman had to take the crates off his van and drive him home.

The following week Pauli called the builders in, and the entire house was changed. The ground floor was extended into the back garden to make a larger kitchen, the old kitchen became a playroom for the babies, and the toilet was made bigger, and a bathroom with a tub was fitted.

On the first floor, a third bedroom was added. Pauli boasted that when he got his son, he would have his own room. The top floor was not left out; a third room was added also with the intention of later making it into a self-contained flat for me. The major work was completed in four months: windows, doors and flooring were in place. I spent every waking hour being the carpenter, putting in cupboards and shelves in the new kitchen and bathroom. Pauli, by then, had the use of his arms, but he still hobbled around with the aid of a single crutch.

We were gathered in the playroom getting ready to hear the evening news on the radio. Pauli got upset because the girls were running around playing, and he had problems picking up the frequency clearly. He made a remark, and Mary told him that he had better get used to it because she was up the spout again. The room was suddenly so quiet; even the girls seemed to understand what was said.

After that night I could hear arguments and raised voices from their bedroom, but I didn't interfere. My brother became withdrawn and sad, drinking too much and not eating as he should. He never confided in me; we never got to talk man to man. Even after knowing that Mary had kept my letters from him. In no time Mary was so big, I began to joke that she was having twins.

Pauli stopped going out with her to the pub in the evenings; I couldn't reason with him; the slightest thing seemed to set him off. I arrived home from work one morning in time to see Pauli getting into an army jeep. I ran to catch up. All he said to me was,

"I am glad that you are my brother, but I am sorry that I may not go back home to Jamaica with you."

Tears came to dad's eyes as well as mine. While he drank some more coconut water, I thought to myself, all seven of us girls grew up with dad being the only man at home and we all shared the same surname. I was almost fourteen when I realised that our family had a skeleton in our closet. Sophia had left home (not for the first time), but it had been two weeks so we were all worried and the police got involved.

On our way home from school one evening Rose and I stopped at a park, it was a little off the beaten track from our home. We saw a girl looking like our sister Sophia from afar and ran to catch up with her. The girl and her friends seemed to know who we were. She had the backing of her friends as they attacked us with the worst foul language and insinuations about our dad. We were confused and, even worse, we were so ashamed that we ran home in silence and never discussed what happened until we were grown and, even then, it was difficult to put two and two together.

I adjusted the pillows around dad's head and he drank the remainder of the coconut water. He took my hand and cupped it on his chest as he relaxed once more. I thought he was done, but he continued.

"I always asked God why he gave Pauli such a raw deal. Not that I didn't have it rough myself, but I had you girls to see me through. I remember that I was left just standing on the pavement that morning not knowing what to think or do next. Still seeing the image of the jeep and Pauli moving away from me and taking away part of my life with him. One of our neighbours called out to me, asking if I wanted her to watch the girls while I went to the hospital. She explained that an ambulance took Mary to the hospital the night before. I got worried, thinking that Pauli may have hurt Mary and it could have been the army police who took him away.

That was how I met Liza. When I got to the hospital I was told Mary was in the delivery room and I had to wait. Liza was speaking to another nurse almost at the top of her voice and was clearly upset about something. I was close enough to hear the whole story as she related it to the nurse coming on duty to relieve her, but as she put her coat on to leave she noticed me, and looking me directly in the face remarked,

'I wish these black men would realise that we black women are not looking for any white man to marry. They let all the white women make fools of them then come to us with their leftovers.'

Weeks later I found out what she meant…

63

Mary had to stay in the hospital for three weeks because she had a caesarean delivery of her third baby. It was the birth of Pauline, who looked nothing like my brother. I didn't catch on to the gossip because I was so used to hearing people passing remarks about us not being brothers. But when I caught up with Liza, who had been trying to avoid me after the first evening, she started apologising for being insensitive and speaking out of turn, etc. Only then did I realise that it was Pauli she had been talking about and caught on. I explained to her that I wasn't like my brother in more ways than one, but I had to do the right thing. Even though at that time I wasn't sure what the right thing should be. But my brother was married to Mary so in his absence I felt staying by her side was the right thing to do.

Whenever Liza and I met we would have great conversations, and for the first time I felt that I had a friend. But another nurse, Jenny, who often came on duty when Liza was going off, started taking an interest in Mary and before the three weeks were up, she was informing me that she may move into our house in order to keep an eye on the baby and to assist Mary. So I was not surprised that a week after Mary was discharged from hospital, Jenny was at our doorstep with her suitcase.

I still stopped by the hospital. Yet somehow I was never able to see Liza, then one evening I spotted her on the high street on my way to work. I jumped from the bus and ran back up the road to catch up with her. Some weeks later I took a part-time job during the days so as to enable me to be off a couple of nights every now and again. That's when I got to spend the night at her place.

I can safely say, even now, that your mother was the first and only woman I ever loved."

Dad stopped speaking for a moment to catch his breath. I looked at my watch; it was well after two a.m., but Dad still had more to get off his chest.

"At home Mary and Jenny were working hard to get me to see that Jenny was the perfect woman for me to be married to; even at the pub they were treating us as a couple. I must have let it slip that I had already found the woman I wanted to marry and spend the rest of my life with.

The following weekend when I turned up at Liza's apartment, the landlady was surprised to see me. She asked if Miss Liza was missing something after she moved.

The place was still vacant, so she let me in. When I went in and saw that it really was empty, confusion hit me. I felt it would have been better to go through the window rather than face the landlady on my way back out. My soap dish, toothbrush and towel were still in the bathroom, so I collected them and rushed out the front door, pretending not to hear what was being asked of me by the landlady. Then two weeks later I received a letter from Jamaica informing me that Grandmother Tata was dead.

The letter was addressed to me but sent to the army base before it was sent to France, reaching me three months later after her death. More misfortunes to add to Pauli leaving."

Dad started to weep; his face was so wet I had to use the sheet to mop up his tears. I consoled him the best I could. It was painful to see him so devastated, but I could feel his pain, having been there in my own short life. Yet my mind was still busy trying to put the pieces of his story together, trying to understand just what my father was telling me. Weeping, he held my hands tightly as he continued.

"Oh Beth, my child, your father, I am sad to say, was an old fool and no match for Mary and Jenny because they were determined. It took them only another six months to march me to the register office. The one thing I got my own way with was not going on the honeymoon weekend they had planned. So Mary and Jenny went off together for two weeks.

I was still in my bedclothes when the doorbell rang early one morning after they left. It wasn't a school day; it would have been the Easter bank holiday. So I took my time going downstairs. I could hear Pauline calling 'Dad, Dad', and when I got downstairs, she greeted me with a basket which she was struggling to hold up to her chest.

'Here, Dad, take it; it's heavy. The lady said to give it to you.'

I rushed to open the door, but not a shadow was in sight. When I pulled at the blanket in the basket, it was you, Beth, and you gave me the sweetest smile. I saw Liza looking back at me. It took me a while to read her letter. You were then seven months old. I realised then what those two had been up to behind my back.

Mary and Jenny arrived home a few days later. Pauline greeted them with the story of the lady who brought Daddy a baby. They both went up the stairs to their bedrooms, avoiding me, and the situation was never discussed. But I spent the next six months going to every hospital in London trying to find Liza. When we finally met, we consoled each other and realised that we felt the same and had strong enough feelings to want to be married and try to make a life together.

So we spent a couple of days at her place making a plan. But I had to return to the house to get you. When Mary and Jenny saw that I had packed my suitcase and was ready to leave, they started a fight, and the police were called. The police held me for a week at the local station, and the next thing I knew, I was in court being charged and then given a three-month sentence.

Liza came to visit but was told she wasn't on the visitors list. She spoke to someone on the outside who brought me her letter. I thought that my life was about to end. She had been brave enough to go to the house and confront Mary and Jenny, but she was no match for them, and they would not give up her child.

I survived the three months in jail, praying for you and knowing that your mother loved me. But the worst was not over. Once I was out, I made my way to Liza's last address in Shepherd's Bush. She wasn't there, but her landlady had been expecting me; she invited me in and allowed me to have a bath and stay the night. Liza had told her all about us, so her advice to me was to try and keep my daughter safe until I got news from her mother.

Liza had taken up a nursing job in Canada, promising to write with a forwarding address as soon as she got settled. Reluctantly I got off the train at Finsbury Park station and walked towards Mary's house. Not knowing if I would see you, or if they would again call the police to get me.

It was the middle of August so the children were on school holiday. As I got to the gate of the house, I could hear the girls playing in the backyard. I walked through the gate leading to the garden, creeping along as if I were a thief. Somehow you were the first to see me."

From the corner of my eye I could see the tiny person, running like babies do, with so much effort in the upper body, yet their feet were trying to play catch-up. The girls spotted me then and ran past you, sending you to the ground as they raced towards me. You didn't cry; you just got back up and kept running.

There are some situations in my life that I can never erase from my mind no matter how old I get. When I remember that day, it is as if it were yesterday. Mary came out to the garden wanting to know why they were screaming so loudly. When she saw me, she instantly went back in and closed the door. I felt like grabbing you at that moment and running. But the neighbour looked over the fence and called out.

'Hello, love, Good to see you. I am so sorry for your loss. Tell you what, I will bake one of my apple pies for you later to cheer you up. Good to see you, love.'

Mary came back through the kitchen door and walked toward me nervously.

'You alright, love? I was just about to call the girls in for lunch. I wasn't expecting you so early, but there's enough to share; best be getting in before it gets cold.'

She took the paper bag from my hand and held the door open while she encouraged the girls to take me inside. I had you in my arms, and your little hands were just about choking me; you held on so tightly around my neck. We sat for a long while around the kitchen table after eating, and the girls were watching Tom and Jerry on the television. I was getting tired and wanted to lie down, so I offered to wash the dishes just for an excuse to leave the table.

'Thanks, love. I should go freshen up your room. Don't be upset, but I haven't been up those stairs; I just haven't found the time.'

I felt relieved when Mary said that, because I wasn't sure even after being served lunch if I was going to be allowed to stay.

'Please don't worry yourself; I am so tired. I am just happy that I have somewhere to lay my head; I don't mind.'

I made my way up the stairs with you following close behind. To my surprise my suitcase was still on the landing outside my bedroom door with your little basket. Instantly the events of that day when I had planned to leave came back to me. I opened my bedroom door, and nothing in the room had been moved.

When Jenny came into the kitchen and saw me the following morning, her reaction was the same as Mary's: she went back through the door as if she had seen a ghost. I later realised that the two women were not on speaking terms from the way they moved gingerly around each other. Each of them tried to be extra nice to me, but neither one of them apologised for sending me to jail. But I put it all behind me, because they treated you well, and I was more than pleased to know that they did not go in my room, and I found all my money and my papers still in my suitcase untouched by them.

I went out the following week. My old firm would not take me back, but I got a much better job, more pay and good hours, and I kept in touch with Liza's landlady. The time went by so quickly; you celebrated your first birthday, and I still did not get a letter from your mother. I heard nothing of my brother either, even though I went to the army base where he was first stationed. My working hours were ten p.m. to six a.m., so you were asleep when I left for work, and most mornings you were still asleep when I got home. The second week in December I stopped to shop for presents and arrived home to see a very large black car parked outside the gate.

My first thought was that my brother had returned. I hurried to the door, which was left open. Mary was coming from the kitchen with a tray in hand, balancing two of her best china cups and saucers and a larger plate containing biscuits. A policeman from the local station, who I knew, held the door open for her. I froze on the spot.

"Oh, morning, Mr Creary, I see you have been doing a bit of Christmas shopping?"

At the mention of Christmas shopping, the girls all rushed from the kitchen. Mary sternly sent them back to finish their breakfast.

"Paul love, you had best get those upstairs; you got some visitors waiting in the front room."

She must have noticed how frightened I was, so she smiled to reassure me.

"Go on then, love; you don't want the girls to get a load of those" (she nodded towards the bags in my hand). "I will make you a cup of coffee; that should get you warmed up."

The policeman also smiled and nodded his head at me.

"Don't worry, Mr Creary, I will keep the little angels occupied with one of my stories while you get on with it."

When I returned to the front room, which was only used at Christmas or on special occasions, as I supposed this was one, a small beady-eyed white man with thick-lensed glasses had just placed his cup and saucer on the centre table. Resting on the floor beside him was a large brown briefcase; his coat and gloves were laid neatly on the arm of the chair. Across from him sat a middle-aged white woman. Her head scarf had slipped down around her neck; she was still wearing her coat and gloves as she sat holding a pink and white baby shawl with what seemed like a baby wrapped in it. They were both smiling at me and said good morning, repeating my name. Mary returned with my cup of coffee.

"Here you are, love. Don't just stand there; they are here to see you, so I had best just wait in the kitchen with the girls."

The man stood up, shook my hand, and introduced the lady, who freed a hand to shake mine. We all sat down, looking from one to the other. He was a lawyer; he said his name and that he was appointed by Liza Beth Murry. Whatever was said after that went in one ear and out the other.

He gave me paper after paper to sign. I read without seeing the words. Then he stood up and shook my hand.

"We have taken along all her possessions, which were willed to you as her next of kin. We are pleased to pass them on to you. She also signed to give account for the chest and the suitcase, and of course your child. Please accept our deepest sympathy. We do realise that this is a lot to take in, not to mention, we dare to say, a big surprise."

With that said, the woman stood up and handed me the shawl. I felt the warmth on my chest. Just then you pushed open the door and ran to me, scrambling up on my lap. The woman gave a little laugh.

"Oh my, this must be big sister Beth; your mummy told us about you. We will be leaving now, but you take care of Daddy and the baby, won't you, dear?"

The policeman shouted on his way out of the door. "Goodbye, Mr Creary."

Mary also left to take her girls to the park. I just sat there with both of you, looking at the trunk that Liza and I had bought on the high street so we could pack what we needed to start our life together. I was in the kitchen making a feed for the baby when Jenny got home later that day.

I thought that she only came in because she thought it was Mary who was in the kitchen, because she had tried her best to avoid seeing me face to face from the time I returned. I didn't make much of it because I thought that she should be ashamed of what she had done, and I wasn't too worried about not having to interact with her. She walked past you in the playroom with Rose, without paying much attention, took her coat off and entered the kitchen. The pot I had been holding, trying to cool the baby's milk, fell from my hand. I could not have been mistaken. Nurses' uniforms were designed for slim-waisted females simply by their cut.

The maternity top she was wearing did little to hide the protrusion of her pregnancy. When she realised that it was me in the kitchen, her hands went everywhere. You would have thought that I had caught her naked and she was protecting her dignity. But her secret was now out. Without a word being said. Of course, once she realised that she could no longer hide it, she just shrugged her shoulders, sucked her teeth and carried on with what she was doing. I was not as brave; I gathered up what I needed and took you both upstairs. Being on the top floor, I had a large enough landing, so I lost no time over the next couple of weeks in turning it into a small kitchen.

After Christmas Mary actually came up to my floor saying she needed to talk. It felt good to have the old Mary back. If only for a short while, I had long forgiven her for her conspiracy with Jenny. The first question she asked me was why, over the years, I stayed by her side even after knowing that the girls were not fathered by my brother. I didn't have an answer, not for myself and not for her. It would be the first time she had made such a confession, which made her cry, but I did not reach out to comfort her. She went on to explain that she had got involved with the new owner of the corner pub. When the baby, who was Pauline at that time, was old enough, she had gone back to working three nights during the week. She would take the girls with her to the pub, and they played downstairs with the owner's children while she worked. He was separated from his wife during those times and had the time to walk her home a few nights. Mary was always a flirt, and it didn't take much before they got involved.

I have to admit that I had always admired Mary for her looks and the easy way she made you feel comfortable. She was tall, with a very nice figure and a pleasant, smiling face, which needed very little make-up, mostly just a very red lipstick, and her hair was light brown, sometimes blonde, thick and always well styled. She would never look down on anyone and was always well put together, and the girls were always neatly dressed and well behaved. Maybe why I stayed was because in Jamaica there was a lady who attended my grandmother's church who appeared to be like Mary. She was kind to me at all times and often had a fruit or a sweet to give me after church.

Men found her attractive, and she had a lot of children, all with different fathers, but the men never stayed with her. But she kept the children altogether; they were always neatly dressed and appeared to be well fed.

I personally was never attracted to white women and would never think of getting married to any woman if she was not Jamaican, even before Liza told me off at the hospital, because I always wanted to return home one day.

I really thought that Mary and Pauli suited each other, and to me they always looked like a married couple.

I never understood why the girls didn't look like my brother at first. It was such a disappointment, which was hard to live with, when I realised the truth and knew that must have been the reason why Pauli left, because he too felt deceived. But I loved all the girls and somehow just never thought of leaving them, except to be with Liza. In Mary's case, I felt she and the girls needed someone they could rely on.

It was on that evening that Mary told me she had the same medical problem as Liza, and the child she was pregnant with would also be her last. She was told by the doctor to have the baby aborted in favour of her own life so that she would be there for her other girls, because it was unlikely, if she gave birth, they would both survive. It was at that point that she said two things which shocked me even more.

The child that Jenny was expecting was also by the same man, which was why they were not on speaking terms. She then apologised to me and to my brother, as she knew that she would not see him again. After brushing away tears with the back of her hand, she took my hands and said,

"I have thought about this carefully, Paul, so please understand that I am sure you are the right, and only, person I could trust with my girls. I do know who the fathers are of each of my girls, but I would not want to separate them, and I don't want for them to be sent to a children's home. And as annoying as Jenny is, I know she is not about to leave you. And she will look out for my girls also; you won't have to worry about the father of her baby. He knows about me, but she is too ashamed to even go back to the pub. It was your Liza who gave me the idea. So I am having this house signed over to you. I have made the appointment with a lawyer already, because this kid is due next month, so I don't want to waste any time, and I will not take no for an answer."

Mary got up and kissed me on the forehead.

"Anyway, my love, I have been chatting long enough, and you will be late for work if you don't get a move on."

Dad's head dropped on the pillow, heavy with sleep. Then he opened his eyes again, resisting the sleep.

"Mary was a good person, and the girls did not turn out too badly after all. And as for you, Elizabeth and Rosemary, I know that Liza would have been so very proud of you both. Don't worry too much about that husband of yours, my love; things will work out; just keep the faith. Love you, my pet."

"Love you too Dad."

Chapter Four

Day Three

I heard the clock alarm, but I was not ready to be awakened; I needed to stay with my thoughts. We were given snippets over the years; each time we had a reason to ask questions which stirred up the skeletons. Rose and I tried to put them together and came to our own conclusions. We knew that, despite all seven of us girls being called, and without a doubt feeling that he was Dad, simply because, for one, we all had the same surname. But once we were grown, we knew for sure that Patricia, Prudence, Pauline and Sophia were our cousins and the children of our uncle Pauli, after seeing an old wedding photo of Mary and our uncle Pauli.

In the photo, Uncle Pauli could have easily been as white as their mother. So that explained why they all looked different from Rose and myself. Jacky, who grew to be dark in her complexion over the years, looked a lot like Mum, although she was tall and big-boned like Sophia. We had a problem sorting out her age, but she was the last child of our dad, we thought. Although as a toddler and up to her teenage years, she had the build and looks more in line with the others. Rose and I were definitely the black sheep of the family. But now Dad had revealed that Jenny was not even our mother.

I could not think anymore. I got up; it was only six a.m. I checked the diary to see if we had a pickup or delivery for the day and called

John to remind him. I again tried to go over the story Dad told but could not concentrate. A knock came from the grill.

"Morning Miss Beth, you know that I don't have a phone miss, so I sorry if I get you up too early. I run into your driver yesterday up in Ochi and him telling me story. Is true mam, Mr Creary dead fe true?"

The question was being asked by our day helper, Gertrude.

"No, Miss Gertrude, you didn't wake me, and yes, my dad passed early Monday morning."

She started crying and went on to tell me of the dreams she had that warned her someone she knew would get sick and die, and how she was going to miss their talks and the little help with her bills, and she didn't know how she was going to manage without him. In the same breath, she wanted to know if she still had her day job.

"Yes Miss Gertrude, I still need you to come in tomorrow, because I am expecting my sisters for the weekend, so I will need some help to get the place ready."

"Oh yes mam, I will be here bright and early, and me really sorry about your father Miss Beth, me sorry fe true."

I had spoken to her through the closed grill on the front veranda. My car was parked to the side, and I remembered that Dad had in his diary to have it checked. I cleared it of my personal items, but it was still too early to call the mechanic. I sat in a chair looking out towards the gate. A smile came to my face and even brought a chuckle: Lloyd was walking up the driveway with a string of fish in one hand and an overnight bag in the other. He was wearing black Bermuda shorts and a white T-shirt.

"You are up early; I was worried that I would be waking you up," he said, looking surprised to see me.

"A doctor and a fisherman, what a combination." I laughed.

"Did you actually catch those yourself?"

He held up the three pint-sized fish proudly.

"I most certainly did. Your father, John, and I have been going fishing once per week for over a year now. Correction: they have been going every week, but I have only managed a few times, and this is my third catch, which makes me a seasoned fisherman, if I must say so myself."

We both laughed. I already had the keys in my hand when the helper knocked; I opened the door to let him in.

"So you and my dad were that close? I had no idea."

"I know, I didn't mean it to be a surprise. He invited me to visit and meet you several times, but I was always putting it off. So yes, I had the privilege of saying he was my friend. I hope that you will not hold it against me. It was not a planned or deliberate move not to tell you from the start. I am here as his friend, and I hope that you will permit me to be here as your friend also—first, by steaming these for our breakfast. They are already gutted and scaled; all I need is salt and for you to enjoy."

I suddenly felt awkward, thinking that maybe I had taken too much for granted. He was just being nice to me because of Dad.

"Permit me to declare my hand, please, Beth."

He had placed the fish in the sink and was facing me directly. I was feeling disappointed, so I shrugged my shoulders.

"I am all ears; plus, I am not to judge. I really do appreciate any help you can offer."

"I am sorry, but there wasn't really an opportunity to tell you before that I was a friend of your father's. I was so shaken up when he died. I honestly felt that he had another few years at least; I even told him as much. And I know for sure that he so wanted to put his affairs in order, and mostly he had a lot to tell you, but you know how parents are at telling their children the truth. And I also have a letter which he wrote and had given to me for safekeeping, which I have in my bag. I was to give it to you after his death. I just wanted you to wrap your head around losing him before adding to it."

He went to his bag and handed me an envelope which had just "Beth" written on it, but it was my dad's handwriting without a doubt.

"Please, can you delay reading it until tonight? I know it should not be my decision, but I am just saying that tonight may be a better time."

I took the letter from him with a trembling hand.

"Thank you, I wouldn't be able to concentrate on reading it now anyway, but thanks. I best leave you to fix that breakfast, chief, fisherman—oh, sorry, then I added sarcastically—Doctor."

He chuckled. "I will answer to all, but I wish to add 'friend' also; am I forgiven?"

"Only if I enjoy that breakfast. You will not even get a tip otherwise."

We both smiled in good humour as I left the kitchen to sit on the front veranda, nervously turning the envelope from one hand to the other. An elderly couple appeared at the front gate. They were calling, but with voices so low, had I not been outside, I would never have heard.

Mrs Budd was wearing a shoulder-length wig with bouncy curls and dark glasses. Her husband wore a white Panama hat, so it took me a while to recognise who they were. I walked down to the gate to meet them.

They were both waving frantically on seeing me.

"Good morning, good morning."

They both echoed together before Mrs Budd stepped forward to hug me and took over the conversation.

"We took a chance in stopping. We are on our way into Montego Bay to the hospital for our regular check-up but could not resist stopping to wish you a happy birthday. I am so happy I persuaded Mr Budd to stop. This is for you, my dear. I do hope you will have a pleasant birthday."

She handed me a fresh fruit basket.

"And I took this prize bloom from my own garden," remarked Mr Budd.

I invited them in for a cup of tea.

"We will have to take a rain check on that, my dear, but thank you all the same. We don't want to be late for our appointments. These things seem to take a full day, as you may know, so we best get going, but I am ever so pleased that we had the opportunity to surprise you."

They turned and hurried back to their car while I waited to wave them goodbye. I had not even remembered that it was my birthday and was delighted and surprised that they even remembered. I walked slowly back to the veranda, admiring the garden planted by Dad. The blooms were so fresh and bright I imagined that they were also wishing me a happy birthday.

There was an empty table waiting for the potted plant, and I unwrapped the gift of ripe bananas, pineapple, watermelon, and soursop, placing them carefully around the potted plant on the table. Shortly after, Lloyd called.

"OK, breakfast is served."

He waved me in through the kitchen door. On the table were two steamed butterfish, plated with cucumber and sliced tomato, and two slices of fried bammy. The aroma of the scallion, thyme and pepper was more than tempting.

"May I be the first to wish you a very happy birthday, dear Beth?"

He had made such an effort; I couldn't tell him that he was not the first.

"Oh wow, I can't wait, but I am not going to eat alone — please, where is your plate?" He placed the other fish on his own plate, and we sat opposite each other and ate in silence.

"So are you going to keep me in suspense? Do I get my tip?" he asked.

"Oh, this deserves more than a tip, it's been the best breakfast ever. I am sold on becoming a return customer (I couldn't help but flirt), which, as you know, is the greatest tip."

He gave me an admiring and serious look.

"Oh, to see you smile is reward enough; you have made my day. And I am happy I didn't chicken out. I was worried you would not be so accommodating, even after yesterday."

"So, what you are really saying is that I am easy to please, right?"

"Nothing of the sort, but I wish to be in your good books, and I would never take your kindness for weakness, my lady."

He blew me a kiss from across the table, and I returned the same.

"It's coming up to nine o'clock. Dad had booked my car to be serviced, so I will drive it to the mechanic and leave it, after which I am expecting to be chauffeured by you for the remainder of the day."

He started to clear the table.

"Where would you like to go after dropping off the car?"

"I have made a list." He laughed.

"Why am I not surprised? A true Virgo, the planner and organiser. Let me wash up, and I am taking the liberty of using your back room to shower, so go ahead and do what you need to, my lady, and I will be ready when you are."

I was about to call Ms Mac, but she called as I entered my room.

"Morning, Ms Beth, me was just saying to me husband that Mr Creary always read the computer box every day, so maybe you could come and look on it to see if any important message on it, what you think, Miss?"

"You are right, Ms Mac, and I will be doing just that sometime today. I have a few things planned, so I will be on the road. I am not sure what time I will get to the office, but I will see you a little later."

I remembered the fruits on the veranda; I retrieved them and washed them before placing them in the fridge while getting the birthday paper out of Lloyd's view. Later, after leaving our mechanic and accepting condolences from all the workers, I got to be driven in Lloyd's sports Jaguar to the bank.

I felt that I should wait on Rosemary so we could go over Dad's accounts together. I made an appointment for the following week with the bank manager. I stopped by the office of the estate agency to speak to Mr Grey regarding the house, even though I had not yet looked over the papers he had handed me on the Monday. He assured me I had time to read and digest, because all the important and legal papers were signed off by my dad.

We ran into the pastor on the high road, having a conversation with a group of people, so we stopped to inform him of our intended visit later that morning. Pastor Fairweather was clearly shocked when he heard of Dad passing. He looked at us, stupefied, shaking his head from side to side.

At the undertakers, we waited for a family ahead of us who had lost a grandmother. There were four children and three grandchildren who could not come to an agreement on any decision that the others made. The manager took them to an area outside the office so as not to have us wait indefinitely.

I was taken by surprise at how efficient and organised the undertakers were, not having been in such an office before.

I selected two of the programmes offered so my sisters would be able to assist with the final decision. The casket I selected I didn't think anyone would have an objection to; except Mum, she would go for the flash and bling, but I chose a light varnished and extensively carved one, which, to me, showed that the builder took some time and care working on it. They offered a choice of fabric and a choice of colours for the lining.

When we were leaving, the family who was ahead of us was still in the gardens, clearly still in disagreement with each other. Lloyd shook his head.

"You know that this sort of thing takes place at most funerals. It's hard to think that people who should be grieving would end up squabbling. I think that you have made some good choices. I hope that your mother and sisters will be more cooperative with you than that family is."

"To be honest, Lloyd, the only person I would be willing to change anything for would be Rose; as for Mrs Creary…"

I stopped myself from commenting further. I didn't know how much he knew and didn't want to appear rude or vindictive. After seeing the pastor, we stopped to have a cold drink and relax by a bar along the seafront.

"Penny for your thoughts. Are you OK, Beth? You are looking so perplexed."

"I am OK, but still feeling at times that this is not for real; maybe after my sisters get here, but at this moment I still feel I am in not such a good a dream."

He took my hand in his.

"I can't say that I know how you feel, but I do know how empty and broken it is to lose someone close to you by death. But I can assure you that I will be here for you and will always be just a phone call away."

I turned to face him, but not really wanting to be comforted.

"I appreciate that; thank you. I really am grateful for your help, and I mean that. But we have two more stops to make, I know you will be working tomorrow, so let's make hay."

We headed for the office. Lloyd sighed.

"This is a shame on me. I have passed this plaza so many times going to work and returning home, but never felt the need to stop, even when my thoughts ran on Paul as I passed."

We turned into the plaza, and neither John nor the van was anywhere in sight, plus the door to the office was closed. Normally Ms Mac positioned herself as a watchdog by the doorway. Lloyd held the door to allow me in.

As we entered the darkened office, the light, which was off, came on, music started playing, and the crowd of people on the inside started clapping. About a dozen people were standing around a large cake placed in the centre of my desk, then someone popped a champagne cork from its bottle.

Ms Mac was the first to come forward to hug me.

"Me know that you mind would be on your father Ms Beth, but his mind was always on you too, because last week him plan to surprise you and ask me to make this cake. So although we know that you must miss your father, he would have wanted you to have a happy birthday and a good day."

Everyone agreed with Ms Mac and started up with the singing of 'Happy Birthday to Me', then demanded that I blow out the candles and make a wish. After being given a drink and a slice of my birthday cake, the conversation went on to giving me sympathy and condolences on the passing of my dad.

I whispered to Lloyd, and we sneaked out.

"That was really nice of the staff to surprise you like that," he said.

"I know, and I made sure I took an extra slice of my cake, but it was a little difficult to stay. Besides, I wanted to check on the computer, and I couldn't do that with the place so noisy. You don't mind, do you? I would love to go to Savoy Mews; I have not seen it on the inside as yet. I guess it's about time I do. But I would want to return to the office later; I really need to check on the emails before returning home, and I am a lot more comfortable using the one in the office."

I searched in my bag for the key to the house when my mobile phone rang.

"Where you is Miss. Beth? I never get to give you my present, and I have dinner for you as well."

"Thank you, Ms Mac, I am not far away. There is something I had to do before it got late. But I do plan on returning to the office to check on the emails. I know that John will be staying late because he has to pick up a client from the airport later tonight, so you can leave the keys with him; I will soon be back."

"OK, Miss; happy birthday again."

"Ms Mac, I really thank you for the surprise; it was really nice of you, and I appreciate it."

We were at Savoy Mews in no time, because Lloyd took a route I was not familiar with. Doc held the door of his car open for me.

"Here you are; please allow me to do the honour. Can I for a moment take the place of your dad? I know it was his wish to present the house to you on your birthday. So Beth, on behalf of your father, happy birthday, my darling."

He held his arms open. I was so overwhelmed and so touched. We were at the entrance of the gate, and I was not seeing the Budd family's car in their driveway.

"You may, kind sir, and I am having the feeling that you have a connection to the location by the route you drove to get us here."

"Well, today seems to be the day of confessions, so I better come clean with my connection."

We sat on the steps of the veranda because I wanted to give Lloyd a chance to say what he had on his mind. He cleared his throat and took my hands as we sat.

"I came to know this house because it was owned by the doctor whose job and position I have inherited. When I was sent from Kingston to assist him, he was in the process of building this house. The lots were still being sold, and only four other houses were already built near the entrance of the estate. I had to live at the hospital cottage with him, so I got to be a sounding board for all his disagreements and all his triumphs. He thought that he was settled at the hospital and that he could make a good life down here for himself and his family. But like most of my patients, I realised that a lot of their problems centred on the fact that they did not have any discussions with their other halves and more often than not made plans without consulting each other.

Which was just what happened in Doctor Barnes' case.

He bought this land, built his dream home and then planned to present it to his wife. But that did not happen. At that time in the eighties, most people were leaving Jamaica due to the politics. I returned at that time because politics was the last thing on my mind. However, Mrs Barnes was no different; she wanted to leave for the US dollars and went ahead with her plans to do so without having a discussion first with her husband, just as he did not discuss his dream home with her. She went up to the U.S. with their children for the summer holidays, got them settled into school, and got herself a job; she, being a midwife, had no problem getting settled at the hospital of her choice. She then demanded that he sell their house in Kingston because she needed the money to complete the purchase of the house she bought in Miami. I remembered the morning I woke up to a string of expletives at the top of his voice. For a moment I thought I was the cause of his outburst.

He wasn't able to attend to his duties that day, so it became my first day being the doctor in charge at the hospital. When I returned to the cottage later that night, he had been drinking all day but was still able to tell me the whole story. That weekend he took me to see this place. It was still unfinished, with no windows or doors, but you could see the beauty of his design. I fell in love with the place, but even when he gave me the first option to buy, I didn't, because it was meant to be a family home. I couldn't live here alone, for one, and two, I had no car at that time. It just wasn't practical. That being said, I already had an idea in my head regarding a private practice, and this house was not practical for the purpose. But to cut a long story short—

Two years later, after he had finished this house and sold his other house in Kingston, his wife gave him the choice of a divorce or for him to pack up and leave Jamaica. So he requested that I try and get this house sold for him, and as a payment he also gave me the use of his car and a recommendation to be his successor. So along with the car I also inherited the hospital cottage. Mr Grey wasn't in charge of the real estate office at that time, but when he took over the office, I kept in touch with him, and between us, we kept the place in order while we waited for a buyer.

A year later, your present neighbours moved in, and around the same time I also bought my place up in Ocho Rios. When your father asked my opinion on the value of a house he was about to buy for his daughter and grandchildren, you can imagine the surprise when I heard the address and realised that he was asking about this place. So you see, it was just fate. I really had nothing to do with it. But I am so pleased that you are now the owner, and I will be happy to show you around."

"Wow, so in some sort of a way I will still have to thank you. This house has been sitting here without an owner all these years, and to think you are responsible for keeping it in good shape, not to mention Mr Budd taking over the garden. This is so unbelievable."

Lloyd laughed out loud.

"And a fitting fairy tale for such a fair lady; your magical gardener has to be a plus. I have not met him, but Mr Grey told me about the garden, and I must say he has done a marvellous job."

We left the steps to walk over to the rock garden. Doc confessed that he had not visited the house in a long while, and the planting out of the garden was ideal.

In-between the large white rocks were selected areas for a bloom of one sort or another. What was a surprise was that the landscape space from the street seemed to take up two plots, but once on the inside of the yard, the rock garden spread over half that space and left room behind it for a parking area to accommodate about three cars before the land rolled downhill.

A green bush hedging was planted along the edge of the rock face, marking out the edge of the property, which disappeared beyond the upstairs building. The property was on a hillside overlooking the roads below and looking out to the sea. We returned to the veranda, which seemed to be the only way into the building.

"Dad had recommended placing a grill around the veranda, but now I can see it up close, I think it would spoil the look." Lloyd agreed.

"When you look closely, you will see that this is security glass. And, see, it slides open to…"

"Wow. This is so interesting; I love it."

The camouflage entrance opened to a high wall with a cascading waterfall which was descending from an opening that allowed in the natural daylight. On either side of the green creeping plants were staircases: the one to the front of the house leading up, the other a shorter set of steps leading down.

I turned towards the side of the building which was visible from the outside yard. Lloyd held the bunch of keys, so he opened the door at the top of the stairs, which led into a sitting room; sheets were thrown over the seating.

Carpets were rolled up. Beyond the sitting area, a short staircase led up to the bedroom and bathroom, which were separated from the living area by a wooden lattice blind. I had first thought it was a large window before going up the stairs. There was no bed, but the walk-in closets and built-in dressers and mirrors were in excellent locations. And a door led to a balcony at the end of the building; one side hung over the indoor garden, and the other had an amazing view looking out to the ocean and overlooking the backyard. This was another 'wow'. I voiced that I could already envision myself sitting out there watching the moonlight on the sea.

"This is so amazing. Your doctor friend must have been broken-hearted to leave this behind."

Lloyd answered absentmindedly.

"His heart was in fact broken, and I am also feeling that he left it right here."

We stood for a moment in silence, looking out on the view, before he turned to face me and said,

"You know, Beth, I appreciate the way you think. When I was offered the house, I could not have lived here knowing that so much planning was put into realising his dream and then not to have been able to live here and enjoy it. Knowing all the efforts he went through to build it with such love.

But we are losing the daylight; let's have a look around the ground floor quickly."

Lloyd led the way down the stairs from the bedroom. We entered a spacious and well-designed fitted kitchen, which was on the same level as the back garden. The space between the kitchen and sitting room was on two other levels up: one was the dining room, which had a large table with matching chairs; on the other level was a reading area with bookshelves on either side of the walls. The sitting room, which was on the same level as the veranda, was a large empty room with window seats at the wide glassed windows looking out at the garden and towards the front gate.

"Wow, who would have thought? This is a prize. I love it, but we need to come back and spend a full day. I was just expecting a regular house."

There was a knocking at the gate. Lloyd asked:

"Would that be your neighbour? I can see an elderly man looking over the fence."

I left Lloyd to lock up and went towards the front gate.

"Oh, it is you, Ms Elizabeth. I did not recognise the car, so I thought I had better check. You can't be too careful these days, you know."

"Good evening, Mr Budd, I came by to show Doctor Cain the layout of the place, but I am afraid we ran out of daylight and time. I need to return to the office before it gets too late."

Mrs Budd was still sitting in the front passenger seat of their car. I again introduced Lloyd before we left to make our way back to the plaza.

When we got back to the office, Ms Mac was seated at her spot by the doorway; her husband and John were standing close to her.

"I am sorry, Ms Mac, but you didn't have to wait on me to get back. You could have locked up."

She came and whispered to me, concerned.

"You not upset, Miss Beth; your father did plan the little surprise for you. I know you would miss him, but…"

"No, no, Ms Mac." I gave her a tight hug. "I just left to show the doctor my new house. Thank you so much for making the cake and setting up the party. I really appreciate it very much; now you best get Mr Mac home. I know he don't like being on the road too late."

With Lloyd's help I was able to retrieve the emails; some I could reply to instantly, others I needed to make a note of, and work through the booking details.

"Well I best get you home, Mr Cain; you have been a tower of strength today. Youay, no way could I have done it without you."

"I thank you for your compliments, Mrs K, but I am driving you home, remember?"

On the drive home, he put in a CD of Ray Charles, so we were both humming to the songs as he drove. But my mind was on my new house. Lloyd pulled up, opened the gates and parked on the driveway.

"It really has been a long day. Would you like a hot drink, or do you need to get an early night?" I asked as I unloaded my bags on the kitchen table.

95

He went to put the kettle on.

"It isn't twelve midnight yet, so it's still your birthday. You sit, I will make the tea, and the news will be on the TV shortly if you don't mind me watching."

We watched the news of the day, then started a discussion on local and foreign affairs. One topic led to another and another, then he asked,

"Why did you decide to stay on in Jamaica with your dad?"

"Wow, that's all of five years ago, almost a lifetime. I realised that it was the second time he was asking, so I thought I should answer as honestly as I could, but I also returned to the story from the start, because without dad I would not have known Jamaica and experienced a rebirth. Dad would have told you that he won a ticket for two to Jamaica from a radio station in London.

We were tuned into the programme the Sunday evening, a week after they had called to say dad had won. We were, that is Rose, dad and myself, still full of excitement and congratulating dad and waiting for them to play the interview of dad accepting his prize. Mum was upstairs waiting for her phone call, which would come every Sunday evening from my older sisters.

But instead of a call there was a knock on the door. My sisters still had keys to the house and let themselves in, the knock was just to warn Mum that they had arrived. She came down the stairs almost instantly with one suitcase, dropped it at the bottom of the stairs and went up for another. Pauline hurried in to pick up that case and returned out the door, holding on to the handle with both hands, struggling as she went, and between breaths saying,

"Evening all, how you dad?"

We were looking at each other open-mouthed and flabbergasted. Then Patricia entered with her nose so high that she tripped on the worn carpet. Mother returned down the stairs with another suitcase.

"Mother dear," said Patricia. "You really have to think about selling this old house; it's getting so tacky, it's not even worth redecorating. Hello Daddy and Rose, 'and in the same breath', and how are you, Beth, my dear? Mother did mention you were home; I must say you are looking well. If you are still around when we get back, maybe we could do lunch. Come along, Mother, the traffic is awful, and you know how badly Pauline drives; we don't want to be late, do we? Goodbye, Daddy, take care."

She and Mum went through the door without another word. Pauline came back in for the other suitcase and hurried to kiss Dad quickly before wobbling her way out with the weight of the suitcase. I turned to Rose.

"What on earth was that all about? Where is she going? Did you know about this, Dad?"

Rose just shook her shoulders and said casually,

"It seems that they are off to Trinidad. Isn't that where Mum is from, Dad? She wanted to show off on you."

Rose laughed and continued, "She didn't think that you would have won the Jamaican trip. Heck, they are thinking that they are having the last laugh; what a joke."

We all had a good crack-up over the way it played out. But deep down I was mad. How could they have been so disrespectful? I had been away more than eleven years and had been out of touch, but what could have happened to warrant such bad behaviour towards Dad?

Rose went to the kitchen and returned with a couple of bottles of Babycham for us and a can of lager for Dad. We forgot about Mum and continued to celebrate Dad's good fortune. Later that week Rose and I went along with him to collect the prize, which came with spending money and hotel fees fully paid for a two-week vacation for two. I had only been back in London a couple of months and was still job hunting. Rose suggested I go along with Dad to Jamaica to find my roots. Because, as she put it, I had no job, so I had nothing to lose. She, on the other hand, had just been given a promotion and was also on probation; plus, she was also attending evening classes to get her managerial certificate. So it was agreed. She drove us to Heathrow, and we hugged and cried before saying our goodbyes.

I was sad, because had I not been in London, it would have been Rose going with Dad. Instead, she was going to be left alone in the house for two weeks all by herself. Our plane arrived in Kingston on a Friday evening. The sunshine was bright, and the landscape reminded me of Africa. We could see the coastline as we made the approach to the airport. The aircraft landed. Suddenly all the passengers were clapping. The lady next to Dad informed him that we had landed, and the clapping was to thank God and the captain for a safe landing.

It seemed a long and tiring process to collect our luggage. We both had two pieces each, but they were separated, arriving a good ten minutes apart. As we stepped out to the warmth of the evening, a taxi driver held up a sign with Dad's name on it. We were taken to a small hotel on Constant Spring Road. Dad used the opportunity to book the driver to take us to Clarendon the following day. He was so eager to see his old town; had we landed in daylight, we would have gone directly to Clarendon.

The following morning we drove out early, but it took a little longer than expected to find the exact location, with new roads, new buildings and some of the old landmarks gone. Trees were overgrown along the roadway, and names of streets were changed (or so Dad thought). But our driver was helpful and patient. Dad found the old church where he and his grandmother used to visit, then traced his footsteps back to the old house, but neglect over the years had left only one standing post and a few crumbled stone steps. Otherwise it was an open field with just an old broken-down shack.

With no one living close enough to the property for us to make any enquiries, he found and traced the remains of the gateway which led up to the foundation of the main house and kitchen. Dad was not able to return to bury his grandmother after getting the news of her death, but he did get in touch with her church and was told she was given a grand farewell.

We searched the area around the house for a grave spot but did not find one. The driver suggested we go back to the churchyard, as she may have been buried there, but we found nothing. Dad was a little disappointed but happy that he was at least able to show one of his girls where he once lived and went to school. Too soon the two weeks were getting to a close. I wanted to see a little more of the rest of the island for the remaining couple of days. The driver suggested we visit Dunn's River in Ocho Rios.

We were to spend two nights, then leave from the guest house directly to the airport. We arrived at our destination very early in the morning to an empty reception area and waited for more than half the day to be shown to our rooms. The lunch served was not more than a sandwich and was not well prepared. Luckily for us there was a white American couple who arrived at the same time as us and were intent on being vocal, demanding the attention of the manager. I was not happy with the situation, considering it was our last three days of our holiday and it was at my request that we left a comfortable place in Kingston to be treated so badly, putting a damper on our holiday which had been going so well.

Later that evening we made our way to the falls, notwithstanding the unpleasant situation, in the hope that it would be sorted on our return. The owner of the complex was present on our return and tried her best to organise what she felt had been a state of overbooking, but she was so flustered and disorganised she was not getting anywhere.

So I stepped in, out of my own impatience and frustration. In no time I got everyone placed in a room and then suggested that she should send out to a local restaurant to purchase our evening meals. I proceeded to take the orders and even went on the road with a taxi to collect food for fourteen of the guests. The manager never stopped apologising. We were told of the problems that the hotel faced, which started the week before, when several staff members got injured in an accident on their way to work. The bus they were travelling in had an accident and crashed. The staff and other passengers were taken to the hospital, leaving the hotel short of a front desk clerk and three other kitchen staff.

The following morning, while Dad and I were on our way to the craft market and the beach, the manager called me to her office and thanked me for jumping to her assistance on the previous day and offered us a discount on our stay. She then asked if I would consider accepting a job as a manager for the complex. Of course Dad and I had a good laugh, and we explained to her that we were on a holiday. Nevertheless, she gave me her card to call her if I had plans to return to Jamaica.

I thought that was the end of it, but it was so funny; Dad simply asked me while we were in the line waiting to be booked on the return flight home the following evening, "Beth dear, maybe it would not be such a bad idea to take up that offer at the guest house. After all, you are returning to the cold, which you dislike, and you have no job to return to, while, by the looks of it, that job is a sure thing. What do you think, why not give that manager a call? And it would be great to have you here when I return."

I looked at dad surprised but my mind went into a spin. If I were really honest, I had been daydreaming about the job offer and had no idea that Dad was seriously planning on returning to live in Jamaica. He patted me on the shoulder and winked.

"Nothing ventured, nothing gained, love. Go on; if the job is taken, we are still in line." He nodded at the line leading to the check-in desk.

"And will continue on our merry way."

I looked around in search of a phone box, then proceeded to make the call. The job was mine; I was to get a cab back to the guest house to start work the following day.

Lloyd clapped and said, "Bravo."

"Good for you, Beth. You jumping in and helping out paid off big time. But I was always under the impression that you and your dad were always together in this business here from the start."

"No, I started working at the guest house while he returned to London. But you had asked why I decided to stay? It was because of Dad why I got here, so his story had to be told. But the short answer is, I felt at home. I am not in a home away from home. Jamaica is my comfort zone; I am at peace, and my heart beats with joy just waking up in the mornings, rain or sunshine. I really would not want to be anywhere other than right here.

And to continue Dad's story, he returned six months later, after he had settled his affairs and given in his notice at work in England. He had also applied for early retirement. He was sixty-five that year, so they didn't have any objections to his application.

Rose returned with him on his second trip but stayed only ten days with us. After she left, I arranged for us to share a double room at the guest house so Dad and I could be together. He had enough funds to buy a comfortable home, so we took our time checking out the prices of properties around the area. It took just over six months to find this place. I maintained my apartment at the guest house because there was a lot of refurbishing and renovation needed to get this place looking as it is now.

Dad started the business small at first, just by being a taxi driver, then little by little he added other things and was doing pretty well. Until a few years ago someone broke in and robbed him. I guess it was the usual thing; he became a target with the fact that he was a so-called Englishman and was assumed to have bags of money. Which, in a way, that particular day he did. I must admit that my dad somehow had that Midas touch; he was good at crunching numbers too.

Before he left England, he also bought a property for Rose because he wasn't comfortable leaving her on her own with Mum and the others. So when she returned to London, it was to her own apartment. The property had a shop downstairs and was rented to maintain the payment of the mortgage.

Dad always had a long-term view on any venture or plans he came up with. He had plans for a business because he bought and took home to Jamaica a van, the jeep which he customised for himself, and the Mini which I now drive. They were all used vehicles in need of repairs. His plan was to take his own time to repair each one himself with the assistance of Mr Wright, who now owned the garage Dad started. I later found out that the reason Dad was robbed was that he had collected a large sum of money that very morning. It was legal money as far as Dad was concerned.

Another businessman he had been working alongside encouraged him to put a sum of cash in a partner draw plan, which was supposed to pay out double each month. Dad thought that it was too good to be true, but, as he later told me, he had an aim in view, so he took up the gamble. He said for more than a year, while driving home, he had taken notice of the "For Sale" sign at the plaza where we now operate the business and started getting ideas. So when the offer was made, he calculated that three months' money was all he needed to make a purchase or to deposit in order to obtain the plaza.

So the day he collected his jackpot, he went directly to the owner of the property and was able to negotiate a cash price towards the purchase of the plaza. He had no idea that he was being followed by a group of men whose aim was to take back the monies, and they didn't bargain on him having a plan to pass the cash on to someone along the way. They held him up by the gate, ripped out everything from the van and still couldn't find the money, so they trashed the house and beat him until his neighbours went to his rescue. It was after that I gave up my job at the guest house and moved in to look after him and got involved in assisting with the business. He didn't tell me about the robbery until a good while after I had moved in, when he felt sure they were no longer interested in finding the money.

But during that time he changed how he did business and who he did business with. He registered the company name, got the computers, and put in alarms around the house, and then he told me his plan. I already had inside information on the travel and hotel business. So we went the route of setting up a travel agency in one of the shops at the plaza, selling tickets and arranging transportation to and from the airports. Later we would even book rooms and plan day excursions to beach attractions and holiday spots we would recommend. The way Dad operated, most people thought we were just another tenant and not the owners of the plaza.

I was distracted by the TV; the Jamaican anthem was being played before signing off, which it did at twelve midnight each night. I got up to turn it off.

Lloyd went towards the kitchen with the tray of empty cups and plates. I followed, and he then said,

"My final birthday duty: I am leaving your kitchen as I found it. I must say I really admire your father. I am only sorry I didn't spend more time with him as a friend. What time will your sister be coming in tomorrow?"

"Jacky! Her flight should be in at six. But that will be on Friday. Tomorrow I have the helper coming to help me straighten up the rooms. But I can't help feeling a little disappointed for Jacky. She had been talking to Dad and making arrangements to be married, so she is actually coming in with her fiancée. Her plan was to surprise me. The last time I saw her was about eight years ago; I was travelling to Switzerland to see my children who were in boarding school over there. There I was, walking towards the boarding gate. A group of flight attendants were walking towards me. A tall, attractive female pilot took off her hat and smoothed back her hair. Her actions reminded me so much of my sister I smiled and kept my eyes on her because of her complexion.

She noticed me, and her face lit up. We ran to hug each other. I could not believe how much Jacky had changed. When we were growing up, Jacky was the tomboy in the family; she was just rough. At five years old she went to the local barber shop and had her hair cut short. I had never seen her in a skirt or dress. At the age of fourteen, when we were developing breasts and wearing make-up, she was flat-chested and totally clumsy. Her friends were all boys, and you could not pick her out of the crowd. She even joined the Boy Scouts, and they did not find out she was a girl until they went camping.

She got into a scuffle with the police, then she went off on a boat all the way to Alaska for months. The police were involved, as she was reported missing, and we gave her up as dead until she just turned up on the doorstep, knocking so loud it would wake the dead. All she said was,

"Sorry, I lost my keys."

She was unbelievable but a lot of fun. So to see her that day with breasts, long hair pulled back into a ponytail, lipstick, and most of all, her complexion and shape had changed completely. And she was now a pilot, actually flying the aircraft, which was not surprising. That day I had to rebook my ticket because we started chatting until I missed my flight."

Lloyd's head was resting on his hand; his eyes gave way to sleep, and his head almost touched the table as he nodded. I laughed as he tried to cover his actions after a jerk of his head.

"Mr Cain, your birthday duties are officially up. You really need to get some sleep, and you will be no good to a sick person if you are not rested."

"I know. It must have been that hot drink; I am suddenly so tired. Beth, you won't mind if I crash in the spare room, please? I don't have an early start, thank goodness. My duties at the hospital start on the two p.m. shift, so it will give me time to get home and change."

"You will have to stay; I can't afford for you to drive home when you are so tired."

He made his way through to the back veranda to the spare room. I turned out the lights and made sure I set my alarm for six a.m., knowing Gertrude would be coming to clean up.

Chapter Five

Day Four

I was up at five a.m., before the clock alarmed. But I was still on the bed when my cell phone vibrated on the bedside table. I answered before it started to ring.

"Hello, good morning."

"Hi sis, morning. Sophia told me she called you to let you know that the twins will be coming with us. The flight should be in on Sunday at two thirty. We are all ready to go here; I am just on my way to my workplace to pick up my cheques and collect our tickets. Have you heard anything from Mum?" Rosemary sounded excited and in a good place.

"No," I replied. "But Patricia called to say that they will be in Jamaica sometime next week and that they will be staying in a hotel in Montego Bay."

"Oh thank God, I am so happy she won't be staying near us. Beth, we have so much to talk about. I can't wait to get there. Looking forward to seeing you on Sunday. Bye, sis."

I got up to pull open the window curtains, in time to see Gertrude entering the street gate. I hurried to unlock the grill.

"Ms Beth, morning. you up early man. The yard well want a good sweeping, so I going to start out here."

She continued in a loud singsong, cheerful voice.

"Me wearing me working clothe already because me have to leave here before twelve o'clock. A send me son to Spanish Town to buy goods from the wholesale yesterday. Him should be on a country bus in Kingston right now waiting to come back down, so I have to meet him at Turtle River to help him with the load. Miss Beth, you never plan to turn out you father room today? Me time short, but Saturday me will get me son to come and help me."

I heard the statement Gertrude made, but did not quite understand it fully, so I dismissed it but continued to answer.

"Just my room, the sitting room and veranda, thank you, Ms Gertrude. I was so tired last night I fell asleep fully dressed, so I will be in the shower. No need to call."

The yard was large enough, so I figured I would be out before she was finished. I had already removed all of my clothes from my wardrobe and chest of drawers and placed them on Dad's bed. I quickly stripped my toiletries from the bathroom and went to shower in Dad's bathroom.

For as long as I had been living with my dad, I had been into his bedroom from time to time but never in the bathroom and was surprised that it was so well lit once the curtains were drawn. A narrow glass louvre window ran along the length of the spacious bathroom. On leaving the bathroom, Dad had a sitting area with his old furniture taken from London: a comfy single-seater chair, a large leather recliner which was his favourite chair when we were children, a bookshelf and a large round centre table placed on an old red carpet rug.

I pulled the cords of the curtain wider, which revealed larger but similar windows to the bathroom, except it had an iron grill to the inside.

Below that was a built-in wardrobe using up the width of the room. There was also a pulley to open the glass window. The fresh air made such a difference; the window was too high to see outside except for the sky, but the cool breeze and fresh smell of the sea, which was not more than a half mile away from our backyard, drifted through the room. We had no access to the beach over the rocks. But a dirt and gravel road ran to the side of our property; the path was used by all who wanted to swim and use the beach. Our yard was separated from the path by a high stone wall. To the back of our property, Dad planted out a thick line of thorn bushes which was as high as the house. In front of the bush was a wire fence and flowering plants.

The garden was neatly arranged with seating in selected places. Our front yard had most of the large trees on the side facing Dad's window. The gate and driveway were quite wide, allowing for two cars to be parked. A row of bright flowering blooms was a delight when I opened my window in the mornings. The remainder of the front yard was paved.

Along the stone wall were tomatoes, peppers, and whatever else Dad could plant—or maybe it would be better to say what would grow. Gertrude was already cleaning my room as I passed. She asked, in her loud singsong voice:

"You sister them coming Ms Beth? Your father tell me him have seven girls, I hope them coming to help you."

So as not to shout, I went back and spoke to her directly from the doorway.

"One of my sisters will be coming in tomorrow with her husband," I replied. "They will be using my room."

110

"Oh, so that's why you move out your things them."

She shouted from the bathroom. I reached the kitchen and started gathering the ingredients I needed. I felt it better to prepare a lunch rather than a breakfast for Lloyd. I was also sweeping and cleaning the kitchen at the same time, feeling a little relieved that Gertrude would be leaving early, for more than one reason. She, 'thank God', continued her work quickly and quietly, and in no time was already working on the veranda.

"You food smell nice Ms Beth, you can dish out some for me in a container, it's soon eleven o'clock, I better deal with the back room."

She was making her way through the kitchen when I stopped her.

"No, I will take care of the back room later, and I still have some things all over the floor. You can use my bathroom to change when you are ready."

"Alright miss, you notice that I never use the electric polisher."

She held up a bottle in hand.

"My sister sent me this from foreign, she says that it is a self-shinning polish for tiles. So me use it on your floor because is board floor I have at my house. I don't have tile, so tell me if you like it when I come back next week."

She left to change and came back with red shoes and a matching red handbag, which she pulled and dusted off from her market bag. The scarf which was wrapped around her head was replaced by her well-styled hairdo.

She covered the container I had shared out with the food tightly and placed it in her market bag, then came closer to me and whispered,

"Ms. Beth, me know that your family big. But a begging you two long sleeve shirt and two church pant for me big boy. Him and you father always get on good, and him even carry him go fishing with him sometimes. But I will have to leave you now, miss, so have a good day."

I walked her to the veranda and closed the grill. Returning inside with the intention of knocking on Lloyd's door, I saw he was entering the kitchen, fully dressed with his overnight bag in hand.

"You beat me to it; I was just about to come see if you are still alive."

"Good morning, Beth, I couldn't sleep any longer. The aroma of your cooking is so sweet I needed to savour its taste."

I laughed. "I see that you were well prepared." I pointed to his overnight case. "I was getting ready to lend you one of Dad's shirt."

"Guilty about being prepared. I always pack for a few days because more than often I have to do back-to-back duties at the hospital. But trust me, I am totally rested. I slept like a baby, and your water pressure here is great; I thoroughly enjoyed that shower. Do you happen to have a thermos flask?"

"Yes, dad has one. Why do you ask?"

"Can I fill it with coffee to take along with me for later? My electric kettle stopped working last week, and I clean forgot to replace it."

I started looking around for the thermos, but he dropped his bag and started to open the other cupboards.

"I will find it; you go ahead and share the breakfast—or I should say it's now lunchtime. What are we having?"

"Well, considering that I am now serving lunch and not breakfast, I fried some slice fish, after cutting them into thin strips, then added some shrimps with lots of onion and scotch bonnet peppers. The side dish will be oven-roasted sweet and Irish potatoes. And the vegetables will be cabbage, string beans and carrots steamed in coconut milk, not forgetting the tomatoes and cucumbers. For drinks, I juice that soursop the Budd's gave me yesterday, and I also baked an apple pie."

"Oh wow, my mouth is dripping; can't wait to taste."

We practically eat in silence, because every now and again I surprise myself and cook a really sweet-tasting meal, which I also enjoy. Lloyd smacked his lips as he closed his knife and fork.

"Thank you, I enjoyed that. You do know I will be a repeat customer," he said, raising his eyebrows and smacking his lips. We both roared with laughter, remembering my own comments of the day before. He left the table first.

"Let me help you to wash up; I like to get to the hospital before the doctor on duty goes off. It save a lot of time knowing for myself how they diagnose each patient. But can I request a take away on my apple pie?"

We tidied the kitchen together and joined in the singing of 'Cherry O Baby' being played on the radio. He returned to the bathroom to brush and refresh his mouth and adjusted his overnight case before collecting the thermos.

I placed the pie dish in a carrier bag along with some ripe bananas.

We turned from the kitchen table at the same time and brushed against each other. If I were sixteen, I would have run from the kitchen with a silly giggle.

If I were trying to seek his attention, I would have used the opportunity wisely. But I wasn't ready. I stepped back, a little too quickly, and then pretended I was reaching for an extra fruit to place in the bag. I turned around only when I knew he had gone out the door. At the gate, I waited until he was settled in his car and had started the engine before I handed over the bag, then wished him a safe journey. I then walked back to the house a little uneasy and restless; no way did I want to follow my heart.

This situation was much too abstruse.

I went directly to Dad's room and started to shift the furniture from the sitting area facing the bathroom, then pulled the bed into a new position, placing the headboard up against the wall opposite the bathroom door.

It was perfect; there was now a massive space at the entrance of the room. My phone rang, sending my heart into a spin, and I was thankful when I heard the motherly voice.

"Ms Beth, I leave some lunch for you, you alright miss?"

I suddenly remembered the e-mails.

"Afternoon, Ms Mac. I am on my way. I was just doing some house cleaning, but I sorted out the e-mails, and I also have some cheques signed to be collected for tomorrow, so see you in a while."

"Okay, drive carefully, Miss. One more thing, miss, please can you return the containers, a running out of them now."

She chuckled over the phone.

I collected my briefcase and made my way to the office and was happy for a few hours getting back into the working-girl Beth. Later, on my way home, I thought of my home in Savoy Mews and the other bedrooms and garden which I was yet to view. I dialled the Budds' phone. They were chirpy as usual, and we kept up a conversation until I turned into my old driveway.

I returned to continue rearranging Dad's room, leaving just the easy chair and centre table. It was a struggle, but I got the recliner around to the back veranda. Mopped and dusted the back room before changing the sheets on the bunk bed. As I pulled the sheets from the bed Lloyd had slept on the previous night, my phone rang.

"Goodnight, my darling."

I froze. "Goodnight yourself, what time is it?"

"Way past ten, my pet. I hope I did not wake you."

"No, you didn't; a matter of fact, I am just about finishing up my house cleaning, so your timing is good."

"Great, I won't keep you long; I have had a very hectic evening, and the crowd came in after six. I am about to hit the sack."

We were both silent, for me because I suddenly became nervous remembering our encounter earlier that day. Lloyd's voice sounded low and sleepy on the other end of the phone when he asked.

"Beth, are you standing?"

I replied, "Yes, I am."

He whispered, "Ok, I am standing behind you, and I have my arms around your waist. I am kissing you ever so lightly on the neck, whispering sweet words in your ear, Sleep well, my pet. Goodnight."

The phone clicked off. I was left standing trapped in a trance with an awesome, intriguing and sweet feeling, and the image of this man holding me in that spot for God knows how long.

Trapped in that position, my mind wandered. I had just turned nineteen and graduated after completing a two-year course in fashion designing.

I had passed my City and Guilds with flying colours and was recommended to take up an internship with a fashion house in France. But it also meant another year's further college work, while I ran errands between fashion houses as part of my work experience. Dad was not keen to send me away from home, given that Jacky had left home under dramatic and trying circumstances, and Sophia was also about to leave home to board with a family in Oxford, where she was expected to study nursing.

My teacher persuaded Dad that I would be just fine because I was her best student and I would make them both proud. So I was allowed to go.

I was on my own in France. It was hard work and lots of late nights. Worse, I did not speak French, and most of my homework, questions and assignments were presented in French. So I suffered most nights trying to translate before I could write my paper. In London I was the bright student and had time to assist others. Here, I was a fish out of water, and, being the only Black student in the class, and worse, I did not speak the language, so I was ignored by my teacher and classmates.

I returned to my boarding house late one evening after being sent across town to deliver couture lace to one of our designers. The canteen at my hostel was closed, so I went across the street to a sidewalk café.

I was tired, hungry and feeling sorry for myself. I just was not getting the translation right. I had ordered a coffee and fries from the waiter without a second glance in his direction. He returned and stood over my shoulder for longer than I felt he should have, and I was about to let him know when he took the pencil from my hand and erased what I had written, replacing it with what I knew were the words I was looking for. Then he said in perfect English:

"Your French is not very good, is it?"

"How about non-existent?" I replied.

"But thank you for the help."

He continued without even giving me a second glance.

"If you leave your notes with me, I could translate them for you and return them tomorrow night. I am working for my friend tonight, but I can meet you here tomorrow."

Someone called "waiter", and he turned to continue his job. Needless to say, I jumped at the chance. That was how I had met David, my husband.

He was from Nigeria and on a full scholarship doing political law and history. He happened to be working that night for another student and friend who was training to be a doctor but was not as fortunate as himself and had to work to pay his way. Whenever his friend had to stay late at the library or on hospital duties, David would volunteer to work for him. This I found out the following evening when I met up with three of his college friends, all from different countries in Africa.

They all spoke different languages, which included some French and, for the most part, very good English. With David in their corner assisting them to keep their jobs while they studied, they bonded as a great team. I was now part of that team and the only female. However, I was also on a full scholarship; my food and board were paid for, and I even got a stipend for pocket money. For a few hours we would meet on most evenings, including Saturdays and Sundays.

Once our homework was done, the main topic of conversation was politics and Africa. And being men, from time to time the conversation strayed to women. They all spoke and understood English, so I was able to defend my female counterparts and was never left out of a conversation. With David translating my notes, I soon moved up in my class to be among the top four. My grades allowed me an internship at a top fashion house for the second year and a guarantee of obtaining full-time employment.

But summer holidays were to separate the group. I was returning to London to prepare for another year from home. David was staying on in Paris to undertake a work-study assignment. He had completed his course of study and was awaiting his results. Two of our friends graduated and were on their way home. The other changed his course of study and was attending classes in the evenings while he took on a day job.

We all exchanged names and addresses as we parted for the summer. Once I was back in London, I realised how much I was missing the group and, in particular, David. When his letter arrived, I was over the moon. His request was that I should return a couple of weeks before my work appointment because he wanted to celebrate his exam results and also my birthday. And he had plans to take me on a trip across Europe.

Of course, I could not let my dad know, not even Rose. I came up with a reason to convince my dad why I had to leave home earlier than planned. He was not happy to be missing my birthday, but he baked me a cake to take on my return to France. When I disembarked from the ferry, David was waiting. We ran into each other's arms like long-lost lovers. I recorded my first romantic kiss. When he reluctantly released me, we laughed like young children, and he took my case in one hand and held my hand in the other while we ran along the crowded sidewalk. I stopped to catch my breath. And asked.

"So are you taking me on a long-distance run around Europe?"

He scooped me up, spun us around before planting another kiss on my lips, then pointing to a road bike with a sidecar.

"Here we are, my princess; I rented this for our trip."

I was terrified but tried not to show it as he strapped my suitcase to the back of the cab and then placed a helmet on my head. I held on for dear life but soon settled down as David showed off his driving skills, moving effortlessly through the busy traffic of Paris, then on to the open road of the countryside. Our journey took us through Paris, to Brussels, to Rotterdam, to Cologne, to Luxembourg, through Charleville, then back to Paris. We would stop for dinner each night at a roadside inn, a guest house or motel along the way. On our fourth night we drove off the beaten track and found a most charming castle by a lake. We spread our blanket on the grass in the warm summer night, drinking champagne from the bottle and eating cheese and crisps. The mood was set, and kissing was not enough. David told me he loved me. I knew that if he felt half as much as how I was feeling, then it had to be love.

We arrived back in Paris and went to my hostel, but I was a day too early, and they would not book me in. So after a lot of pleading, even an offer to pay the extra, I was still turned away. He had no choice but to take me to his place. I sneaked into a five-star hotel where David's family owned a four-bedroom apartment. The bathroom was almost the size of my apartment at the hostel. It was then I was told he was a prince. Yet he gave me as little information as he could about his family, except that he never saw his dad, who he thought had no real interest in him anyway. He lived with his uncle at the apartment. That night I was expected to be extra quiet so as not to make my presence known. The thought of a prince from Africa meant very little to me. I only knew about the Royal Family in England. I dismissed most of what he told

120

me. In the weeks that followed the start of my new term, we were no longer able to meet in the evenings as we did before the summer. His friends were no longer in Paris, and we were both working and more often than not having to do overtime.

Our only spare time was on a Sunday. He would arrange a meeting at a different hotel each weekend, where we would have breakfast and then spend the remainder of the day in bed if it was a rainy or cold day. On a nice day we visited the plaza. He insisted that I try on shoes or dresses just to see how I would look. I fitted rings and necklaces, pretending we wanted to buy. On two occasions he did present me with a pendant and a charm bracelet which I didn't view in the shop, and when it was his birthday at the end of October, he gave me an engagement ring.

I was overjoyed at the gesture but kept it a secret from my family, for no particular reason. But it just seemed as if it were just the two of us and no one or nothing else mattered. But too soon it was the end of November, and he had just a week remaining in Paris. I was invited to be with him at his graduation, after which we would have just two days, and he had to return to Kenya at his mother's request.

He showed me the ticket sent by his mother and the letter requesting him to return as soon as possible. No other explanation. I requested the three days off work, but my boss wasn't having it; we were preparing for a fashion show in December. I was allowed to be off on his graduation day, provided I worked the following Sunday. I had made myself a simple dress which fitted my budget and was quite sure that I would be as stunning as always. David wanted us to stay at a hotel on the Tuesday night; the graduation would be at two p.m. on the following day.

After dinner in the hotel dining room, we later returned to our own room, where he presented me with a couple of packages. I was told to fit them in the bathroom for my own satisfaction. I was not to allow him to see me, because he wanted to be surprised the following day.

When I opened the packages and realised that I had been presented with a complete outfit. An absolutely exquisite peach chiffon dress, with a pearl-beaded empire-line bodice. The skirt falling just above my knees. Strappy stiletto high-heeled shoes and a matching beige pillbox hat with a short lace veil, a pretty little lace bag and gloves. It all fitted perfectly.

I laughed at myself. Now I understood why he insisted on me trying on all those dresses in the mall. We were to dress for breakfast the following morning. He wore a brown woollen three-piece suit and just happened to find a peach shirt to match my dress. We certainly didn't go unnoticed.

After breakfast he said he wanted to meet up with a fellow graduate, and he insisted that we walk to the location. When we entered the building, if there was a sign, I did not happen to notice, but I sat in a small waiting room while he spoke to a clerk at the desk. Soon we were led into a small prayer room. It was almost a miniature church, with a large cross in the stained window. There were candles and flowers at the altar. We sat in silence. Each time I tried to whisper to him, he would place a finger to his lips. A young couple joined us, the young woman holding a young baby in her arms.

The young man with her I recognised as one of our friends from the café and waved.

We were interrupted by a white male, well dressed in a dark grey pinstripe suit. Behind him, a white woman followed, wearing a grey suit with a very nice scarf arranged around the neckline. She carried a black book and a folder in her hand. The man nodded towards us, and David took hold of my hand, and we stepped forward. He turned to face me, and in that instant I realised what was about to take place.

We were married. His friend and his wife were our witnesses.

We left the registrar's office and went to have lunch. A lot of congratulations and excitement was all around us when people became aware that we were newlyweds. The graduation went off well, and we danced the night away. I was taken to his apartment late at night. He had expected his uncle to be there, but the apartment was empty, so we made the most of it for the night. We were still in bed when the door to our bedroom opened the following morning. I heard David shout in surprise.

"Dad?"

I melted under the sheets. I refused to leave the room because all I had to wear was the dress I was married in, and it just was not appropriate. So my suitcase was sent for from the hostel before I was able to have a bath and change.

"Well, good day to you, Elizabeth. My dear, I have to apologise to you and my son. I had every intention of attending his graduation, but a last-minute meeting with our ambassador last night prevented me from doing so. David informs me that you are my daughter-in-law; permit me to congratulate you."

The man standing in front of me was a giant of a Black man in every way, and he spoke the Queen's English with perfection. I held my hand out timidly, but he drew me to his chest, smothering me and announcing with certainty.

"Welcome, my daughter. As soon as David takes you home, we will give you a proper wedding ceremony."

I was then introduced to the other four giants sitting around the dining table, with David assuring me that they were forced to wait for me before starting the meal. David appeared still happy, winking at me every chance he got; likewise, the men all continued to pat him on the shoulder each time they got up to refill their plate from the abundance of dishes laid out on the side table. His father did most of the talking.

"David I know that your mother will be disappointed at not having you home with her, but with your knowledge and training…You can be my right-hand man in Nigeria. I have been given the opportunity to be assistant to our ambassador in London. This will give our company an advantage, and by the end of my five years, our company will be the biggest Black-owned business in Nigeria. I know you will do great things with the company. Your older brothers I have no confidence in and would not allow them to be part of the company regardless of what their mother thinks. Now, Elizabeth my dear, your passport will be ready for you to travel in the morning. You and David can travel home on the jet; I won't need it in London. I love to roam around in London;

it's my favourite city, just as Paris seems to be my son's favourite city." he said, giving me a wide grin and a wink.

Most of what was said after that went in one ear and out the other. But after what had been our lunch… The men all gathered in a section of the sitting room and began shuffling papers around and were clearly discussing business, all speaking in a language I wasn't familiar with. I made myself comfortable in another corner of the room, wondering if I would still have a job to go back to… and how I would explain being married to my dad. The marriage certificate in my hand said clearly that I was now Mrs David Kworori. I was twenty-one years old on my last birthday, so I had no need for my dad to consent, but I am sure that he would have thought that one day he would have walked me down the aisle.

A few hours later, four of the men gathered their cases and shook my hand before leaving.

His father took one last swallow from his glass and stubbed out his cigar before holding out both hands towards me. As an obedient child, I walked into his arms.

"Bless you, my daughter; I know that my son will make you happy. And when, or I dare say if, his mother arrives in Nigeria, don't be too worried; she is more bark than bite." He roared with laughter.

He kissed me on my forehead before releasing me, then turned to do the same to David. "As soon as I am settled, son, we will celebrate."

Then he was escorted to the door, and his cases were given to a waiting bellboy. The man remaining was his uncle Steffan, his father's youngest brother. He took David to one side of the room, and they sat deep in conversation, with David being on the receiving end, nodding in agreement with what was being said. Later that night David again tried to explain his family and his position in his family, but I still could not take it all in. The following morning we were stepping onto a private jet on our way to Nigeria.

Day Five

A noise coming from the backyard woke me. I was still in the back room, sprawled out and entangled in the bedsheets. Once I released my body and was able to look out through the back veranda,

John was busy stacking up chairs and folding tables up against the shrubs.

"John. Good morning, what is this all about?"

"Good morning, Ms Beth. It's for the domino games tomorrow night, miss, but I had to drop them off today because I have a pickup in MoBay in the morning. Sorry if I woke you, but I wouldn't get another chance."

"That's okay, John. When you get to the office, please remind Ms Mac that I will be going into Kingston later today, so I won't have time to stop."

I returned to the room and allowed my body to drop with a thud on the bed, feeling as if I had been swimming for hours and had been dragged from the water just in time before my body gave out.

I took a few deep breaths and did hand stretches to relax. The house phone rang, and I ran to the sitting room to pick it up.

126

"Thank God! I have been trying your other numbers, and they kept going into voicemail. I am Debbie Stewart; I went on a road trip with you last year. Is this PauliMay Travel?"

"Yes, we are; how may I help?" I asked.

"Sorry for the late notice, but I have to attend a funeral in St Mary this Sunday, and I need a pickup from the Norman Manley Airport. Can you help? I am booked on the six o'clock from Miami later today. Please say you will be able to pick me up."

I took her details and assured her that I would be there. But to drop her off in St Mary would mean returning home via the Junction Road, not the best route for night driving, but with my sister and her husband travelling with me, at least I would have company for the rest of the journey home. I reached for the diary to check that I had not missed any of our appointments. Thankfully the only one on the books was for John. So I relaxed and started to plan my day. First, I wanted to visit some furniture shops in the town before heading to Kingston.

The space I vacated in Dad's room was large enough to accommodate a chest of drawers and a dresser, but first I needed to complete the job I started the night before. I hurriedly made up the bed in the back room, trying hard not to think about Lloyd. I was having my coffee when the mechanic returned my own car. We chatted for a while, and he offered to wash the Jeep while I got dressed. Dad always said never collect a customer in a dirty car.

Later, at the furniture shop, I found a dresser and chest of drawers which fit in with what was already in Dad's room, and the salesman insisted I also take the rug on display for a bargain price. I agreed only because I could afford it, but I didn't think it was a bargain at all and told him so.

He just laughed and told me that I should not be afraid to spend some of my husband's money. The conversation would have gone on all afternoon, with him pointing out some other things he was sure I needed. He was interrupted by a shopper who recognised me and started making enquiries about the funeral arrangements for Dad. On hearing about my father's death, I was offered a further discount on the rug.

I made my way through Fern Gully with deep concentration on the road, as there is always a driver willing to take his chance around one of the blind bends. The winding road took me over the hills, to the River Road and through Spanish Town in good time. Both flights were expected to land within twenty minutes of each other, but that was small comfort, as more often than not the time spent retrieving the luggage and being searched at customs would spoil the wait. I was pleasantly surprised when Jacky strolled out behind the group of aircraft attendants. She stopped at the exit, looking intensely at the waiting crowd. I shouted, "Sis," and waved to her.

She blew me a kiss and went back on the inside. Another ten minutes and she was walking out with her husband-to-be. He was pulling two large suitcases while she carried a number of smaller bags. They already looked like the ideal couple. Both were golden brown and also similar in height.

We hugged and kissed after being introduced. He had a deep bass voice and spoke and acted sweet and gentle towards Jacky. I explained that we had to wait on a passenger who had called me at the last minute and apologised for having to travel with her part of the way.

"That's understandable; no need to worry about us, it's your job," remarked Jack.

I was happy that Dad had the foresight. He had a luggage rack made for the roof of the jeep, which came in handy, because Debbie arrived with three oversized suitcases. We got help from men who were waiting on the pavement to strap them securely in place before heading through Kingston then over the hills of St Andrew. A little over an hour later…

"We are coming up to Devon Pen. Debbie, is your home before or after we enter the square?" I asked.

Debbie replied after my second attempt at the question, after rubbing her eyes and yawning aloud.

"You would need to turn left as we enter the square," she said, clearing her throat a few times.

I did so ten minutes later. There were several cars parked in the square. The shops were still open, and a few vendors and groups of people had gathered outside the shop doors. The narrow lane was dark and lonely, and I was more than happy when she instructed me to pull up under the upcoming street light, which was so dim I wasn't sure it even served a purpose other than a mark for her gate.

I stopped the jeep and turned off the engine but kept the headlights on. No house was visible in the dark. The minute she opened the door to step out, a pack of dogs rushed towards the open door barking. She screamed and closed the door. My sister became frightened and concerned.

"Oh my God, Beth, be careful; stay in the vehicle."

I pressed on the horn, which made the dogs bark even louder.

"What is your mother's name, Debbie?" I asked.

She told me, and I lowered my window to shout.

"Miss Gracie! Miss Gracie!"

As loud as I could manage over the racket the dogs were making.

A light shone through the thickness of the bush.

"Is who that, who is there?" came a reply.

Debbie shouted back.

"Is me mama, is me Debbie."

Several windows and doors became visible as squares of light shining through the darkness. Shadows of men, women , and children were coming towards the jeep. The dogs were told to stop the commotion and were shooed away. Miss Gracie came towards my window.

"Debbie me daughter, me so glad fi know you come, you uncle a try fi call you phone for over six weeks now and he can't get you."

She broke down crying. Debbie got out of the vehicle to console her. Someone asked.

"Where you suitcase, what you bring?"

I pointed them to the rack on top of the jeep, and the younger boys were on top in no time. They loosened the ropes, and the suitcases were moving off into the darkness. Debbie returned to the jeep to collect her handbag and handed me an envelope. Her mother returned also with a market bag of ground provisions.

"Thank you miss, and God go with you. Take you time and get home safely."

I started the engine and carefully turned the jeep around with just about everyone giving me instructions like, 'Touch back a little bit more, bend up the wheel now, come forward little more, etc.' When I got back to the square, it was still abuzz with people.

"Sis they do great fry chicken at that restaurant. Would you like me to get some for you and Jack?"

She slipped gingerly from the arms of her sleeping husband.

"Poor baby, he is still asleep, but go ahead; I would love some."

She stayed in the jeep while I loaded up with three boxes of fried chicken and cold drinks for the continued drive home.

"Wait, Beth, let me get to the front with you so Jack can have all the seat to stretch his legs. He has been going nonstop for days, travelling from Australia to New Zealand, then to England, from London to New York, then to Miami to meet up with me before getting here, so, poor baby, he has had a long trip; no surprise he is flaked out."

She settled herself into the passenger seat, unwrapping the festival which came with the chicken.

"So, how much further? These roads are so dark and narrow, and the drivers have no manners. Why don't anyone dim their headlights? It's so rude."

I laughed, because it's a constant cry, even from the same drivers, who complain when they are unable to see. But I am spared because the jeep is high, so I am above the gleam of most of the oncoming lights, and when I am in my Mini, it's a left-hand drive so I am also at an advantage.

I spread a towel over my lap to catch any crumbs, took a long sip of my cola champagne, and said a short prayer to myself before continuing our journey.

"Well, we are halfway there, and thankfully, the roads at this time of the night are never busy, so we should be home in a couple of hours."

"This chicken is so good. And look at you. I am impressed at your driving. I guess you had lots of practice driving in Africa."

We both laughed.

"Funnily enough, in Africa I was never allowed to drive out anywhere on my own. We had drivers to take us everywhere."

"You are kidding me. So you really were – sorry, are – married to a prince? I don't mean to pry, but what happened? Dad said you have been here in Jamaica for as long as he has, so what about your kids? Don't you have any plans to go back?"

"It's a long story, sis, a very long story."

"Well, I am all ears. If we are only halfway, then we have a long journey ahead. Care to share?"

For a moment my mind went blank, and I said nothing. My thoughts were jumping from one incident to another because I had not been able to even think through my story from the start without leaving out parts, and I wasn't sure even now that I was over the hurt. But I felt the need to tell Jacky something.

I knew they say the beginning is always the best place to start, so:

"David and I met and were married in Paris." Jacky laughed.

"That is also a surprise. How did you get to Paris in the first place?"

I explained to her how it was and why it was.

"Anyway, the very same day we got married, his father sent us to Nigeria. David was to sit in for his father, who was given the position of assistant to the ambassador for Nigeria in London.

He stopped in Paris to brief David and also to prevent him from travelling to Kenya, where his mother lived. When his parents were separated, his mother took their first three sons under her wing. But his father insisted that the young David should have a chance to spend time with him in London, where they were living at the time. David was then ten years old. David's mother was a high-ranking queen mother and head of her tribe in Kenya and was an independent woman with a lot of power. His father was the son of a King in Nigeria and equally powerful. (David remembered that his mother always said that they were two bulls in one pen.) Later, when his father took on a second wife, David asked to live with his uncle in France.

After hearing his story, I often thought that David got married to me in order to have a reason to stay on in France. But his father's new position happened by chance, so as things changed and moved without a plan, so did we.

So I was the king's daughter-in-law and wife to the head of a prominent oil company overnight. The problem was that I had no idea that my husband was living a double life. He had returned to Nigeria before starting his degree in Paris. His mother took that opportunity to have an arranged marriage for him to a girl from Kenya who was his own age. They got together each summer when he returned for summer holidays. They had two girls together, but he wasn't ready to settle down, so he spent another three years in France until he met and got married to me.

My saving grace was his father's mother; she took me under her wing as soon as we got to Nigeria. When she found out that we got married without my family knowing, she asked for my father's address, then took me back to England to apologise for me, and she apologised on behalf of David and even offered to pay a dowry for me. It seemed funny at the time, but Dad was pleased that I was under her care.

David often travelled to Kenya to see his mother but never offered to take me. His excuse was that he had not planned the trips; they just happened. The fact that she never asked about me never bothered me. Our children were four and five years old and were being home-schooled at the request of his father's mother, the only grandmother they knew. She took me to lunch one day and explained that she went ahead and enrolled them in a boarding school in Switzerland. She did this because she did not think the schools in Nigeria would give them a rounded education, and should they want to return to London to attend university, or if I, for some reason, would want to return to live in England, it would be in all our favour.

So she convinced me that it would be best for me, also because should I return with my husband to Nigeria, I would be expected to take up duties which would take me away from them.

So I travelled with her and the kids to Switzerland. We spent six months while they settled in; they loved the school, and their grandma was more than pleased. However, David's father was not ready to return home after his post was up in London. He stayed on in London, and we stayed on for a further three years in Nigeria.

Then Grandmother took to bed; she wasn't able to stand for long without the aid of a stick at first, and then she wasn't able to sit for any length of time either. So her bedroom became her boardroom, and she assigned me to be her personal assistant. I was expected to be dressed and ready for a day's work at six each morning. One morning, as I made my way to her apartment in the palace, I realised that everyone else was also heading in the same direction. The staff waited outside, but David and his uncles were standing around her bed. Someone was trying to call David's father on the phone. She took my hand and smiled. She wasn't in pain, and her voice was as strong as ever.

I remember she said calmly that she had decided to return to her ancestors' village until it was her time to go, as she put it. She had summoned her youngest son, Uncle Steffan, who lived in Paris, to return home and take her in their private plane.

So at that time, we said our goodbyes. That was the last time I saw her. They had no phones out in the village, but I got a letter every now and then. She died a year later, but I wasn't asked to attend the funeral. David's father returned home and handed me a box and a letter addressed to me from his mother and then told me they had laid her to rest. After that, everything changed. David went back to Kenya.

I stayed on in Nigeria because he said that our house was being built and he wanted it to be comfortable for me and the kids, so we spoke a lot by phone. I only saw him on occasions when he had to do business at the office.

Two years went by, then his only remaining brother died in a plane crash. (The other two had suffered similar fates: one died by drowning and the other in a car crash.) This brother had been a tyrant. He was well known, and his death was in the papers for weeks because he crashed on the mountains, and they had to arrange for climbers to go up and return with his remains for burial.

David's second stepmother, his father's third wife, had returned with his dad to Nigeria. They brought their young son, so David now had a three-year-old brother. His father's new wife brought a breath of fresh air to my life.

We became the best of friends. She was only five years older than I, and she was born in England, so we had no problem bonding. When the funeral was arranged, his father wanted to go alone, but Carol insisted that as wives of both father and brother, it was only fitting that we should be there.

After ten years of marriage, I was about to meet my mother-in-law for the first time. Carol, of course, was about to meet her husband's first wife. Little did I know that the same would also apply to me.

Carol and I were asked to share a room, being told at first that the men were also sharing. Our meals were taken to us for the first two days. We were told that the family had a lot of rituals and meetings, so we were to remain in our room until we were collected. That did not happen.

Our advantage was that Carol understood the language, although she did not wish to speak it. Her father and mother were Nigerians and lived in England. We got ready for the funeral service and left our room. Cars were parked all over the grounds; no one knew who we were, but we got a drive to the church. Carol suggested that we sit at the back of the church until we are able to get the attention of either David or his father. So we sat and watched as her husband walked in with his first wife, followed by David Junior and his wife. They were led to their seats, and the service began.

Outside the church, after the service, we hitched a ride to the cemetery and watched the burial from a distance. Carol started to cry, only because she felt that she did not belong there and was sorry that she had insisted on attending. David's uncle Steffan had spotted us and drove us back to the palace. He didn't think it was a good idea for us to be there, and we stood out like sore thumbs, dressed in our western outfits like fashion models."

I felt my hands tighten on the steering wheel of the jeep. Guess for the second time, the first being when I had to be hospitalised in France. It was sinking in that I had been through hell and back.

I almost choked on the chicken. The memory of that moment made me so enraged. And to think that I had to spend time in hospital to recover. I choked up, and I couldn't stop the hot tears from clouding over my eyes. David's betrayal tore my heart from my chest and left me so empty. But I took a deep breath, cleared my throat and continued telling Jacky my story.

"That day, I was without shame. I was so ready to attack David at the graveside. His uncle called in two of the security guards who practically carried us away. They sedated me and Carol and returned us to the room we were sharing in the palace."

My eyes clouded over again, and at that point I could no longer see the road ahead, just the vision of that night in the palace. Jacky leaned across and placed her hand on my shoulder.

"Oh my God, how awful and cold for you, Beth. That couldn't have been a good feeling."

I unintentionally let out a scream. Thinking about it was making me mad with rage.

Just then, another car coming from the opposite direction flashed its bright headlights, blinding me further. I blinked just in time to see a deep pothole and swung the jeep to escape from it at the last minute. But by swinging the jeep so fast, Jack fell from the seat to the floor of the jeep as my foot went flat on the car brakes. I suppose that Jacky saw it coming and braced herself to stop herself from going over the dashboard. Jack was the first to react; he was out of the vehicle thinking that we had hit something.

I did not realise that I was still holding on to so much anger until that moment. Both Jacky and Jack rushed to my side because I kept up the screams between sobs. They began to touch my body all over, asking where on my body I was hurting. I managed to take a few deep breaths and control my outburst.

"I am sorry, guys; it's just that my emotions got the better of me, I am okay. Sorry for shaking you up. Let me get us back on the road. I am just happy that there wasn't a vehicle following behind me."

I took the jeep off the road and parked for a while on the lay-by while we adjusted the luggage back onto the back seat.

"Well, that's one way of waking me up," said Jack. We all laughed. Jacky gave him a kiss. "Honey, we brought some chicken earlier; it's cold but pretty tasty."

We sat for a moment while Jack ate from his box of chicken, and while I took a short walk to cool my head.

My phone rang. Jacky was closer to the Jeep and my bag, so she answered.

"Good night, this is Beth Creary's number. Can I take a message?"

"Hi, good night. Are you her sister, Jacky?"

"Well, yes, I am. To whom am I speaking?"

"Please let her know it's Doctor Cain. I was just saying goodnight. Are you still on the road?"

"Yes, we are, but we are okay; we should be home soon, I think."

She told him to hold on so he could speak to me.

"Good night, Lloyd. Yes, we are okay. No, hardly any traffic; we are just coming into Galina. I know, but I had to drive in this direction because I had a passenger getting off at Devon Pen."

"Okay my pet, keep your eyes on the road. My doctor didn't turn up for duty tonight, so I am on a double shift. It's okay so far; good thing I have a full set of qualified nurses tonight. You be safe; I will stop by your house on my way home later, okay?"

We said goodnight, and I composed myself to commence the rest of our journey home. Before long, Jack went back to sleep, and I turned up the music on the radio. Jacky started humming to the Kenny Rogers song being played.

I was still more than half an hour away from home; it was such a comfort to have had a call from Lloyd. It placed a balance back in my mood and thoughts. I had long tried to bury the hurt I felt that day in the graveyard. I did not hate David or ever want to see any harm come to him. I just wanted to know why he felt the need to hurt me. I could not get it out of my mind, so I continued to put the pieces of my memories together without speaking about it to Jacky.

After the funeral that night, Carol was deep in sleep, but I was so restless I needed to find David at all costs, so I left our room. Earlier that morning, as we walked through the palace, I had noticed that staff members all wore a white draped headdress. So I took off the white silk pillowcase and ripped it at the seams to cover my head and face, slipped on a long black skirt, then took a few of the towels from the bathroom and walked slowly as a maid, instead of dashing toe first, walking as if I were a model on a runway.

A few persons looked in my direction, but I was happy no one spoke. The place was massive; I trembled as I stopped at each door, listening for any sounds that might help. I came to an archway which separated one section of the palace by a grass lawn. There were about six people in an open area, and there were no guards or servants around. I trod slowly across the lawn; David was sitting in an armchair, his father standing and pouring himself a drink, while four women sat close together at one end of the room.

When I pulled the scarf from my head, the younger of the women stood up, frightened, and placed herself behind the older woman's chair. I went towards the woman who was sitting, simply because I knew I was to pay respect by bowing, but the old woman got up and slapped me so hard across the face. My only reaction was to return the slap. David's father came to my rescue and placed himself between his wife and me. She spat at me and pulled the cloth from my neck with such force that the fabric cut my neck, all the time cursing me with all the expletives I had heard in the streets over the years.

She reached for me and grabbed at my blouse. Her husband was holding my arms from behind, so I kicked out at her. She was a big woman and grabbed my leg, pushing me back against her husband, who stumbled and fell, still holding on to me. The room became crowded with people after that, with hands and feet hitting me from every direction all over my body.

A woman screamed, and their attention was drawn away from me to David's father. I scrambled to my feet and ran, somehow finding my way back to my room like a scared rabbit. I slammed the door shut and locked it with the key. Carol was still asleep. Nothing happened.

I sat by the door until morning. After she got over the shock of seeing me the following morning, she assisted me to shower and change. Two days passed and no one came to our room. On the third night, we huddled together, trying to make a plan. Then came a knock on the door. The person asked to speak to Carol. When she opened the door, he asked her to pack her case because she was to go with him back to Nigeria. She insisted that I should go with her, but we were stopped at the entrance of the palace, and I was asked to return to my room by orders of the queen's mother. Carol tried to argue. Not being able to speak the language myself, I could only rely on what she told me.

But at that point neither Carol nor I knew that the older David Kworori (her husband) was dead. The guards did not touch me; they just pointed me back to the car. I watched as Carol got into another car on the other side of the gate, and the car sped away.

The driver of the car I was in spoke on the phone before turning the car around, and I was asked to step out, firmly but politely, and was marched back to my room. I remembered that we had finished the last of the water and food over the days we were locked in and asked if they would take me some. They just repeated the words I spoke and smiled at me. Rather than lying on the bed, I pulled up a chair close to the door and waited.

My suitcase was taken along with Carol's to her car, so now I didn't even have a toothbrush. Early the following morning, the door burst open. I had dozed off. Although startled, I remained seated as the two women entered. I was a sitting duck. They were able to tie my hands behind my back and my feet to the chair, and one took out a pair of scissors. I screamed, and they found something to gag my mouth before cutting my hair down to an inch of my scalp."

After that they cut away my clothes and left me in the room wearing nothing but the gag covering my mouth and whatever was holding my wrists and legs together at the back of the chair. There I sat all through the day waiting for the door to open. All I was hoping for was to ask for some water. In the dead of night I watched as the door opened slowly. I was in full view of the doorway. A male figure stepped in and switched off the room light, leaving us in pitch blackness. I remained still, wondering what was next.

My imagination took me to the unthinkable. The weight of the blanket from the bed went over me, and I was suspended in mid-air, still sitting in the chair. The person started to run, and I bounced to and fro, up and down like a rag doll. I was placed on the floor on my side. Still wrapped in the blanket and getting hotter and hotter, I could feel other things being thrown over me, and then movement. I was in or on a vehicle. I passed out.

When I woke up I was lying on a cot in a room so small I could touch the walls without getting up from the plank I was lying on, but my hands were no longer tied and the gag was gone. I was still without clothes except for the covering of the blanket. Too frightened to move, I remained on the wooden plank until the daylight entered the room. There had been no sound except for animals and birds throughout the night and into daylight. Hunger and thirst made me slowly get up.

The door was almost touching the wooden plank, and there were no windows, just two open spaces left in the mud wall. I was thankful that I was not afraid of creeping things because lizards of all sizes were running over my head. When I stepped off the cot, my feet knocked over some plastic bottles and landed in a tray of fruits. I had three bottles of water, two packs of biscuits and fruits and nuts. The space was suddenly again pitch black.

I somehow slept through the noise of another night.

The following morning and throughout the day I drank most of the water and ate all the fruit. I did not touch the door. It was night again, and I could hear the engine of a car getting closer until it stopped outside the door. My name was whispered.

"Beth, Beth, it's Steffan."

The door slowly opened, and a hand came in holding a pair of jeans and a white shirt.

"Put them on quickly; we haven't got much time."

I slipped into the jeans and shirt even though I felt that they were too big and as if they were already worn and dirty.

"You can come in; I am ready."

But he just grabbed my hand and the blanket, and we ran to the van, where the engine was already revving. He drove at speed through the bush and without headlights. We got to a river where he exchanged the van for a boat. I was told to lie down, and he threw the blanket over me.

I could feel the movement of the boat, but the water hardly made a sound. We came to a stop, and I waited, shivering with fright. Not in my wildest dreams could I ever imagine what was happening to me. Then came a gentle tap on my shoulder.

"Beth, wake up; it's time."

He pulled away the blanket; it was first light, and the freshness of the morning breeze cooled my face.

"Come on, hon, we have to move."

I stepped out of the boat onto dry land, but I had no shoes on.

Steffan bent in front of me.

"Come on, I will have to carry you."

I got on the back of this older but strong and courageous man, and he carried me for more than a mile to a waiting helicopter. Carol was at the apartment in France waiting for us to return.

After a lengthy bath and a substantial meal, Uncle Steffan, Carol and I went on to discuss the events of the past weeks.

The Queen Mother and my husband's first wife were not happy that we had the audacity to attend the funeral without an invitation. They felt it was not fitting to be in the same space as them; in fact, they thought we were disrespecting the family because we were not accepted as part of the family, and we were not even considered to be married. We had not done the regular rituals of the forefathers and elders. So we were total outsiders. Uncle Steffan was saving our face from disgrace when he took us away from the graveside.

He thought that a better way of distracting us would be to send for Carol's parents, who were on holiday in Nigeria at the time. He knew that I would have willingly gone along with Carol.

However, because I had provocatively confronted them in their own space and brought disgrace to their house at such a time of grieving for their oldest son, things worsened.

The following night, his brother, my father-in-law, was hurriedly laid to rest. This happened because he had a heart attack late on the night following my interruption, while the two wives and husbands were having arguments regarding us (us being Carol and myself). All the clans and family had already travelled for miles to be at his nephew's funeral, so the decision to bury David Senior in haste meant that they did not need to make another plan.

So when Carol's parents arrived at the gates, Uncle Steffan was not expecting David Junior's wife to be home. She was told of the visitors and asked the guards not to allow me to leave. Steffan overheard her plans for me later that evening, plus her intentions of having me charged with the murder of my father-in-law when the queen mother returned.

He acted as quickly as he could to get me out without putting himself in a suspicious and difficult situation. Carol was the one who was more alarmed at Uncle Steffan's statement.

"That is so not right. David was past eighty years old; he had two heart attacks and bypass heart operations in the past year.

When we got married in London, I thought he was only fifty, because he looked so good. But he was far from healthy."

"We know that, Carol," said Steffan. "But David kept his health close to his chest; it was between you, me, and his doctor. But to have Beth take the blame for his unfortunate demise would have been wrong, yet under the circumstances, and with the queen going along with such a plan, trust me, it would have turned nasty. I had no real powers to give orders in the queen's house, and I could not have allowed David junior to take charge of the situation; he could not manage those two women. I know I did the right thing in getting Beth out of the palace and out of the country."

That was when I broke down. I lost it and had to be sedated. Uncle Steffan booked me into a nursing home. Carol stayed with me in Paris until I recovered, then we returned to London together, parting only when I insisted on going to my dad's house alone.

I had just passed the sleepy town of Oracabessa and turned into our driveway. Dad always insisted on us leaving the gate open when we were out at night, and as the car approached the veranda, it activated a number of lights to instantly come on in the yard. This, he felt, would deter any would-be robbers. Well, for me it's comforting—being able to see around me even if I was being observed. Cutting the noisy engine of the jeep brought the others awake instantly.

After all the luggage was placed in the house and the grill and gate locked, I asked, "Anyone for a hot drink?"

"No way, sis, just point us to our room."

Jack was on the bed as soon as he let go of the suitcase.

"See what I mean? Go get some rest, sis; see you later."

We hugged and kissed before I closed their door.

Chapter Six

Day Six

My phone rang at eight o'clock.

"Morning, Ms Beth. A just checking that you reach home safe, miss. Everything alright?"

"Morning, Ms Mac. Yes, all is well, we got home about one last night, and the journey was okay, thanks."

"All right, miss, I know we might not see you today, but I will call you if anything is going on that we can't take care of. Say hello to your sister for me, my dear."

"Thank you for calling, Ms Mac. Have a good day."

I pulled the curtains and opened the window over the wardrobe.

A stream of light and a welcoming whiff of fresh air flooded the room. I lay for a moment to savour and breathe deeply, thanking God for a new day before I showered and changed. When I left my room, Jacky was ahead of me in the corridor on her way to the kitchen, wearing a short mini skirt and a matching coloured tank top. She had a towel drying her hair.

"Hey, morning, sis. Hope you slept well after that crazy road trip last night. You deserve a medal for getting the jeep around those narrow bends, and in pitch black, I don't know how you did it. Sorry we weren't much help, falling asleep on you."

Jack was already in the kitchen, over the stove with a frying pan in one hand and a spatula in the other. His boxer shorts were covered by my frilly apron. He turned to kiss me on the forehead.

"Morning, sis. And she was driving stick shift; don't forget that. You have my admiration there. Trust me, I have always said it the best way to drive."

"Well, thanks, but no thanks; I am more comfortable just pressing gas in my automatic," Jacky remarked.

I asked, "What's for breakfast?"

"Oh, I found some lobster in the fridge, so I am serving up some of my favourite fish cakes and bacon. Sit yourself down; I am about to dish up. I must say I love your kitchen, Beth, if only because I was able to find everything I wanted at my fingertips."

"He is just having a go at me, Beth; I am guilty of having the worst-organised kitchen. Matter of fact, I can never find anything in my house."

We all laughed and tucked into Jack's fish cakes, which were quite tasty.

"Beth I was admiring your mural in the hallway. I must say some of those locations are impressive. I hope you will have time to take us on a tour before we leave. I would love to drive that jeep, as long as it's daylight."

He added with a laugh. Jacky then asked,

"What will you do, Beth? Do you think you will continue the business, or will it be too much for you to manage?"

"Oh, I definitely will be keeping Dad's business open; we have been working together for the past three years. I know all his clients; I pretty much know our financial standing. I don't think I should have any problems maintaining them. My only regret will be not having Dad sitting beside me on those long drives and someone to console me at the end of the day when I get pissed off by a pathetic tourist."

Jacky got up from around the table to hug and kiss me.

"You will do fine, sis; you are the strongest person I know. Except for me, of course."

That was an icebreaker which led into memorable Jacky antics.

"How far are we from the sea, Beth? I could have sworn I could hear the sound of water splashing on rocks in the early morning before the traffic drowned out the sound of nature."

I described our location to Jack and offered to take them to the beach later that evening.

"But first I need to do some laundry; I don't want them mounting up when the crowd gets here. But come along with me; let me take you on a guided tour of our home and grounds."

After our tour, Jack and Jacky returned to the kitchen and I to the laundry room. No sooner had I finished hanging the washing on the line than came a loud blowing from a truck horn at the gate. Jack and Jacky were now in their hammocks under the trees while I directed the delivery men into the house.

An hour later, with the new furniture comfortably arranged in place and the four new fans placed around the apartment, the two guests were clearly deep in sleep in their hammocks under the trees.

I started the evening meal. Satisfied that drinks and salad were also in place, I collected the laundry and was in the process of folding it away when I felt the brush of arms girding my waist from behind.

And the warmth of soft cheeks against mine, followed by a whispered,

"I always finish whatever I start."

His lips found mine and locked. For some unknown reason my mind drifted to 'warm New Zealand butter, salty and smooth, while my body was immersed in refreshing cool river water.

I giggled and Lloyd pulled away.

"You are laughing. Why?"

I told him and he roared with laughter.

"So, I was a fisherman and chef; now I am butter and river water. I can't wait to find out what's next, but please, can you return some of my butter?"

I obliged, and now the butter was dripping and hot. We were pulled apart by the siren pitch of Gertrude calling from the front veranda.

"Ms Beth, is me Gertrude, Ms Beth. Ms…"

"I can hear you, Gertrude."

I replied, adding volume to my own voice. Lloyd still held me around my waist and was looking at me with wanton passion. I said what came to my mind.

"You know what they say about rubbing butter on a puss mouth."

"No! What is it they say?" he asked.

"I laughed. I don't know, but I will tell you when I find out."

I replied, pulling myself away to attend to Gertrude, who was waiting in the front yard with a very large galvanised tin (which Jamaicans called a kerosene tin) on her head. Her son was standing some way away with a large crocus bag.

"Good evening, Ms Beth. Mr John asked me to come and start the cooking early fi the man them later. Me son have a bag full of breadfruit fi roast, and me have sprat fi fry and some 'mack a back' fi mek fish tea. But me would a like fi turn out you father room first before me start the cooking."

"What do you mean by turning out, Gertrude?" I asked.

"How you mean, Miss? You have to move the bed and lean up the mattress so the duppy no tek set and come back."

"Duppy?" I repeated, shocked at the thought.

But I saw the funny side of it. "No, you won't need to change anything; besides, my sister and I will be sharing the room tomorrow."

"So you not fraid a duppy miss?"

"No, not of my own father's anyway, he would only be there to protect me."

153

"I suppose that you right Miss, is true you talking. Mr Creary love you fi true. Alright Ms. we going round the back to mek up the fire and mek a start."

Jack and Jacky were clearly woken up by Gertrude's loud voice and were making their way to the house. I stopped and waited for them.

"You guys must be hungry, I have dinner ready."

"I am starving Beth but we need to get a shower and cool off, give us a half hour okay."

I returned to the kitchen, but Lloyd was not there so I called. He answered from the laundry room.

"I am here; I interrupted your folding, so I am just finishing up for you. Hope you don't mind, but I have to get to the bank in town before going home. And I have my own laundry waiting to be done."

"You are going to have dinner with us first, though? I have cooked enough."

"Love to pet, but would you mind just dishing some for me to take home and have later? I just called the bank to let them know I am on my way. So, where is your sister?"

"She went to take a shower before dinner, sure you can't wait?"

"Not today, my love; I am out of cash, and I also have some bills to pay, so a rain check, please."

"You won't refuse a cup of broth while I am sharing. It's not the usual Jamaican soup, just something to warm you. My dad always liked a cup of hot drink before dinner, so I have gotten used to preparing a

154

warm drink. Ms Mac made sure she brought Dad two carriers so there was always one at the office and one at home."

I opened all four compartments, placing pumpkin rice in the top, peppered steak in the second, mixed veg in the third, and two large slices of my freshly baked banana bread at the bottom. Lloyd placed the empty cup in the sink before kissing me on the forehead. He held the carrier with great care as we walked to the gate.

"You drive carefully to Mobay tomorrow, my pet. I will try and make time to meet your sisters on Monday. My duties at the hospital will be running back to back until next Saturday. The good thing is I will be nearer to home, working out of St Ann's Bay Hospital for next week. Thanks for the hot drink; it's warming my tummy just like the butter."

We both laughed as he blew me a parting kiss. Gertrude met me part way as I walked from the front gate.

"Ms Beth, you have that thing for me yet, ma'am?"

For a moment I was puzzled, then I remembered what she had asked me for.

"Not to worry, Ms Gertrude, I have not forgotten, but it's best to wait until my sisters leave. By then I may have a few more things, okay?"

"Yes, Miss. Ok, no problem."

"Wow, sis, I saw you walking to the gate with that good-looking hunk. Was that the good doctor?"

"Yes, that was Lloyd, but he had to get to the bank before closing time; he said to tell you guys hello."

Jacky gave me a push with her elbow.

"Oh he can say hello to me any time. I hope you are thinking of keeping him close to home, he is for sure husband material."

I only smiled and pushed her gently into the kitchen ahead of me.

"Come on you two, I am starving, help me set the table."

"What's going on in the backyard? I went out to pick a lemon, and there are two people out there building a wood fire in the middle of the yard."

"That's our helper Gertrude and her son; they are preparing for later. Some of the workers and a few of Dad's friends will be coming to play dominoes and have a get-together in memory of Dad. Apparently, it's the 'done' thing when someone dies to visit their house every evening until the funeral, but we were able to talk them into having it just for tonight."

"Oh that's a nice way of showing respect; it will be like a campfire party. I should enjoy that," said Jack.

Later that evening John turned up with ice, bottles of rum and a bunch of water coconuts to use as chasers for the rum. They set up the tables and chairs. Mr and Mrs Mc along with some of the tenants in the plaza, showed up. Gertrude did a great job with the cooking and serving and was happy to be in charge. Halfway through the evening, Ms Mc stopped the domino players to conduct a prayer meeting.

She closed the evening's gathering with a simple announcement informing the gathering that it was time to leave and allow Ms Beth and her sister to get some rest. No one protested.

The men all gathered up the tables and chairs and collected all the used plates and cups. Satisfied that they had restored the garden in good stead, she ushered them through the gate. John and Gertrude waited while I locked the front grill before bidding us goodnight.

We sat for a while on the front veranda.

"It was a good evening sis, I love your Ms Mac, and she is definitely a character."

"Oh that's because you weren't speaking to our little Miss Gertrude," remarked Jack.

"She came and complimented me on how nice my shoes were, then in the same breath said, 'But your foot and my son foot is the same size, you could leave that shoes for him so him we have something to remember you by!'"

We giggled and exchanged more of such occurrences and cracked up with laughter at each one.

"You guys, I am getting cold out here, let's relax in the sitting room."

"Beth, cold really? Are you alright sis?"

"I am fine, thank you, but this kind of cool breeze will give me a cold. You are free to use the fan if it's too warm in the sitting room for you."

Jack stood up first, stretching his long frame before pulling Jacky by her hands to her feet.

"Come on, J, besides, it's a lot cosier inside. I am going to fetch that last bottle of rum punch, and I have to help myself to some more of that roast breadfruit and fish; I really enjoyed that."

Jack went off to fetch the drinks and food, but I really wanted a hot cup of Milo, so I followed to put the kettle on.

"Any good show on TV, Beth?"

I laughed. "Sorry, Jacky, Dad and I only ever watched the evening news."

"Oh wow, really?"

Jacky slipped off the settee and made herself comfortable on the carpet on the floor. The sight of her doing so brought back memories of when we were children and one particular evening, which was lost in my memory until that moment. I reminded Jacky.

"Oh my goodness, yes."

I remembered that night. Dad went off to work; Mum was nagging him to take the night off and take her to some big dance going on somewhere. They had a big argument, and then after he left, she got dressed and called a taxi. We girls were all supposed to be sleeping. Do you remember that the day before, Mum had taken the strap out and was so mad that she scarred poor Sophia's hands and feet because the three musketeers told her it was Sophia who had stolen her money?"

Jack asked curiously, "The three musketeers?"

"That was just one of the names for our three older sisters, Patricia, Prudence and Pauline," we told him in unison.

"I won't ask why; continue your story. I have a feeling this is going to be quite interesting," said Jack.

I picked up the story: "Jacky came upstairs to the bedroom I shared with Rose. And because Sophia was upset with the others, she was sharing a bed with me. I wasn't sleeping, so I saw when she walked in with a bottle of white rum in one hand and a bottle of cream soda in the other.

She told me her plan, then went back downstairs to wake up the others. Of course, they were willing victims. We selected some of Mum's mini dresses and her shoes, and we got dressed up with her wigs and make-up. Jacky poured out the white rum straight without mixing it and served it to the three musketeers; to Rose and me she served the lemonade. Sophia was still in a bad mood and didn't want to join in. The others were as drunk as skunks in no time because they thought they were drinking Dad's prize lemonade, so they filled their glasses to the brim. Prudence started cussing and carrying on awfully, Pauline was sick all over Mum's pretty dress, and Patricia was out cold.

We dragged them back down the stairs by their legs, not caring that we were bumping their heads on the stairs. We placed them in the sitting room where, as children, we were not allowed except at Christmas time. Jacky continued,

"I took out some of Dad's records and scattered them over the floor and turned on the player, poured the remainder of the white rum over their dresses and closed the door."

I continued, "Then we went back up to the top floor to our bedroom; Jacky and Sophia got into bed with us. Later, when Mum came home from her party, she was so tired she went straight to bed. Dad got home from work and made breakfast for us before calling us down to get ready for school.

This was his routine each day, before he went to get his rest and before preparing again for the next night shift. The three musketeers did not show up for breakfast, so he went into their room and didn't find them. He came upstairs and found us four getting our uniforms ready for school. We happily went off to have our breakfast, but Dad could not find the three musketeers. Mum came down ready to grab Sophia, because we had left a few of her dresses and shoes out of place deliberately.

She screamed at Sophia, calling her names. Mouse couldn't take it any longer; she told Dad it was Patricia who brought her friends to have a party in the sitting room. So Mum and Dad rushed to the sitting room.

I wished that we had an instant camera back then; it was such a sight. Dad was so mad; he let them have it. No one went to school that day. Of course, we were so innocent – we were all the way on the top floor; how were we to know what they were up to? Mouse cleared herself by saying that she went down to have some water during the night and that was when she saw them.

Jack asked, "Okay, the Mouse you refer to would be Rose. So why was she called Mouse?"

We both laughed, then shared different stories of Mouse with Jack.

"And the three musketeers?" he asked.

"Because they were always together and scheming, always getting Sophia and Jacky in trouble. That was one of the good names; we also called them 'the piss pot pansies'." Jack cracked up with laughter.

"Please tell me that you have grown out of this sibling rivalry; I dread to think what might happen at your father's funeral."

Jacky gave him a kiss on his forehead. "I promise you that it will never come to that, my darling."

I added, "Not to worry, so much water has gone over and under that bridge. I am in such a better place about Mum; I have this covered."

Jacky got up to hug me. "I love you, sis, and we have so much to catch up on. I can't wait for Rose and Sophia to get here."

"You and me both, Jacky, and trust me, we have a lot to sort out before the funeral. We'd better get some shut-eye. Oh, I have a request, Jack. Would you mind driving the jeep tomorrow? It's four coming in, plus luggage, so I am going to also drive my own car.

The roads are fifty times better going to Montego Bay than the ones we drove on the other night, and hopefully you won't mind driving behind me. I know how men are when it comes to women drivers."

"On the contrary, Beth, you are an excellent driver, and I am looking forward to using a stick shift again. Oh, by the way, why was Sophia accused of stealing your mother's money?" Jack asked.

Jacky explained as they hugged and walked to their bedroom.

"It was so unfair; Sophia was invited to her friend's party that weekend. Weeks before, she took on a part-time job. On her way to school she would also collect three toddlers from their home and drop them off at a day centre, then in the evening she would collect them and return them home.

I knew this because she had asked me if I thought it would be a good idea. She used her pay to buy herself a dress for the party. She was all dressed up and ready to go. Mum asked her where she got the dress, and before she could answer, Patricia told Mum she saw Sophia take the money from Mum's purse. Mum reached for her purse and checked it and found that money was missing. It all happened so fast. Sophia's words went unheard. She was attacked so badly not even Dad could stop Mum until she had gotten rid of the demon within her."

"Oh my goodness, that is so sad. I had a friend in Baltimore whose mother would beat him brutally, and for the slightest thing. He frequently ran away from home to crash at our place.

But I am happy to know you looked out for your sister Sophia. And now I also know not to get on your bad side."

"Don't you worry, my darling; I know that you would never lift a finger to harm me."

They kissed and hugged as they closed their bedroom door.

I felt good inside and happy that Jacky was the way she was then and was even more pleased to know how things have worked out for her. I know that Dad would have loved Jack. They had a similar taste in the love for smoking a pipe. For Dad, though, it was a ritual done only before he retired to bed.

He would signal by taking out his leather pouch from his desk drawer, cleaning and tapping the pipe. No words were required to tell me he needed his space. It's funny how men find ways of excluding women from their space. With David and his father, it was a cigar and cognac after dinner.

No female would interrupt their evening sessions. I stood for a while admiring Dad's portrait before blowing him a kiss, then went off to bed.

Day Seven

I showered and dressed for the drive to Mobay, opting not to go first to the kitchen. I also decided to use a smaller handbag, and while swapping the contents over from one bag to the other, I realised that the letter Lloyd had given me from Dad was still unopened. I was about to break the seal when the house phone rang.

"Good morning, Elizabeth, my love, and how are you this morning?"

"Mrs Budd! Good morning to you too. I am very well, thank you for asking. How is that handsome husband of yours?"

She laughed. "Please don't tell him that; his head can't get any bigger than it already is, my dear. He is presently closing the garage gate. I am in our car as I speak, we are on our way to church, but it's so much better to call early before we go our separate ways. I believe you had mentioned driving to Montego Bay to pick up your sisters today."

"Yes, I am. I was just about sorting myself out to prepare for the journey."

"Here comes Mr Budd now; I will let him speak. You have a safe trip, my dear."

Mr Budd's baritone roared from the other end of the telephone.

"Good morning, good morning, pretty lady. How are you doing this morning? We just wanted to wish you a safe journey and a pleasant day. Oh, and before I forget, between our two gardens, I can safely say we have sufficient flowers to fill the church for your father's send-off, so please allow me to cut them when they are needed, won't you?"

"I will, Mr Budd, we will be seeing the pastor sometime tomorrow to set a final date, so I will be sure to let you know."

"Okay, my dear, you drive carefully now. Bye."

While I replaced the extension phone in the front room, I could see movements in the front yard and opened the window for a better view.

Jack and Jacky were washing both the jeep and my own car simultaneously and, in the process, splashing the soapy water like children at play on each other. I was still watching in amusement when the street gate opened and John walked in with a large string of freshly caught fish from the seaside.

Dad would always go to the beach early on a Sunday morning to catch or buy fish to serve as dinner for us during the week. I had forgotten about it and was so thankful that John did not. He had stopped and was having a conversation with Jack when I got to the veranda.

"Morning, Ms Beth, you getting plenty help to wash the car this morning, Miss."

He laughed as he handed me the fish along with a folded Sunday Gleaner.

"I was wondering if you wanted to use the van today Miss, it will be a few of you travelling."

"Thanks John, but Jack will be driving the jeep, so he will be able to take the luggage, I feel we should be fine."

"Okay, Miss, but do you have any idea when the funeral will be? The butcher will be killing a goat and a pig on Wednesday. Ms Mac wants to prepare the goat meat and put it in the freezer, then her husband would be able to jerk the pork the day before the service or early on that morning. And then we want to know how the grave digging will work out; we will have to prepare some food for that too. Will you be burying your father at the big graveyard, or would you want to put him to rest around the backyard, Miss?"

"Oh my, I haven't thought that far, John. But the pastor did mention that he has a spot in the churchyard. I thought that the undertakers would have done all of that."

"Yes, they do miss, but grave digging always draws a crowd, so we need to have the ladies cooking while the men work. And I would need to get some money to buy the sand and cement and a little money to buy some rum and to pay the diggers."

"Tell you what, John. Why don't you make out a list for me and do an estimate of the funds? My sisters and I have an appointment with the pastor in the morning. I will stop at the office after seeing him. By then we will know the date and time and can make all the other arrangements. Thank you for taking the initiative; I really appreciate it."

"Miss Beth. Your father was my boss, but he was the most honest and helpful person I have ever known. He was there for me when my wife took sick, and when she died, he stood by me like a brother, and I never needed to ask him. So God would take away my blessings if I never stood by you for him. I hope that you will allow me to say a word at the service to pay my respects."

"Yes, John, of course you can, and please, just write down everything; my sisters may want to know what is happening too."

"Okay, Miss, I will see you tomorrow; drive carefully."

I was touched and felt blessed to have people like John and Mrs Mac around me, who were caring and thoughtful.

"I see that you too are having too much fun; there is more soap on both of you than on the vehicles. Do you need me to fix breakfast?"

"Morning," they both sang out. "We are good."

Jack came running onto the veranda to escape Jacky and handed me the keys to both vehicles.

"I have checked the water, oil and the tyres, but we are going to have to top up on petrol. I see you are already dressed. Come on, J, we had better go get ourselves ready."

Jacky was still in a playful mood and tugged at his shirt as she ran, leading the way back to their room. Above my head I could see freshly opened ackees.

So I got out the picking stick and ended up picking mangoes, limes and a couple of sweetsops before returning to the kitchen. I packed the cooling container with fresh fruit and a few packs of biscuits and peanuts. In the icebox at the back of the jeep, which Dad built under the back seat, I loaded it with soft drinks and a few Red Stripes. I checked around the backyard to make sure nothing was out of place, then checked on the outside lights, closed up the open windows and fetched my handbag from my room.

The letter I placed under my pillow, promising myself to read it before going to bed later that night. I sat in the cool of the garden before dialling Lloyd's number.

"Good morning, my sweets, How are you? Have you started your journey?"

"Good morning, Doc. No, but I am about to; just waiting on the two lovebirds to show themselves. Did you get to the bank on time yesterday?"

"I did not, but it pays to have friends in high and low places. I was sneaked in through the back door."

"I hear you." We both chuckled, then he asked,

"So how was the domino party last night? They didn't keep you up too late?"

"It was great, and no, Ms Mac made sure they packed up and cleaned up by twelve midnight. Surprisingly, it turned out to be a great evening.We all had a good time, and Jack and Jacky were introduced to breadfruit and sprat, not to mention rum punch Jamaican style."

"Sorry I missed it, but I had to get some order back into my life. I had allowed some business to back up on me. By the way, thanks for the meal. I really enjoyed it."

"You are most welcome, but I can hear someone calling you in the background, so I will let you get back to what you were doing."

"That's my gardener; he turned up pretty early today. So he should be just about finished cutting the lawn now. Sweet Beth, please drive carefully. Ok, I will call you later. Kiss, kiss."

"Back at you, my love; catch you later."

The two lovers were still in their room, so I reached for the Gleaner and read it page by page slowly, paying only the slightest attention to them when they finally emerged on the veranda dressed in matching blue shorts and T-shirts, still kissing and cuddling and in no rush.

Waiting for people, no matter who, has always had a bad effect on my psyche. For no reason I get in a bad mood. I have been trying to control my feelings and emotions, so the fact that I appear calm on the outside makes me feel good that I could still smile. It was after ten o'clock, and I had planned to leave at nine, with intentions of stopping at the Green Grotto Caves for breakfast along the way.

Jacky had gotten in the jeep with Jack, but on leaving the petrol station, I asked that she drive with me because I had a lot of questions on my mind and I wanted to vent. She reluctantly changed cars.

We travelled for a few miles before I started a conversation. I was happy that driving would at all times relax me and also calm my spirit.

"Jacky I am really sorry that Dad will not be at your wedding; I know that nothing would have pleased him more."

For a while she did not reply. I looked over at her face, which appeared troubled, then she said.

"I know that. And I also know that Paul knew that I was not his daughter, but he always tried to do the right thing by me. And in the last few months we have been able to have real conversations. I will miss that."

"How long have you known that he was not your birth father?" I asked, surprised. She pulled the recliner on the seat and slid her body down.

"My God, it was such a long time ago. I always hid in the front room just to get away from you guys, then banged the front door to make you all think I was coming in from the streets."

She laughed, then sighed.

"One day I was in the front room; I hid behind the settee when I heard Dad talking to someone, and they came into the room. At first I was puzzled at the conversation, which did not make much sense, then the man said.

"I will always be in your debt, old chap; it was so selfless of you to agree to keep Sophie after Mary died. Of course you know I was in no position to let the world know I had been a bad boy, so to speak. I came clean to my wife, of course, but we agreed not to let the rest of her family in on the secret.

After all, old chap, she controlled the money in the family, so there was no need to overturn the apple cart. But now that she is gone, and of course, the other kids knew about Sophia all along, you know yourself that my older daughter and Sophia can't be told apart; it's so remarkable that they should be so alike.

My wife's family accepted my story and agreed that I could adopt her under the circumstances. Sophia will go directly to the hostel, of course, but with her visiting us at the house on weekends, it won't be long before she fits in. I must say though, old chap, you have done a remarkable job in raising her. We will always be grateful to you, Paul."

Dad then asked him, "What about her sister? Have you given it any thought?"

"Good lord no, no offence, old chap, but at least our Sophia will fit in with the family, but that girl... I was told by Mary and not her mother, you know, and I know that Mary would not have said so if it were not so. But it would be too much. Sorry, old chap, but I will have to let sleeping dogs lie on your Jacky."

Jacky became angry at that point and swore.

"Oh good gosh, did he really say it so coldly? Honey, I am so sorry. Was that why you left home? I can't remember the details, but I know you and Sophia left home almost at the same time."

She brought the back of the seat up.

"Beth, there were so many secrets in our family. It took me a week back then, trying to put it all together. It was not until Sophia was packed and ready to leave that I confronted Dad. Then Dad told us the lie that she was being adopted so she could get into nursing school. Her father and the sister who looked like her came to pick her up. Mum didn't come down to see her off. Then when they were gone, she came into the kitchen and was arguing with Dad, and then she made a sly remark. That's when it hit me: I was really that man's other daughter.

I stayed home from community college the following day and hid in Mary's room. You know, it was always kept locked, and we were told ghost stories to keep us out. I read through all the important-looking papers and some letters and all sorts of stuff. And the birth certificate of the three musketeers clearly said, 'Mother Mary and father Paulie', then on Sophia's it read, 'Mother Mary and father Matthew Ogilvie'. I could not find any papers for you, Rose, or myself.

So later that evening when Dad went off to work, I searched his room. Your papers were not hard to find because he was always reminding you of your basket, so that was the first place I looked. Sure enough, it clearly states the father's name is Paul, and I kept reading over and over, the mother's name is Liza Beth Murry. Thinking how funny it was that they split the name Elizabeth. But you and Rose both had the same mother, and it was not Jenny.

171

I could not find my records, so the only other place to look was in Mum's room. It took me two days. First, I found her passport and her own birth certificate. Jennifer Brown, born Spanish Town, Jamaica. Of course it did not dawn on me that the name belonged to her because we were told she was from Trinidad. But the photo was clear. And when I finally found my own papers: Jacky Brown. (No father) born in Streatham, London. I remembered that Streatham was also Sophia's place of birth, and she was born only a week before I was.

I still remember how sick, confused and unwanted I felt. Why was I the only one who didn't have a father's name on my birth certificate? And why was I the only one to have Jenny as a mother? Of all people, she hated me so much and never gave me the time of day. I never ever remember feeling so rejected. I took my papers, packed my bag and left.

I slept on the streets for a few days, then I remembered that ship at Blackfriars where we were taken on a Boy Scout outing. There was a bigger ship in the docks that day. I waited until dark and got aboard without being seen, then hid myself away for three weeks, stealing whatever I could find to eat at night. I almost froze my butt off; it was so cold. I had no idea where the ship was going, and I really did not care.

As far as I was concerned, no one loved me or wanted me, so I needed to get away and show them that I could do whatever on my own. When the ship finally docked, I left in the same way I got on, in the pitch of night. After two days without food, I saw a friendly face walking the streets and decided to beg. I was sent a saviour in Nickalus.

Thank God he spoke English, and he also had money."

172

He had also travelled as far as Alaska via a long-distance trailer to get away and find himself because his family found out he was gay and was not prepared to accommodate him. But they were not going to let him starve, so he was allowed to withdraw funds each month from a bank account to support himself. He had a tiny apartment which he kept quite clean. He couldn't cook, so he spent most of his time eating cheap food and getting drunk. When he allowed himself to stay sober, he was able to paint and draw excellent portraits. We went around unnoticed until one night when he left the pub where he drank most nights. He was followed home by a thief who tied us both up, beat us and stole all we had, or rather all he had.

I mean all, they emptied the place. For a while he was unable to remember his name or where he was from. The beating left him in a stupor, with a large cut on one side of his head and a broken arm. So it meant we had no money. I took a job washing plates and sweeping the yard at the local guesthouse. Lucky for me, they still thought I was a boy. The winter was getting to be awful. I took the chance and got us a one-way ticket to Germany, getting a ride from a guest who took a liking to me. Most people would commend me for looking out for my older brother when he got drunk. There was this one night that I had to fight like a man. But that very night something triggered Nick's memories, and the following morning he got dressed and was able to walk into the British High Commission office and give them his details. They made some calls, and he was sent money for us to travel to the south of France, where his family had a villa. Things went well for us once we settled, and he wasn't drinking half as much.

I wanted to attend a college to learn to fly but had no papers. Nick came up with the idea of us getting married. It meant sending back to England for my birth certificate before we were able to be married. But it allowed me to get an identification and a passport. However, that training course was just to fly light aircraft without passengers. But I was hooked, I wanted to learn more. Other things were changing for me, Nick started to take an interest in me sexually and I couldn't object because I was his wife. The thing was, I knew when he left me at night where he was and who he was with. But at that time I didn't allow it to bother me because he was always interested in me and showed me a lot of love and wanted me to fulfil my own dreams.

Then he suggested we move to Canada, but insisted that we go under one condition, which was that I dress like a wife, meaning I was still being called his little brother.

That was how the transformation came about. Not too long after we were settled, Nick got cancer of the bowels. The news almost coincided with me getting my aviation pass and finally being able to fly commercial planes. But I had to stay home and nurse him for a year because he deteriorated so quickly. One morning after we had breakfast and I gave him his bath."

Jacky started laughing. "You know what he asked me to make, of all the things I was able to cook? He asked me to make him a cup of cornmeal porridge. So I did; he drank it, took my hand and said thank you, then closed his eyes.

I looked in his room at lunchtime; he was still sleeping. I went back at four and then had to call the police because I couldn't get him to wake up. His family all managed to get to Canada for his cremation and were ready to accuse me of all sorts of ridiculous things. But his doctors stood by me. In the end they released his life insurance to me. We owned our apartment, but I felt I needed to move on, so I moved to Atlanta. And the rest, as they say, is history."

She again reclined her seat and gave out a loud sigh, and I could see the tears running down her cheeks, but she was laughing. Which made me laugh too.

"That just sounds like the type of adventure we all expected you to have," I said. "But you mentioned something about Mum. About her being a Jamaican? I don't understand."

Jacky sucked on her teeth and said something under her breath.

"Me neither. When I started corresponding with Dad again, I told him, or rather asked him, who my real parents were. And he told me that when he got married to Jenny, she said that she didn't know she was pregnant. But he had always thought that she had given me his name because I went to school as Jacky Creary. I then told him about her passport and birth certificate.

When I found them at first, I didn't know the difference between the islands. But with what I now know, I found it impossible for her to be both Jamaican and Trinidadian at the same time. So Dad hired a detective to prove me wrong, and it made it worse, because he also found out that they had no record of a marriage between himself and a Jennifer Brown. From Trinidad or Jamaica."

"My god, this one takes the cake. Why on earth would she have told Dad that she is a Trinidadian? It just doesn't make any sense."

"Jack is blowing us, Beth, slow down."

"Oh, that is because he is thinking that I have missed the turnoff for the airport."

I pulled off the road and stopped. He was waving and pointing to the sign, then shouted, "We have just passed the sign saying Donald Sangster Airport!"

I shouted back, "You are right, but we still have an hour before the flight comes in, so I thought I would drive through the town to show you around first. But thanks for being so observant."

Jacky went over to hug and kiss him.

"Baby, we should stop at a restaurant or somewhere to have a drink and something to eat. You okay with that?"

"Don't worry, guys, there is food and drinks packed in the vehicle. It's Sunday, and you will hardly find any place open in Mobay. I will find somewhere in the town to stop so we can unpack the basket and eat."

I pulled in on the top of the hill overlooking the cricket ground, and we were refreshed while we watched a group of young men playing football in one section while others were working on the cricket pitch, maybe for a match later that evening.

"There is a plane coming in now; by my watch it's dead on time."

I pointed in the direction of the British Airways gliding smoothly past us on the way to landing. We waited for another hour or more at the outside of the airport until Jacky sprang from her seat.

"My goodness, is that Sophia? She hasn't changed a bit; she is still knock-down dead gorgeous."

We rushed towards the exit as the others struggled with suitcases and bags. Jacky's greeting to Sophia was, "Well, look at you, stunning as ever; you haven't changed a bit," and Sophia's remark was,

"My word, Grandma, where did you get those breasts? My, how you have changed!"

A few other smart exchanges brought laughter before we all did a group hug. Then Jacky introduced her husband-to-be, and Sophia introduced the twins before we made our way back to the car park.

"Ok everyone, there is food and drinks; take what you need before we start the drive back home."

The journey back to Oracabessa was a lot quicker, and we made it without incident, as I drove into our driveway with my sisters all sleeping. Even Rose, who was so sure that she would never sleep in the front of a car. Jack got most of the luggage to the rooms, and it was an instant hug and good night. Rose was fast asleep on my side of the bed by the time I settled Sophia and the twins. It was only ten p.m., and I was in no way ready for my bed.

I took the letter from under the pillow and found a comfortable spot in the sitting room. My phone vibrated, and I turned it on to read the messages. Two were work-related and two from Lloyd. I dialled his number.

"Goodnight, my pet, Are you home? How was the drive?"

"Good night, Doc. I only just had a chance to look at my phone. The drive up was good, hardly any traffic. We are home and all are asleep except yours truly. But I promise that I was going to read that letter from Dad which you gave me last week, so it's now in my hand and has been for the past twenty minutes; it's still sealed, and my hands are shaking."

"Beth, baby, take a deep breath."

His voice was almost a whisper and calming as he spoke again.

"Pet, close your eyes. Settle yourself for a moment, then look out on the ocean. The waves are slowly coming towards you, ever so gently. My darling, they will always come to you. Read your dad's words, and if you need me, call, ok? Kiss, kiss."

I switched off the phone after saying,

"Thank you, goodnight."

The first line read: 'My dearest Beth, you are reading this, I know, because I was not given the time to speak face to face, but I had to pen it in black and white for your future benefit.' And also I really needed to put it together in a way that cut to the chase and put you clearly in the picture. It took me a while, but tonight my mind is clear. First I will state the facts, but at the end of this you will understand the bigger picture. I am so sorry I waited this long to tell you. I know that over the years, with Rose and I being left at home and always spending so much time together, she got the story little by little, but please allow her to also read this letter.

On the next page, the letter got formal with time and date and address and phone numbers, also with reference to Lloyd being his doctor and witness to the official papers signed by his signature and another person.

'I, Paul Junior Creary and being of sound mind; this is my last will and testament. My lawyers have been instructed to read all legal papers after I am laid to rest. But before that, I want to know that when you walk into that church, your minds will be also at rest. God bless you, my dearest Beth. Just this week, I paid down a deposit on that home you so like in Savoy Mews. That property, along with the Plaza, now belongs to you. The rent from the plaza can adequately repay your mortgage, and I know that you are able to maintain yourself without being dependent on any other.

Our house here in Oracabessa is owned jointly by yourself, Rose, Sophia and Jacky.

Rose is the sole owner of her property in Islington, London, England.

It's my wish that you will continue the business at PauliMay. It's an excellent source of income, and I know you enjoy the work.

There are no obsolete guarantees in life, Beth, but I wish you every blessing on having your children by your side. Your uncle Steffan made arrangements for them to speak with me over the telephone at my request, so yes, I can say that I have met them. And you have every reason to be proud; they are marvellous children.

Jacky has plans to get married in Jamaica. If I miss her wedding, please look in the trunk in my bathroom; you will find a present I selected for her. I am thankful that she already know her own story and has made peace with herself, and one day her birth mother and father also.

Sophia, bless her heart, is a good soul and a gem. I know she will always be there for you and Rose.

Rose my little mouse, would have been told bits and pieces from time to time and may have put the bigger picture together for herself in some sort of way.

The house in London, where you girls were born and grew up, was the property of Mary's mother. And when she died it was passed on to Mary; she in turn passed it down to me, and so it is now in my power to pass it to her three daughters, Pauline, Patricia and Prudence. You may be wondering, what about Jenny? It is unfortunate, but I can say without a doubt. She deserve and will get nothing from me. It was with such sad and utter shame and much disappointment that I found out that we were never married, and to top it all, she had the nerve to live with us all these years and have us believe that she was a Trinidadian, only to find that her true birthplace is Spanish Town, Jamaica. And it can be proven without a shadow of a doubt. Had I been in London when I received that bit of news, maybe I would not have lived to write this letter. But that is, as it is, my love. I have been blessed to have you and Rose, and for that I have to give thanks to God that he was able to lead me to Liza. I promised myself that if I were unable to tell you face to face, then I would write my story because you need to know, and I know that you will understand.'

The story that followed was almost word for word what Dad told me on the Sunday night before he died. I still read it through line for line, even though the hot tears swelled in my eyes from time to time.

It was past three a.m. I was drained and trying to comfort myself when Rose appeared at the doorway.

"There you are. I thought that we were sharing a room?"

"We are, but you were sleeping on my side of the bed."

She threw a cushion at me before coming over to hug me, and we laughed together.

"I could do with a cup of Ovaltine; do you have any?"

"Not Ovaltine, but the Jamaican version."

I told her I would make us both a cup of Milo. We left the sitting room for the kitchen. I placed the kettle on the gas burner and started to take out the cups. The kitchen doors opened from both sides of the room, Sophia from one end and Jacky from the other. This brought a loud chuckle from all four.

"Do you remember when Dad used to make this drink with hot milk, and each time he would turn around, we would wet our fingers and dip them in the tin?" said Jacky.

"Except that I was the only one who ever got caught," Sophia said, laughing.

I was thinking that it was so funny that we were all in the kitchen at that time of the morning, so I asked,

"How come all of you are up this time anyways?"

They replied in unison, "Dad woke me up!"

We all looked at each other with rolling eyes before we burst out laughing. With cups in hand I said, "Come with me to the sitting room, girls. Dad woke you all for more than Milo." I took out the letter while they made themselves comfortable.

"I know that you all know some of what you are about to hear, but after reading this, it will be nice to know that we all are on the same page."

I gave the wads of paper to Rose, making sure to place the will for last. No one commented until Rose was through reading.

Jacky clapped and commented,

"Good to go, Dad. That conniving so-and-so deserved nothing, not one red cent."

"Why do you think she lied about being a Trinidadian, though? "I just can't see a valid reason," Sophia remarked. "And what is even worse, she got Dad into thinking they were married. Why would she have done that? Why? And Beth, how do you and Mouse feel about her not being your birth mother after all these years?"

"Well, I can't wait to see her face when she knows that we all know the full story," said Rose. "I really do not think I want to be given an explanation."

"My God, why am I the only one who has to call her mother?" said Jacky.

"She has been everything but a mother to me; she was always mean. Dad was the one who fed me and looked out for me. Even when he knew all along that I was not his child. I could not give a fig's ass if I did not have to see her again. As far as I am concerned, I have no mother."

Jacky started to cry. And that set us all off. We wept together, hugging and consoling each other, each individually but collectively feeling the same pain.

"Mum, Mum, where are you?"

I opened my eyes and instantly looked at the clock on the wall; it was seven a.m.

"In here," I shouted.

Jack and the twins appeared through the sitting room doorway to find four grown women huddled together on the settee.

"So you guys decided to have a pyjama party, and we were not invited."

remarked Jack, as he sat on the carpet close to Jacky. The twins jumped on the settee, between and on top of their mother.

"Is that a photo of Uncle Paul?" One of them asked, pointing to a photo hanging on the wall.

"Do you have any more, Aunty?"

I reached for the half dozen photo albums with photos we had taken over the years. We all spent time looking through, laughing and reminiscing over each snap until they got bored.

"Oh good Lord, it's after nine, and we have a ten o'clock appointment with the pastor!"

Everyone rushed from the room to get washed and dressed for our day outing. With no time to make breakfast, we grabbed fruits, water, and biscuits as we left. We were able to leave the house by ten thirty, and were thankful that the pastor was also running late and he got there at eleven.

"So we were all on time," said Jack, grinning with amusement.

Pastor Fairweather hugged each person as they were introduced.

"I must say Mr Creary has a very attractive family, and it's good to see you all. Please rest assured that your father will be sadly missed; having been such a good and faithful servant of the church and this community he adopted. Let me take you to the burial spot before you settle, and it will also give my secretary time to prepare my own tribute."

While we walked through the church grounds, he reminisced.

"You know, the very first time I met Mr Creary was right under that black mango tree. The Men's Fellowship had a meeting for the planning of our church hall which is shared by the basic school. Mr Creary supplied us with most of the building material and even laid a few of the blocks with his own hands. So although the spot will be a little way away from the other graves, I think it would be fitting to give him that spot, and while I am about it, I should make sure my name is right beside his. I couldn't want a better friend in heaven."

We all laughed. I was again made to feel special knowing that Dad was loved. I informed him,

"Pastor, John will be making arrangements for lunch and refreshments and wanted to know which day they could dig the grave."

The pastor replied,

"Wednesday or Thursday would be in order, and I will ask our caretaker to fill some drums with water because the water pipe is a good way off. But John can go ahead and make his arrangements; I will let the staff in the office know to keep an eye out for him."

On our walk back to the church office, I called John and also let Mrs Mac know that we would be stopping by the office later that evening. Rose and I followed the pastor into his office while the others stayed outside to eat the mangos they had picked along the way.

Pastor Fairweather started the meeting with a prayer. Then he suggested,

"I don't know if you have selected your choice of songs, but I know that the choir would love to sing 'The Lord is my Shepherd' to a special arrangement which Mr Creary always requested. Also, the children would like to show their appreciation and perform their school song, and then, of course, I would love for you to print my tribute on behalf of the church and school. And I am preparing to conduct his service this Sunday if it's convenient to you and the family."

Rose and I nodded in agreement.

"Ok, my dears; Sunday at one o'clock, following our morning service, and of course the church hall is available for the repass, unless you wish to have it done at your home. Also, I must add that it is a custom of the church to request that the collection of the offering for the funeral service be donated to the church building funds."

"All of that is fine with us, Pastor, and we will accept the church hall for the repass. John is also planning for the nine-night at the house on Saturday evening. Please feel free to come."

We got up to leave.

"One more thing, Mrs Kworori. Another custom of the church is to have a prayer meeting with the family of the dearly departed, in the church or at your house; that will be your choice."

Rose immediately said she thought it would be best at the house so he would be able to bless the house also. We agreed on a time for the meeting before we left.

Next stop was the undertakers. Everyone wanted to view Dad's body, so we waited for the undertakers to prepare the room while we went over the programme to be printed and the choice of colour to cover the inside of the coffin. When we left, we were all teary-eyed and a little shaken up from seeing the lifeless body of one so dear. We brought soft drinks and sat by the roadside for a while before deciding that Rose and I should leave the others and see the bank manager together.

All of Dad's accounts were in order; thankfully he had no outstanding bills. The purchase of my new home was done in my name using a mortgage from the Plaza, which was also transferred in my name, so all I needed to do was put my signature on the paperwork. The transfer of our present home to my three siblings and myself was in its final process at the land title office. A lot of the other financial information given to us, Dad had already told me, even when I was thinking that I did not need to know all that information. But I now saw the importance of Dad taking so much trouble to put me in the picture. We left the bank after almost an hour and made our way to the PauliMay office.

Ms Mac was beside herself, hugging and kissing everyone and holding on to Sophia's hand as if they were glued together. Taking her to each of the shops in the plaza, introducing her, basically showing her off as Mr Paul's white daughter. We were there until closing time, Ms Mac making sure she fed them with as much Jamaican food as they could eat. We then took a drive through Ocho Rios in the late afternoon to evening, stopping for dinner at one of the many hotel restaurants in the area.

During the dinner, one of the twins requested,

"Aunty, can we please go to the beach tomorrow?"

"I will definitely second that," said Jack.

"We have been seeing a lot of sun but no beach and sand," Rose said. "Is everything sorted now, Beth? Do we need to put any other things in place before the funeral?"

"No," I replied. "I think that we have taken care of everything today. The rest of the planning is up to John and the other staff members; it's mainly cooking and catering, so we should be able to spend the day at the beach tomorrow. Then on Wednesday, we can visit Dunn's River Falls."

"Please, can we go to that pork place?" asked Rose.

"That would be Boston in Portland, OK; that will work for Thursday."

"On Friday, can we go see your new house, Beth? I am dying to see what it's like," remarked Jacky.

"No problem, and that reminds me, I should call the Budd's to let them know the updates , also Rose please can you help me later, we need to send out emails to inform our clients of the date for the funeral service, I will deal with the phone calls."

The twins started to sing.

"Yeah we have a holiday plan."

Sophia reminded them that they were not on holiday but in Jamaica to show respect to their uncle and to bond with the rest of their family.

They answered as children do.

"Yes, Mother, but surely you could not fault us after taking us to such a great place and not expecting us to enjoy ourselves also. And we really need to go back to England showing off a tan!"

Needless to say, it brought laughter back to the group and closed off the day on a pleasant note.

Rose completed the emails in no time. I left messages on the phones of the clients I was unable to contact in person. I also had a message sent to me by Carol, whom I had kept up to date with everything. She did not meet Dad in person, but often when she called, I would pass the phone to him. She became his daughter number eight. But I knew it would be too much to expect her or Uncle Steffan to make it to Jamaica at such short notice. After I showered and changed for bed, I first called Lloyd.

"Hey, how are you? How was your day? And how are your sisters and others?"

I ran through the events of our day and told him of our plans for the remainder of the week.

"You did remember to put me down on the programme, right?"

"Yes, I did, and we decided between us that Jacky and Sophia should read Dad's eulogy. Rose felt that she will be able to sing; she has a pretty good singing voice. I don't think I could keep my voice from cracking up, so I am happy just making sure it all goes well.

But I know it's late and you need your beauty sleep, Doc. Also, I have another important call to make before I turn in, so you get some rest, and I will speak to you tomorrow, OK?"

Lloyd replied, "Love you, my pet."

After he hung up, it took me a while to relax. Those are the words Dad often used after we said goodnight. I went to the kitchen for a cold drink before returning to the sitting room to call Carol. She was the first person I had called after leaving the hospital following Dad's death. Uncle Steffan was so shocked on hearing the untimely announcement. He, in turn, called me and has sent me a message every day since that Sunday. Carol and I had kept in touch at least once per week after I made the decision to return to London, not wanting to remain in Paris and be reminded of David at every street café. So over the years, while I have been in Jamaica, she has been the bridge, always giving me an update on the children. And when she and Uncle Steffan started getting intimate, she confided in me. They had also managed to take control of my children after an incident with David's first wife, who had decided to visit the children in Switzerland and wanted to take them out of the boarding school.

"Oh Beth, I am so glad that you were able to call. I am about to leave for the airport, and Steffan had to go to Nigeria on business, so I really didn't want to miss speaking to you before I left. Have you made any further arrangements regarding your father?"

I brought her up to date on our arrangements and what was going on with my sisters and me. We terminated the call because she said she had an appointment to pick up her son. She wished me good luck and goodnight.

On Tuesday we set out for the beach and spent the day at the White River beach. For the remainder of the week, we spent the days according to plan.

On Saturday morning, I felt that I should remain home while the others visited the beach behind our house. They decided to walk for the adventure.

About midday, an open-back truck with a few men drove up to set up an outdoor kitchen and to put out the domino tables and chairs for the function later that evening.I was happy to have followed my mind and remained at home. Another truck came by with food, ice, and other items.

While I stood at the gate allowing them to go to and fro, a car drove up with two women at the front. They were looking around and returning their eyes to a paper on the dashboard as if they were confirming the address. I stepped out onto the pavement close to the car.

Prudence noticed me and got out from the passenger side.

We hugged while the other woman looked on.

We were later introduced, after which she offered her condolences regarding my father.

Prudence went to the boot of the car and took out her case, then returned to have a private conversation with the driver. They kissed and said goodbye. The woman waved at me before starting the car, then shouted back the question:

"When is the funeral?"

I told her Sunday. She then asked Prudence when she would like her to come back and collect her. Pru took some time to answer, so she said:

"Tell you what, call the hotel and leave me a message when you are ready, OK?"

Pru nodded her head in agreement, and the woman drove off. We watched the car for a while before turning to hug each other again.

"It's good to see you, Beth; it's been a while. You are looking great."

"And so do you, Pru. I like your haircut. Hope I am not speaking out of turn, but was that the Sam as in "Husband Sam"?

She just nodded her head 'yes' but looked uncomfortable and turned to pick up her bag. To put her at ease, I walked around her and led the way while I gave my approval, telling her:

"I like Sam, she seems nice, and looks as if she knows her way around."

For whatever reason, I did not take her further than the veranda. We sat and talked while I served her a cold glass of lemonade.

"So are you alone? What happened to Rose will she be here?"

"Oh Rose and the others are already here, they all went around to the beach. I stayed behind to allow these people access to the yard to prepare for the nine night later."

"I have heard about that. Sam and I went to one which was kept for a relative of her mother last week. It was quite interesting. But I didn't walk with my camera, so I will make sure I am at the ready tonight. You mentioned the others, who else is here?"

"Jacky with her expected fiancé, and Sophia with her twin girls and of course our Rose."

"What about Mum? I thought that they would be here, they did say they were coming in on Wednesday?"

"That was the last message I received also, but it seems that they have lost their way."

I said, shrugging my shoulders while I answered. I also got up to open the gate to the veranda for the twins who were running a race towards me.

"Look what I found Aunty!" "No mine is better look at mine Aunty!"

They kept up the excitement, showing me a starfish, conch shell, brainstone, driftwood, and a handful of other treasures they picked up along the beach, until the others joined us.

Sophia and Rose slumped down in the chairs closest to them, just casually saying hi to Pru. When Jacky joined us, she called out in surprise.

"Prudence, is that really you? You are looking great, girl. Love that haircut. Where are the others?"

"Thanks for the compliments; I have to return the same. I would not have recognised you at all, Jacky."

Jacky pulled her up from the chair and hugged her. Then introduced Jack to her.

Who said hello but excused himself, saying that he was still wet and could not hug her. The twins also said hello and went off to the fridge for cold drinks. Sophia then asked Prudence:

"So where are the rest of the musketeers and Jenny?"

"As a matter of fact, I expected to see them here. This is the house where Uncle Paul was living, right?"

Pru placed a lot of emphasis on her statement, so Sophia answered her crudely.

"Right! But it is also Beth's home. Why do you ask?"

Pru cleared her throat and sat up in the chair.

"Well I remembered Mum asking that Beth should wait until she got here, so mum could make arrangements for the funeral. So I am surprise to hear that there is going to be a funeral on Sunday when she is still not here. How could you go ahead with a service tomorrow and mother isn't even here? I don't understand why the rush. Mum is going to be so pissed."

"Not as pissed as I am right now, Pru. said Jacky angrily.

"First of all, Beth don't have to wait on Jenny for anything; she and Rose have all the right to make the arrangement for their father to be laid to rest."

"I am aware that he was their father, Jacky, but Jenny..."

Before Pru could finish the sentence, Jacky got up and pulled Prudence up from her seat by the front of her blouse.

"Don't even mention that woman's name; she is nothing to Uncle Paul, and if I was Beth, I would not want her near me. She is my birth mother, and thank God that is all she is. If there was a way to change that, I would gladly do it. Don't you ever disrespect Beth; this is her house. Jenny has no say in the matter."

Jacky pushed Pru back down in the chair with as much force as she had pulled her up, then walked away. After we all collected ourselves, and even more so Prudence, who was now as red as a carrot, cleared her throat and covered her face in embarrassment.

"I am sorry; I have not been as close to Jenny and the others in the last five years. Clearly there is something going on that I have missed."

Sophia got up and took Pru's hand. And, as she is noted for, also changed the subject.

"So will you be staying for the funeral tomorrow? Come on, come with me; you can share my room. The girls are sleeping on my bed anyway, so there is plenty of room. Come on."

Sophia took up her bag and led her to the back bedroom.

I sat for a long time watching the activities transforming in the yard, more people joining and the festivities taking shape. Rose was curled up in a chair at one corner of the veranda, where she had fallen asleep. I took out my phone and called Lloyd; he was expected to be off work from two p.m.

"Oh Beth, I am glad you called. I am not going to make it this evening, I'm afraid; my relief doctor is held up in Kingston with a patient. The matron also had an emergency and had to take a few hours off. I have to continue running the ward to give them both a chance to get some rest before they return to take up their duties. So you will have to tell me all about the gathering tomorrow, but how are things going so far?"

I filled him in on what was happening in the front yard as we spoke and that another of my sisters had turned up but did not mention what had taken place. Then I could hear his beeper going off.

"Please save some of the sprat and breadfruit for me; I have got to go, hon. Speak to you later. One other thing. Can you drive with me tomorrow, please? I will come to collect you so we can travel to the church together. Will that be OK?"

"Yes, I would love that. Rose can drive my car; I would love to go with you."

"Great, looking forward to that," he replied. Kiss, kiss, Beth, my love, have a good evening."

I continued watching the frolics of the grown men roaming around in the garden until I also dozed off. The clapping of the dominoes on the table drifted into my dream. Jack and Jacky went out to join in with the games. Sophia, the twins, and Pru followed with her camera.

Rose woke first and went inside to change before she too got into a game of dominoes with the men around a wooden table. She woke me for the prayer being given by the pastor. I kept looking out towards the gate for the Budd family but saw no sign of them. They had been at the prayer meeting the night before, so I expected that they were tired.

Also, it seems that Mr Budd had a problem getting home after taking a wrong turning. I called to make sure they were home and safe and almost panicked when, after an hour, they still were not answering their house phone. It was only a fifteen-minute drive to their home from where we were. Apparently their eyesight is not as it should be, and the bright headlights caused them to turn off the main road, which took them through a section of the town they were not familiar with, but thank God, after directions, they were able to find their way home.

I finally went out to join the others when a group of three men started to chant and play on their colourfully decorated drums.

It was electrifying. I could have stayed up all night with the sound of those drums. Unlike the previous Saturday night, Ms Mac just said goodnight and left, and then others left in their own time. When it was only Gertrude, John, and a few other men clearing up the used cups and plates, the drummers stopped playing to collect food they could take home. John took everyone home except Gertrude, who had asked to stay the night, as she would not have been able to get a taxi from her home; the road would be without the usual traffic, being a Sunday morning. She insisted on cooking a pot of ackee and saltfish for the following morning's breakfast before turning in. Rose and I cleaned up the kitchen and sitting room before we also gave in to sleep.

Chapter Seven

"Sunday morning I woke to the loud and rumbustious singing voice of Gertrude in the backyard. She had chosen a spot in the backyard to read her Bible and sing her choruses. I listened while I lay in silence, singing along with her in my mind. My own bedside clock alarmed later at half-past seven, which woke Rose. She got up and stretched a hand across my back to turn it off.

"Morning, sis. You ok?" I asked her.

"I guess so. Hope it will be a good day for Dad," she answered.

"Hope so too. At the moment I feel like running to somewhere—anywhere—but I know that I should just count to ten and breathe slowly. By the way, sis, can you drive my car to the church today? Lloyd asked me to accompany him in his car. I think that he may want to read through his tribute to dad for me before the service. Also, I have not seen him all week, so it would be nice to relax with him for a moment."

The door to our bedroom opened, and Sophia walked in.

"Morning, sleepyheads. Beth, your helper has been keeping church from five o'clock this morning; when will she stop?"

"Your guess is as good as mine, sis. I had no idea that she even read the Bible. Most of the time people are afraid to cross her because she will spin you in webs of cloth."

"Excuse me?"

I explained to Sophia about Jamaican swear words, but she still did not understand, so she changed the subject.

"Beth, love, we have a problem. I thought that I had chosen two nice dresses for the twins to wear to Dad's service, but your Gertrude informed me last night that they are not appropriate—or, as she puts it, 'Them too dressy, dressy'. You and the girls have about the same waist measurement. Do you happen to have a couple of skirts that they can borrow? They already have matching white blouse."

"I can't understand how you manage to keep so slim. Even Rose is fatter than you now, Beth."

"That is because Rose still cook enough for two and then has to eat Dad's share as well."

We all ended up in a pillow fight, joined in by Jacky, who had also entered for a chat—even when she scolded us for being too happy. Then came a male voice trying to be serious.

"Well, this is the last thing I expected of you ladies so early in the morning. What brought this on?"

"I guess it's just Dad telling us to stay strong because he is in a good place," I said. "But while you are all here, ladies—and Jack—Ms Gertrude has asked me to give her son a few of Dad's old shirts and trousers. Take a look and see if there is anything you want to hold on to before I start giving his stuff away."

"That helper of yours is something else. I am sure she has already picked out the exact outfit she expects to get. Every item of clothing I put on, her remark is always the same, 'dat would look so nice on my big daughter.'" Rose scoffed; her comments are now predictable.

That comment brought another bout of laughter, as I scattered Dad's clothes on the bed, while Sophia fitted on one of Dad's pinstriped long-sleeve shirts. We all agreed on how good it looked on her, so we each tried on a shirt of our choice, then viewed ourselves in the mirror. Jacky sent Jack for a camera to take a photo for the memories. We also found two skirts for the twins from my wardrobe, and for Gertrude I placed in a bag four shirts and trousers, a jacket suit, and a pair of shoes from Dad's stuff to present to her.

"By the way, Beth, I hope that you won't mind; your letter was still in the sitting room, so I gave it to Prudence earlier this morning. I think that she would understand best if it came from the horse's mouth, so to speak."

"Amen to that. It's fine with me. I really don't want to get into it with her or the others, so when her sisters and Jenny turns up, she will be able to explain it all to them. I am good with that."

The others agreed.

"OK, I can smell the breakfast, so let's go eat," said Rose.

Prudence and the twins were already around the table. I remembered the Budds and called their house.

"Good morning, my dear Beth. Mr Budd only just drove in; he took the flowers to the church as soon as he was up this morning."

"Good morning, Mrs Budd, please tell him thanks for me, and I will see you both at the church. I just called to check that you were both okay. I did not see you last night, but I realised that you may have been a little tired after doing your weekly shopping. But I won't keep you. Bye for now."

The family left the dining table in time to get dressed for the day. I showered but kept on a loose-fitting house dress while I washed the dishes and left the kitchen in order. No sooner had I finished than Lloyd's car pulled up at the gate.

I knew because of the comments coming from my sister, who was already on the veranda. And by the time they all welcomed him and introduced themselves, I got myself together and was ready to go. It wasn't possible to miss the surprised look on his face and my sisters' when I said,

"Good morning, Doc."

I also got a 'wow' from the twins but had no intention of drawing further attention to myself. I ushered them out while Gertrude and I locked up before driving off in a convoy of three cars to the church. Lloyd kept glancing over towards me, which started to make my heart flutter, but I kept my cool. When we drove into the church parking lot, he reached over and held my hand, which still rested on my lap.

"Beth, we need to talk before you go in." I did not know what to expect, nor was I thinking it would be anything that I couldn't handle.

"Your uncle Steffan called me late last night."

My eyelids went up; I was more than surprised, but I waited for him to finish.

"He was given my name and number by your father. He arrived in Jamaica late last night but felt it was better to call me rather than get you up so late. I picked him up from the hotel this morning and took him here, so he is waiting for you in the church office."

Of course, I was out of the car before he had a chance to complete the sentence. When I entered the church office, the first face I saw was Carol. I screamed and ran to hug her, and from the corner of my eye, Uncle Steffan's figure was approaching. My emotions got the better of me, and I could not keep back the screams of sheer joy and excitement, even worse when I felt smaller bodies and hands hugging me from behind and knew for sure that they were of my own children, Mario and Monai. My sisters heard my screams, and soon the office was full of laughter and crying. I wore no makeup because I did not want to end up looking a mess, knowing that I would not hold back the tears during Dad's service. I washed my face once I was able to calm down. The bathroom was to the side of the office, and Lloyd had not left my side. He had a small towel with which he tapped the water dry from my face as gently as if he were holding a newborn baby. In the midst of all that excitement, he kissed me so deeply I held on for dear life because I was drowning in happiness.

The pastor gave us some time for the family to reunite and was himself taken up with the events of the day. The music from the hearse carrying Dad's coffin could be heard from the churchyard, so we were told to prepare ourselves for the service.

We followed behind as the choir led the way through the centre of the church, followed by the pastor and Mr Wright, playing his

202

saxophone. While he continued to play, we all paid our respects to Dad by walking around the coffin, each person stopping to say our last goodbye before taking our seats.

After we were seated, Mr Wright continued his playing at a lower and slower, reverent tone, setting the mood for the service. The pastor started by saying:

"We are here today because our lives have all been touched by the living of Mr Paul Junior Creary, who was sent to bless us and help us on our own journey through this life! We want to thank him, and we want to let his family know that his body may be lying in the box before us, but his soul will live on in our hearts forever. Because Mr Creary was a man of his word and a man of God, who never stopped doing whatever was in his power to help others."

After completing his opening prayer, the pastor took up his seat in the middle of the row behind the lectern, and the organist played while the children marched up and took up their positions to sing their song in tribute to Dad. The saxophone played as they marched back down again, and John went up, followed by Gertrude and Ms Mac. Then the Budds sang a duet. What was a surprise was that one of the shop operators from the plaza gave a tribute on behalf of the others and spoke glowingly about Dad. He also gave me an envelope containing cash which was collected on Dad's behalf.

"The church organ started to play. 'O Lord my God when I in...' we all sang. Rose went up to read Dad's favourite Psalm, Psalm 26: Judge me, Lord, for I have walked in thine integrity. I have trusted also in the Lord; therefore I shall not slide... Verse one to verse twelve and last. The organist played I Come to the Garden Alone... We all sang.

Uncle Stefan gave his tribute and greetings to the family. We all sang There is a Place of Quiet Rest... Lloyd gave his tribute and spoke lovingly of a father and a man he will always call a friend.

The organist played, and we all sang When Peace Like a River... Jacky read the eulogy. The second lesson was read by Sophia, Ecclesiastes 3:1–15, which read: *To everything there is a season, and a time to every purpose under the heavens...* to end.

The choir gave their rendition of The Lord is My Shepherd... to the arrangement which was Dad's favourite, and then Pastor Fairweather said his tribute on behalf of the church, followed by a short sermon.

We were all asked to say a silent prayer of farewell to the memory of Paul Creary before we sang the last hymn, Be Not Dismayed... The pallbearers took up their places: Mario and Monai leading, followed by John and Mr Budd, then Mr Grey and Miss Gertrude's son, Lloyd and Stefan. It was a short walk which seemed to have taken forever. The church choir walked ahead of the family members and were singing low and serene, I Am Coming Home to You, Lord Jesus...

At the graveside, the pastor gave his last farewell and closed with *'ashes to ashes and dust to dust'*. All family members placed a white carnation on the coffin before it was lowered into the grave. John and the men from the plaza took up shovels and started to replace the soil over the coffin. The tears rolled hot down my cheeks. Mr Wright started to play Dad's song in a slow, mournful way. I found my voice and raised it high:

Roll Jordon Roll, Roll Jordon Roll, I want to get to heaven to go meet me Jesus and fi go hear River Jordon Roll. Roll, River Jordon.

The sopranos in the choir picked up Roll River Jordon. The bass singers repeated Roll River Jordon, before everyone joined in to restart the chorus. The men moved their shovels to the beat, and the drummers added the rhythm. I saw Dad with his arms around my children singing along.

There were no more tears. My soul was at peace.

All of the seamless arrangement was at the insistence of Prudence, who followed the plan listed out on the programme and kept everyone in line as she snapped away with her camera, holding for eternity the memories of such an eventful day.

The drummers took over at the repast and kept us all moving to the rhythm of our ancestors, while people who knew our dad came to say their last good wishes to the family and collected boxes of their choice of food to take back home with them. A table was prepared for the family to partake of the evening meal by Miss Gertrude and Ms Mac. Seated also were the pastor, Mr Grey, Mr Wright and the Budds.

While Lloyd kept his eyes on me, I kept my eyes on my children, almost as if I were daydreaming. How possible was it to have had such a perfect day?

We all fitted into the three cars and made our way back to the house. We hugged, kissed, laughed and talked over drinks until the children got restless. Carol's son Dominic came to ask her:

"Mum, Mario and Monai are going to stay the night with their cousin. Can I please stay too?"

Rose heard the request and quickly gave the answer.

"They can all stay in our room, and I will move in with Sophia and Pru."

My fate seemed to have been sealed, so I asked:

"Oh, so you are kicking me out too?"

I hugged and kissed my little sister as we all shared the joke.

"It's ok anyway, because I want to go back to the hotel tonight with Aunt Carol and Uncle Stefan. We have a lot to talk about; I hope you won't mind?"

I was asking for my children's approval, but everyone answered so instantly, which brought more laughter. I packed an overnight bag and left Jack in charge of the locking up.

At the hotel I asked Uncle Steffan, "You won't mind if Lloyd stays on with us; we are sort of an item!"

"Oh, we are?" Lloyd questioned, raising his eyebrows.

His lips were slightly parted, which I so wanted to kiss at that moment.

Steffan said jokingly, "Not a problem; Carol and I are sort of an item also."

Carol held out her hand to show off her wedding band as an explanation.

"Wow, this is great. I am so happy for you both. I was so caught up with all that has been my day of perfect bliss; I did not take notice."

Uncle Steffan continued explaining further, "I have recently accepted a new position across the waters in Singapore, and I couldn't see myself leaving her behind and certainly would not have asked her to go with me as a bedmate. We will be serving as husband and wife starting next month."

More hugs and kisses followed, then an announcement from Carol.

"I asked the room service to bring up something special."

She went to fetch a small table and placed it closer to where we were sitting.

"Beth, remember when we last parted company in London we said when we again got together we would celebrate with…"

The knock came right on cue.

"Baileys and ice cream,"

I told her, clapping my hands together, so happy that she had remembered. The unexpected treat was an ideal ice-breaker. We were all relaxed in a perfect intimate setting.

"Please tell me, Uncle Steffan, how did you manage all of this? And to get here at such short notice."

He hugged Carol, who was seated under his arm on the sofa.

"Oh Beth, I had been brainstorming and testing various plans since you left us in Paris. You know that I never want to leave a paper trail of any of my assignments which would cloud the situation. So I had to move slowly and think clearly. But having some friends in the right places also helped.

A year after you left, as you know, David's wife visited the children's school with the intention of taking them back to Kenya to live with her. Of course, this was a plan for her to try and get back at you. She told the headmistress that their mother had died and she was now their guardian.

Of course, if you remember, when they were enrolled in the school, it was my mother, yourself and I who were present on that day. And in your absence, I was to be the next person in charge, not David. She was not aware of this. But the Head got the children together anyway and left them with her in her office while she called me on the phone from another room.

It went without saying, of course; I told her in no uncertain terms that she should not allow them to leave the school in the care of the stepmother. And if necessary, she should allow David's wife to speak to me on the phone. When she returned to the office, however, the children asked to speak with her, and they did so in German, not English. It was clear that their stepmother did not understand.

They explained to their head that their stepmother had been discussing with her friend, who had accompanied her, in a very unsavoury manner what she was about to do to the children when she got to take them home.

What their stepmother did not know also was that David had taught the children his mother's language, so they were able to understand her every word. While the stepmother boasted of being in charge, the Head returned to speak with me, and between us we were able to contrive a plan, which explained that it was impossible for the children to leave school during the term and also that I would personally take them home during the summer holidays. After that incident, of course, you know that I had to come up with something more permanent to prevent the children from ever going back to Kenya.

It was your father who gave me the idea (God rest his soul). The children were registered into the school using your maiden name, because I remember my mother having concerns about how well you would accept the custom of David being able to marry more than one wife and thought that you may not want to live in Nigeria or Kenya. Should you want to take the children back to England, then you would not have a problem. It was a matter of getting them British passports. Of course, you know my work schedule, and also I didn't want to rush it and create a larger problem on my hands.

Over the five years I've had to make sure that when they return to see their father during the summer holidays I was there, and also work out how to tell David without also telling him that you are still very much alive. I have learnt that his wife is an exceptionally evil woman and would do everything in her power to cause mischief if she knew that she had been outsmarted. He still doesn't know anything about this; David has accepted an invitation for us to meet up in New York in a month or so, thinking we have a planned business merger to discuss. At which time I will figure out how much I can disclose to him. They were expecting the children to return to Kenya at the end of this month and would not start to make any enquiries until then.

One other thing in our favour is that the headmistress retired last term, and unfortunately the school will also be closing down due to unforeseen problems on their part. So the paper trail will be quite thin, knowing that they had successfully graduated and were presumably being taken home by their father. I would not normally use the name Kworori, but at their graduation, because it was also a termination of their schooling, I did sign off on their forms using their father's name. However, they left for South Africa in the names of Creary and as very much British subjects. I used the private jet from there back to Nigeria. We travelled first class from Nigeria to London, then New York, and onwards to Jamaica. Of course, all of this started a couple of weeks before Paul died. I had called him so he could speak to the children when we arrived in South Africa. So my dear Beth, your children are home with you to stay."

I was speechless and remained motionless, lost for words; my heart was full to bursting, so I cried. Uncle Steffan laughed and commented that Jamaica must have something to do with my crying so much, because during all that I endured in Africa I was fearless, and he never saw me cry once.

I replied, "That is because I can only cry happy tears, Uncle Steffan. I don't cry when I am sad."

"Actions of a true warrior. When your back is up against the wall, you brace and come up with a strategy."

He hugged me and kissed my forehead. "You deserve to be happy, my darling Beth. And your children need to be with you. I am happy that I have been able to be a part of making that happen."

Lloyd, who was sitting opposite, got up to hug and congratulate me on getting the children back home at a time when I would most need them close, and he offered to assist me in getting them into a school or college as soon as they were settled. Carol joined in the group hug.

"Beth, my sister, I could not be happier for you. The children understood everything. When we explained to them what we had to do, they were with us all the way and regretted that they may not see their father again but were willing to choose you over him and would never want to live with his wife or accept the customs of the palace. So you should have no reason to feel guilty about them being away from their father. When you get a chance to speak with them, you will realise that they are quite balanced and grown up in their thinking. They are happy being here and being back with you."

Carol brought out a case filled with all the legal papers, passports, and school reports for the children. We went through them, commenting on how well the children did in school and that they were to be commended. Unnoticed by us, the sun had started to compete with the night light from the sitting room.

Noise from outside the balcony alerted us that it was already daybreak.

"Oh goodness, I was wondering why I was feeling so hungry. Can you believe that we went through the night and not realise it?"

Carol laughed and got up to pull the drapes, letting in the first light of the sun. I remembered at that moment that Lloyd had stayed up with us.

"Oh no, Lloyd. Are you off today? What time should you be at work?" I asked, concerned that I had kept him up all night, but he gave me a reassuring hug.

"I am good, my sweets, working from two to ten today."

"Well, you had best go get some rest anyway. Carol, you don't mind Lloyd using the spare room to rest a few hours?"

"Not a problem, but it's already six-thirty, so we may as well make our way to breakfast first."

After breakfast I left the others to sleep while I took a taxi and returned home. Jack and Jacky were wrapped together in one hammock under the tree in the front garden. They saw me first and shouted, "Good morning."

"Please be careful and reinforce the ropes for your weight; I don't want to see either of you in a cast. Good morning, did you both have a good night's rest?"

"Good morning, Sis. Not to worry, I made sure to adjust for our weight. Jacky would need more than a cast if I were to fall on top of her."

We all laughed. The children, who were already playing round the backyard, heard my voice and rushed me before I got to the steps of the veranda.

The questions came fast, but I answered each one as I made my way to a seat on the veranda.

"Okay, my question: did you all make your beds?"

They looked from one to the other and slowly said in unison, "No!"

I held up the suitcase with their change of clothes.

"So bed first, then a shower, and maybe…" Before I could finish speaking, there was an uproar at the front gate. I shooed them inside while I went to speak to the young man who was knocking on the gate and shouting with enough noise to wake the dead. By the time I got to the gate, suitcases were being placed on the sidewalk, and two white ladies were fighting to detach themselves from the back seat of the taxi. While they adjusted their hats and dresses, another person exited from the front passenger seat, wearing sunglasses and a wide-brimmed straw hat, throwing back the pink scarf with an air of flamboyance.

Of course the woman turned out to be none other than Jenny. Our eyes met.

"There you are, Beth. I am so happy that you are here; it took us ages to find the place. Pay the taxi, will you? We were not able to change out any of our pounds. The bank was not open when we left Negril this morning."

She walked deliberately around the back of the taxi, avoiding me, and entered through the gate. Pauline and Patricia were still in the process of fixing their hair, dresses and shoes. Knowing that Pauline was the one who always held their money, I asked her if she had a ten-pound note. She went in her purse and handed one to me, which I in turn gave to the taxi driver, who looked at me with his palm open, waiting for more. In my best Jamaican accent, I reminded him how much the fare from Negril to Ocho Rios was and pointed out that he had more than double that amount in his hand.

213

As I turned my back to him, I was practically choked by Patricia's elbow around my neck. She felt that she was now able to greet me. Pauline followed with a similar gesture, then greeted Jack and Jacky, who had left the hammock and were standing by the gate. The visitors all strolled off, leaving their suitcases on the pavement.

Jack, being a gentleman, stepped through the gate to assist. I indicated that he should please place them on the inside of the wall close by the gate, because I didn't think that they would be staying.

"Oh Beth, my love, be a dear and fetch me some cool water or an ice-cold drink; the place is so hot, and that drive was the worst; it's a wonder we got here in one piece."

I took note that she no longer had a Trinidadian accent.

Rose, Sophia and Pru joined the rest of us on the veranda.

Rose commented to Jenny that it seemed she had lost her manners along with her accent, because she had not greeted any of us with a decent good morning. She was shocked at Rose's comment and tried to cover by saying that it was the heat and fatigue of the journey.

For a moment there was silence, but it seemed like an hour, except for the swishing sound of the makeshift paper fans from the visitors. The children came out to join us and broke the silence, wanting to know who the new arrivals were. Jack and Jacky used the moment to escape to their room.

I asked the children to refresh themselves with some drink and food and allow the adults to talk.

"Prudence, my dear, I am dying of thirst. Don't you have anything to drink?"

I realised then that I had not given her the drink she had asked for. Prudence reluctantly left the veranda for the kitchen and returned with three glasses of lemonade. They drank as if it were their first and last drink of the day and returned their glasses to the tray. Exhaling loudly as she replaced her glass on the tray, Jenny kicked her shoes from her feet.

"I must say, I did not expect to find you all here; we were hoping to have the place to ourselves for a few days."

"Really, and why is that?" Rose questioned.

"Because I had asked Beth to keep the place closed up until I got here, it's so important to sort things out and put things in order after a loved one's death."

I looked at Jenny with disgust but said nothing. I could see Rose's fist clenching, but Sophia stood up, pushing back her chair because Jenny's shoes were in her path, and spoke first.

"Why would you want her to close the house until you get here, Jenny? This is where she lives!"

Jenny, dismissing Sophia's question, got up from her chair and took off her dark glasses and hat, dropping them on the seat behind her.

She looked around as if surveying the property, then commented.

"Really! Then you had better show me around. How many bedrooms do we have?"

Prudence also stood up, but only so she could be face-to-face with Jenny.

"You have a nerve, you know that. Do you even know that Uncle Paul was buried yesterday?"

Jenny looked around at me, shocked. Pauline and Patricia both voiced, "Never!" in unison.

Jenny then made a move towards me.

"How dare you, Elizabeth? I told you to wait until I got here, you..."

Pru did not allow her to complete her statement. She pushed Jenny roughly in her chest, sending her falling awkwardly down on the seat.

"You are the one who has the gall to turn up here with great expectations and without any sympathy or remorse. You should be holding your head in shame. In fact, you have no place here. If I were Beth, I would have put you back in that taxi and sent you back to wherever it was that you are coming from."

Patricia and Pauline both stood up to rebuff Prudence. But she was so mad; with one movement of her left hand, she sent them both back to their seats.

"Rose, please bring Uncle Paul's letter for me."

Rose practically ran to the kitchen to retrieve the letter Prudence had been reading before Jenny and the others got to the house.

Not even a breeze could pass through the thick cloud of air on the veranda until Rose returned with the sheets of paper. Prudence took out the sheet containing Dad's last will and testament and read it out loud.

"See, Jenny, Uncle Paul was not a fool. He knew who you were before he closed his eyes, and thanks be to God. Elizabeth and Rose knew who their mother was and why she is not here today. Sophia and Jacky know who their father is, and I know that Uncle Paul was never my father, nor was he the father of those two. My problem is Jenny. Who are you? Jacky is here, and she might want you to be here because you are her birth mother, but you have no business to give instructions to Beth. So I suggest that if you have any shame at all left in you, you should just shut the f… up and thank God that I haven't socked the teeth out of your mouth. Beth, please, can you call us a taxi? I think we should book into a hotel and give you guys some space."

I reached for my mobile phone without hesitation and called John to pick them up and arrange a place for them to stay. In no time, he was at the gate. Prudence went in the house to get her bag, then came back to hug me.

"Beth, I will drop off the video and the photos as soon as they are developed. Thanks for allowing me to take them and be part of the service."

She hugged my shoulders and kissed me on the cheek. I could see the tears welling up in her eyes, and then she asked,

"Beth, we are still sisters, aren't we?"

"Of course we are, my darling; nothing has changed. We have all just grown up and are better informed. I will be in touch. Take care of yourself and your husband. Love you."

I watched the van drive off as it made its way towards Ocho Rios.

The children, restless and hungry, returned from the backyard. Rose got them to arrange and set the dining table for the breakfast which she had prepared but was unable to present, so it was now brunch. Sophia was engaged on her phone and seemed to be excited about what she was hearing.

I sent to call Jack and Jacky from the bedroom so I could give out the announcement of Uncle Stefan's invitation to dinner later that evening.

"So what are you so happy about?" I asked Sophia as she joined us in the kitchen.

"Daddy is here; he is in Montego Bay. He came in an hour ago but said he was tired and needed to get a couple days sleep before coming to see us. He said to give you his love and that he was sorry to miss out on Uncle Paul's service."

The twins had a host of questions for their mother and didn't allow her to sit before replying to their request. We were almost at the end of our meals when Jacky announced.

"Guys, I am sorry; I almost forgot to tell you, what with all the excitement with the musketeers. We had a call from my wedding planner early this morning asking if we would consider filling a slot on Wednesday, which would give us, and them, time to prepare for Jack and I to be married come next Sunday at four p.m. They are asking that the wedding party book in at the hotel on Wednesday, and we would have until Monday midday to leave.

Our honeymoon is already booked for Port Antonio; I confirmed the date, but I have asked them to see if they could also accommodate us as a family. Jack feels that we should all honeymoon together."

A big 'yeah' came from the twins, which confirmed a yes for all of us.

Chapter Eight

It was heart-warming to see Lloyd sitting alongside Carol and Uncle Steffan when we arrived for dinner at the hotel later that evening. The comfort was in knowing that he was already accepted as part of the family.

While Jack and Jacky announced their good news, they also offered invitations to Carol, Uncle Steffan, and Lloyd to join us in Port Antonio.

After dinner, while walking through the gardens, Lloyd and I exchanged some intimate moments where I accepted his offer to spend that night at his home.

I truly believe that we had all experienced an unforgettable family bonding over dinner at the hotel that evening. My children whispered to me that it would be Uncle Steffan's birthday the following day, and they (the children) would be surprising him by baking a cake and presenting it during our meal the following evening. They requested that they (all the children) be allowed to sleep over at the hotel to carry out their surprise. Carol, Sophia, and I arranged and got them settled in bed before making our way home, with Rose driving my car while I accompanied Lloyd to his home.

It was way past one a.m. and raining when we pulled into his driveway. As we ran from the car to the shelter of the hallway, I shivered and made my request in an attempt to get warm.

"Wow, the rain have left me chilly. How about a hot cup?"

"So you don't think I will be hot enough to warm you!" Lloyd jested.

"No worry, I need one as well. You go on up; I will put the kettle on, and I have a ritual to shower down here and leave all the burden of the day right here at the doorsteps, so I can enter my comfort zone of peace and rest at the top of those stairs."

"Sounds like an interesting concept. Go wash away your burdens while I prepare the comfort and replenishments."

I replied, dropping my shoes at the bottom of the stairs alongside his own and running up the stairway. I opened the only door at the top of the landing and was about to search for the light switch when a dimmed blue light came up slowly and offered a soft, quiet glow to the room. I smiled because the light was over and around the bed in the centre of the room. A very spacious bed, which was neatly spread with a white sheet trimmed with a darker border at the edge, with matching pillowcases placed diagonally at the four corners.

I glanced around the room. Glass windows almost covered one wall of the room, and the blinds were still open to the dark of the night, giving the room a romantic atmosphere that only the stars on a dark, rainy night could give. An open door on the opposite side attracted my attention because another light had come on, which was a lot brighter than the bedroom.

I assumed it would be the bathroom, so I headed in that direction. In my handbag was my emergency overnight case containing all I needed for a couple of days away from home.

The warm water on my cold body was soothing, and I was tempted to put my head under the shower but reminded myself of the length of my hair and the time it would take to dry out, as I did not travel with a hair dryer.

My locks were long, almost touching the middle of my waist. I parted them in two and braided two large plaits.

I was not a Rasta, but nor was I a Christian. I knew that I was mindful of a God and found comfort in accepting the religion of kindness and love towards my fellow human, and more so, I was extremely conscious of being an African and Black.

Growing up in London, we were often called names by the white children, even when our family was mixed race. But it's common for children to call others names and bully those who they thought were the weaker ones. So I didn't think much about being different. As a teenager in Paris, I often felt uncomfortable going into certain shops and quickly found the ones where the staff were not as blatantly prejudiced. As I travelled through Africa, and even worse, South Africa, blacks knew their places; there, everything and everyone was discriminated against if you were not white.

In Jamaica, discrimination is reserved for the poorer class of persons, be they Black or brown, and for sure, Rastas were the lowest of the low unless you were a singer like Bob Marley."

One thing I had always believed was that God had my back, and I know that He has always made things right somehow. Before returning to Jamaica and hearing about Marcus Garvey and the constant chant of the Rastas to read a chapter a day, I not only read a chapter, but I read the Bible from cover to cover more than three times, returning to a few of the books from time to time for comfort or reassurance but never as a practice.

The sound of the bedroom door closing snapped me back to the image of the woman facing me in the mirror, so I made a last swish of the mouthwash and deposited it in the sink before wrapping one of the bath towels around my chest. Lloyd was seated on an easy chair, which was placed in one corner of the bedroom close to the window. He had already dimmed the light over the bed, leaving the window blinds open, the stars lighting the room. Beside the chair was a standing night lamp and a low table which served as a bookshelf. He had a similar towel to mine wrapped around his waist and, realising that I was about to sit, spread his legs to allow me space between his flanks as he handed me a cup.

"Hot Ribena? I have not had this drink for years. Dad used to give us this drink at Christmas time." Lloyd's remark was, "I was introduced to it by a nurse I spent time with in London a few years ago."

He laughed when I turned my head quickly to face him.

"Oh, so she was warming you up for…?"

He gave me a wide-eyed look while showing me a flash of pearly whites.

"Nothing of the sort; it so happened I took her some rum from your dad, and she in turn sent him something called Lucozade and a couple bottles of cider. Mind you, she did ask me if I wanted to stay the night. He chuckled. I had a doctor colleague waiting for me in the car parked at her gate; we were on our way to a place called Bristol for a two-day medical lecture. In the short space of twenty minutes she certainly made an impression."

He bent to place his warm lips on the back of my neck, which sent shivers down to my toes. I held my composure. I remembered seeing the parcel with the bottles of drink along with a pink envelope bearing Dad's name on the back seat of his jeep and wanted to know if he was going to visit someone at the hospital after seeing the Lucozade bottle. Dad almost blushed, explaining at the time that they were a gift sent to him by a lady who had been a friend of my mother and with whom he kept in touch. My thought at that moment was to try to send a message to her informing her of his death. But the sensation of Lloyd's warm body made me pull in my belly and reminded me that he was very much beside me.

"Penny for your thoughts!"

He kissed me on the tip of my ear and then breathed his hot breath over it.

I turned to face him.

"I was just wondering what kind of impression I will leave with you."

I said, as I placed my cup on the side table and turned with the intention to lie on his chest. His movements were so fast and unexpected as he pulled me up with ease with both hands on my waist and straddled my legs over his body on the armless reclining chair.

I was thrown into the deep end of a fast-moving stream and was drowning in the pleasures of love. We both came up for air, screaming but not wanting to be realised; as if we were trapped in a bottle, we rolled to the floor. His body was as light as a feather, but his weight was beyond measure.

Later, as we watched the stars through the open blinds, we laughed and kissed. I asked about his family.

He replied, "I have none, but I would like to be a part of yours. Will you accept me as a life partner, Beth?"

"OH, are you are saying I left you with such an impression?" I laughed, not taking him seriously but wanting so much to believe he was feeling the same as I did at that moment.

"You are impossible, you know that." He kissed me deeply before continuing.

"But I love the way you think about life. Your sharp wit, your sweet voice. I loved you from the way your father talked about you. So much so, I was afraid to meet you after he told me you were married. I thought that maybe you would still be in love with your husband. But I had not seen you with a ring, and you never spoke about being married or mentioned him even when you spoke of the children constantly. That day when I stopped by your house the day after your father died sealed my faith. That was when you left the deepest impression on me. And now, I don't want to live my life without you, and I could not be happier for you now that your children are here.

"And I must tell you I love them too. They are great kids; I would not want to let them forget their father, but I want to help you secure a future for them. Will you allow me?"

"Well, I can't speak for my kids, but if you continue to blow my mind as you just did, I have nowhere going."

We sealed it with several kisses before I had a chance to ask.

"Why was it that he had no family?"

He played with my hair for a moment before answering.

"I grew up in the Maxfield Park Children's Home in Kingston. The first time I was made to feel special and happy was when I passed my exam to enter high school. I didn't think I did anything out of the ordinary, but the teachers were making it a big deal. During that time at the home, we were being visited by an overseas group of doctors and nurses who were offering dental and medical care to the children's homes around Jamaica. And one of the things about Jamaicans is they think that all things were created in the U.S. of A. My housemother felt that I was so bright that if I were to be taken to America, my life would be made. I had no idea who started the idea or discussion, but I was taken to America by one of the nurses.

I left a country filled with all Black smiling faces and was dropped into a cold, cold forest filled with all white faces. I was never sure if there were people behind some of those faces. My biggest puzzle was why this white lady insisted I call her "Mum".

He sighed deeply and closed his eyes, as if trying to blot out bad memories.

"I will fill you in with all the not-so-fine details later on, but the short of the story is: I was not allowed to go back to school or even to travel any distance from her house unless she was close by. I was her housekeeper for all the years I stayed with her. One Christmas we went to town for my sixteenth birthday. A circus and funfair was in town. She gave me a sum of money and told me to meet her back at the car park in two hours.

I was so happy to see other Black people; I went to be part of their group and was having fun until a redneck police officer wanted to do what they do best. He insisted that we were up to no good and we had to turn out our pockets. I was beaten up and carted off to jail because I could only have come by the money I had in my pocket if I had stolen it. So off to jail I went and was there for two weeks before Nurse found me.

She was told by her so-called friends to move to another town, even when we had no close neighbours for more than five miles on either side of her house. But she took their advice, thank God. For reasons of her own, she also brought a young Chinese woman to live with us after the move. The woman was older than I, maybe in her late twenties. Her belly was fat and ready to have her firstborn. We were told that we needed to find out about each other and were given a list of the most important questions regarding each other that we needed to know. A year later we were taken before the magistrate with her baby in her arms to be married."

At that point in Lloyd's story, I felt the need to change my position from being on the carpet. I returned to sit in the chair and drank the remainder of the now cold Ribena.

He joined me, pulling me back against his chest.

"Don't worry, I am no longer married. Nurse only arranged the marriage so that I could get my green card. A few months later I was also given a Jamaican passport and the file from Maxfield Park with my records, birth certificate, and family history. She just went ahead and planned my life without thinking that I was capable of thinking on my own, assuming I had no common sense, treating me as her house slave — which, unfortunately, I was just that.

On reflection, I am happy she did. A few months later I was given the choice of returning home to Jamaica or moving to another city to start life on my own. My wife was paid off for a job well done and was already gone. As luck would have it, I didn't have a chance to return at that time, because Nurse was admitted into hospital after crashing her car while driving me to buy my return ticket to Jamaica. It turned out that she had a liver problem which had gotten worse, and she was given limited time to live.

Her personal doctor at the hospital where they both worked was of mixed race. He seemed to know her well and was very sociable to me. He was also quite discerning. He heard me calling her 'Mum', put two and two together, and gave me the low-down on what to expect from her condition. He also knew that our situation wasn't an accepted one among the white population but felt that he should assist me to make the best of it. I nursed her for almost a year before she died.

But I am running ahead of myself."

Lloyd got up and assisted me up from the easy chair.

"Come, let's get comfortable on the bed. Would you care for a stronger drink?"

I went to make myself comfortable while he opened what appeared on the outside to be a regular cupboard but which revealed a small fridge, similar to those you would find in a hotel. He held up a wine bottle and a tumbler-shaped glass.

"Hope you won't mind sharing a glass; I normally drink alone. But I need to show you my baby photo. Then I can go back to the beginning of my story and the question you asked."

He handed me a well-worn hardcover brown book, which he took from the bottom of the table beside the bed. I read out loud the title: *Reader's Digest Family Medical Encyclopaedia.*

Lloyd chuckled and remarked, "That book became my only comfort and friend for over a year until I got the courage to request that Nurse bring me some old newspapers or magazines to keep me company, because we had no radio or television in the house."

He replaced the towel around his waist, poured out a full glass of wine before sitting on the side of the bed, and then sighed deeply.

"One of the things I have been able to observe in my practice is that when my patients get to the hospital, they are so consumed with the pain that they are blinded by it. I believe that my job as the doctor is to go back to the moment before the pain started and figure out, was it a drink or was it something they ate, etc.? I said that in order to explain that I started where I felt the pain and not at the start of my story."

He placed the bottle and glass on the bedside table, then took out a tattered grey folder from the back page of the book, and then joined me on the bed.

"Here you go, my first photo. I was nine months and two weeks when that was taken."

I remarked instantly, "Why were you upset with the cameraman?"

He then flicked the page and showed a woman who appeared to be asleep.

"That was my mother."

Again I remarked, "She didn't seem too keen on having her photo taken either." I laughed.

While I flicked from one page to the other, he made himself comfortable behind me and pulled me back to rest on his chest.

"Well, you are right about me not being happy; that was my first photo but my mother's last. That was taken after they cleaned off all the blood and placed make-up on her face. She was dead!"

I could not have been more shocked.

"Oh my God, Lloyd, I am so sorry; I had no idea. Me and my big mouth. I really am so sorry. Sorry for your loss."

He squeezed me tightly and kissed my forehead.

"It's ok, Beth, I am not that sensitive, and you were not to know. But you asked why it is that I have no family, so I really should have told you that I lost my mother the day after she took me to the clinic to get my shots and then while crossing the road to return home. She was hit by a truck, which broke her back, legs, and shoulder, but she held on to me so tightly that even when she was thrown up in the air and landed, I was still locked in her arms."

I turned to do the one thing I could at that moment.

I kissed him deeply because there were no words to express how his statement ripped through my heart. We just sat in silence for a while until he continued his story.

"Those photos were taken so they could be printed in the newspaper. The hospital was trying to locate a family member or for anyone to come forward and identify my mother. She had in her purse my birth certificate and my clinic card, so they knew who I was, and they had her name, Janet Cain, but the only address was Linsted Post Office. I was told that I remained in the Kingston Public Hospital until I was a year old before they sent me to the children's home. No one knows what became of my mother's body. I was only told the full story at the age of eleven years."

And at the same time as the nurse who adopted me was being told my story, I just happened to be present in the room. My housemother thought that I was bright and intelligent enough and that if I were able to get to America, I could achieve my dream (or hers, because at that time in my life I didn't dream). It was the summer holidays, and I should have been preparing for entrance to high school, but, as she told me when I was able to speak to her after returning to Jamaica, she said that she had tried to find a sponsor to pay my school fees but was not having much luck. So she mentioned my circumstances to the group of medical technicians who were visiting the children's homes all around the island at the time. And she happened to engage and impress one of the nurses to take me along with her when they were leaving to go back to the United States. I am not sure how Nurse McLeod managed to get me out of the country, but she did.

My memories of that time were that I left warmth and a feeling of belonging for a cold, unloving house in the woods, with no mango trees. I felt only despair, loneliness, and a lot of disappointment."

Lloyd exhaled heavily and rubbed his shoulders with both hands, moving his neck from one side to the other as he got up from the bed.

"But can I fill you in on the bad parts at another time? After all, I am hoping that we will have the rest of our lives to talk."

He turned towards the bathroom, but I could see the tears welling in his eyes. On his return he drank the full glass of the white sparkling wine, then poured another, which he handed to me, then held the bottle to his head.

As I sometimes did when my children were young and I had my hands full, I would use my toes to perform simple tasks. So as I watched Lloyd with such a sad look on his face while he sipped the wine, I reached over and with my toes pulled the towel free from his waist.

My heart pounded so hard I held up my hand as if to stop it from leaving my chest; I had felt the power earlier but thought that it was all in my mind. And now I stopped myself from saying "Wow" out loud.

Our eyes locked as I handed him the glass, which I emptied of its contents. When my marriage broke up and I returned to my father's house, I was feeling so rejected as a woman and was in no hurry to give myself sexually to another man until the day I saw Lloyd walking up the driveway with his overnight bag in one hand and a string of fish in the other. That was the day I knew he had my heart.

I was more than surprised when our bodies made the first contact but told myself it was just me dreaming. No one could be better than David. The ecstasy was too much. Only God could make a way when He wants to bless His children, I mused to myself.

I could feel the warmth of the early morning sun streaming through the window and, at the same time, Lloyd trying to leave the bed while trying hard not to disturb me.

He answered his pager phone, "Good morning, Matron. I am really so sorry, but I will be there for the two p.m. shift. No, everything is fine; something came up unexpectedly. Yes, I will see you at two."

I waited until he replaced the pager on the bedside table, then made my move.

"So you are telling me this came up (I had taken hold of his joystick) all by itself unexpectedly?"

The heat from the sun through the window was getting hot, and so were we. I kissed him while bearing down so he could rise even higher.

At twelve o'clock we lay in the bathtub while the cold water cooled our bodies in the heat of the noonday.

"No, don't make up the bed; I want to come back to you when I get off work."

I pushed him gently down the stairs.

"You are going to be late; go on ahead. I will lock up and take a taxi home."

He took a spare bunch of keys from a kitchen drawer and placed it in my hand while we exchanged more kisses as he went through the front door. I watched as he drove out and knew it would not be for the last time. Upstairs, before we left the bathroom, Lloyd took off his college ring and placed it on my finger as he asked me again to be his life partner, insisting that there was no way he would ever want to be with any other woman after me. He laughed as he said, "This stick has found its hoe."

We laughed together at his statement. (A common Jamaican saying is that "Every hoe has its stick in a bush.") I now laughed to myself as I remembered and then voiced out loud to myself:

"I could not have found a better stick."

I was indulging in my satisfied thoughts when the bell from a postman's bicycle rang out in urgency. The sound was coming from the kitchen door, on the side opposite from the side Lloyd used as an entrance. The ringing bell was so persistent I had to investigate. Immediately, as I pulled the curtain to see from the window, I saw the postman waving at me frantically and, with all thirty-four, showing me his widest smile. I pulled the towel closer to my chest and searched the bunch for the key to the door.

Dad taught me to read the brand on the lock and then find the corresponding key, not to start by trying each key individually. By the time I opened the kitchen door, the postman had made his way onto the walkway to the grill gate of the veranda.

"Good afternoon to you, miss. I have a register slip for the doctor, and I know that he has been waiting for an important letter, so I didn't want to drop it in the postbox. Because I know that he is a man who work so hard that he may not have the time to check his box for a couple of days sometimes. I am glad that someone is at home."

He handed me the slip along with a stack of other mail.

"Good afternoon, thank you. Have a nice day."

I placed the letters and the postal slip in a position on the kitchen table where I knew Lloyd would not avoid seeing them. With keys in hand, I went back through the kitchen door to survey Lloyd's property. The gate the postman had used appeared to be the front of the house and the main entrance. The grill fencing, painted in black, was high and thick, surrounding a very large manicured grass lawn, which extended to the end of the road, then turned, showing it was a corner lot. The veranda, which ran the length of the house, was so wide it could have easily been mistaken for a dance floor. A very large double door led to an enormous sitting room, which was retrofitted to look like a library with bookshelves running from floor to ceiling all around the room. The books were neatly arranged, and some were still in boxes. Office tables and chairs with computers and other items were still wrapped in paper and cardboard boxes. There was another door at the end of the sitting room, but I decided to take the stairs, which were partially hidden, tucked away in the corner.

Up the stairs to a wide passage, I was amazed to see four well-spaced doors, leaving me to assume that they were four bedrooms. In a previous conversation with Uncle Steffan, I overheard Lloyd telling him how lucky he was to have found a five-bedroom house in an area so close to the town centre. As he said with delight, it was perfect and suited the purpose of his dream to one day have his own private clinic. And he could not wait to get the approval from the government to proceed, because he already had a plan. While I stood on the staircase, I envisioned a nurse in white walking towards me. I smiled to myself and returned through the double doors of the front room, then retraced my footsteps to the kitchen, making sure I secured the lock on each door. I could hear the last few rings from my phone coming from the bedroom, so I raced up the stairway and redialled the last number.

"Hey sis, what time are you planning on getting here, or should we meet you at the hotel?

"Hi Rose, Please wait for me; I need to come down to the house and change. Is everything OK?"

"Yes, all is well. The others are resting as we speak. I managed to get hold of a few people on the phone in London, so I am good, and oh, your driver John, he brought a lot of luggage and a few crates. Apparently they are for the children. Jacky suggested we put them in the room she is using considering that we are all leaving here tomorrow. But all is well, so see you in a few."

I took a shower and got dressed, gathered my things together and was about to straighten up the bed when I remembered Lloyd saying that he wanted it to remain unmade. Downstairs in the garden I could see a small patch of a rose garden. I had a choice of red, yellow, or white. The yellow, being the best of the lot, I cut, but I also took a red and white bud, flaking its petals from the doorway up the stairs to the bedroom, then placing the yellow stem in the middle of the pillow after placing it in the tumbler glass with water. Making sure to place a bright printout of my lips on the outside of the glass completed the touch I was working with.

The walk to the main road was short, and getting a taxi was no problem, so in no time I was home. Rose was seated on the veranda in what I can now call her favourite chair, her attention focused on the newspaper. She greeted me first.

"Hey Beth, what sort of salary do you earn? Would you say it's manageable, pretty good, or hand to mouth?"

"Wow, well, good day to you too, but I would say it's manageable. Why do you ask?"

"Well, I told you this morning that I was talking to the man who rents the store downstairs from my house (he is from Greece, by the way), and he was saying that his daughter was joining him in London because they have arranged a marriage for her, and he wondered how long I would be staying here and would I consider renting her my flat for a couple of months until they got settled and could find somewhere suitable."

There was nothing I could say at that point, so I encouraged her to continue.

"Well, the reason I am also asking, is that I would also love to buy a car for myself. So I need to know what kind of rent I should charge them, and if my salary here would keep me in the style to which I have become accustomed."

I stared at her wide-eyed, and of course we had to have a good laugh before we went into a serious talk about money and Rose's future plans.

We were joined by the others and had a very rewarding heart-to-heart conversation, which led to Rose selecting the car of her choice from a newspaper advertisement and other information on how she would obtain it. She then made a decision on renting her flat full-time, and maybe the best move of all was that she would be living at the house and joining me in the business at PauliMay Travel Agency.

I marvelled at the way our lives were changing for the better at every turn. But as I gave thanks, I was also mindful; my request to God was to keep me humble and focused. Dad always told me, "You wait and see, pet; things will soon take a turn for the better, and don't feel bad because you deserve it."

Uncle Steffan and Carol were enjoying a drink by the pool when we got to the hotel. The children were nowhere in sight.

"Here, Beth, your son instructed me to have you call him when you were all here. You can use Steffan's phone because it is on roaming."

She handed his phone to me, and I was about to call when my own phone rang.

"Hello, my darling, I can only get away for a couple of hours. The two student doctors are just about sleepwalking. They worked all last night into today. I will be on my own tonight until Matron gets here in the morning. So I can only wish Steff and Carol a good evening and then dash. I am about to leave now; where will I find you?"

"I will meet you at the parking lot, say in twenty minutes."

I then went to find the children to see how they were getting on with their surprise. I was given instructions on where to find them.

"Wow, this looks great. Your aunt and uncle will be more than surprised. Listen, guys. Uncle Lloyd has to work tonight; as a matter of fact, he is at work right now but taking some time off to be here, so can I ask that we allow him to be the first to give his wish so he can leave and get back to work?"

A big "Oh No" went up from all, but they understood and agreed. Later I walked back to the car park with Lloyd, after getting a waiter to fix three takeaway boxes for himself and the other doctors.

I could see the strain of tiredness and stress on his face but kissed him and wished him a safe drive back to the hospital.

The hotel was putting on a stage show that evening with Jimmy Cliff and a few other local singers, which would make it a perfect night for Steffan and Carol. The show would start at eleven and finish after one o'clock. So Jack suggested that we stay the night, considering that we would all be leaving for Portland after breakfast the following morning.

We were able to book a double room which we could share, and we did just that. Rose reminded me that we needed to check on the office computer before leaving for Portland.

"Beth, when we get back I will have to reprogramme those computers so we can get the same information from wherever we access it."

"Can you really do that? I thought that they worked like the cell phone; each one was personal!"

"No, and I can lock the information so no one else can get in and use it without a password. Don't worry, it's not that hard to learn; I will take you through step by step."

We drove into the plaza, while the others continued their journey home. Rose called to someone from her side of the car window as we drove in.

"Mr Wright, good morning."

We parked and were joined by Mr Wright and a younger-looking version of him, who appeared to be of mixed race by his skin tone. His face, showing the first signs of a suntan, was glistening in the sun.

"Morning to you both. I did not expect to see you, Beth," said Mr Wright, who pushed forward his son ahead of him.

"We just left your house; I wanted you to meet my son Winston. He has decided to return to Jamaica to live but insisted on going around the world before he got here, so unfortunately he missed your dad's funeral."

Winston shook my hand, then Rose's, as he declared that.

"Your dad happens to be my godfather, by the way," Mr Wright offered an explanation. "Winston was here with his mother and me when I first returned to Jamaica. His mother got sick, and you know our health system out here; she had to return to England for treatment, but Winston stayed on with me because he was doing very well at the local school in a teaching job. Your dad was good enough to sponsor him back to England when things got bad for us, to allow him to get into university and better himself. But Jamaica is in his blood, so he is now back for good."

We greeted each other as fellow returnees. I already knew about Winston from Dad and knew that he would return to spend summer with his dad each year. Mr Wright and his English wife returned to Jamaica in the early sixties, long before Dad. But they were homeless and jobless, living in the deep countryside and just getting by. He and Dad met one day when Dad took out the Jeep for a test run and ended up with a punctured tyre. Mr Wright, who was walking and making his way back to his house, stopped to assist Dad.

As they say, the rest is history. His English wife had to return to live in England. Mr Wright remarried and had another two boys who were doing very well at the local high school.

While I spoke to Mr Wright, Rose made copies of the information from the computer and at the same time was deep in conversation with Winston. They were speaking in German to each other. When we parted company, they exchanged phone numbers.

"Well, I had no idea! Interesting, good for you, sis. Sprichst Du Deutsch? Like French, I seem to learn just enough to get by. I am happy that you are good at languages; it will be a plus with the tourists."

She slapped me playfully across my shoulder.

When we arrived at the house, John already had the jeep loaded with all the luggage, leaving space for just Jack and Jacky. Rose had her case packed from the day before, but I had to hurriedly pack what I knew would keep me looking good for a week. Having had a lot of experience over the years of living with holiday lovers, I had learnt to look my best living from one suitcase. After locking up and securing the house, Rose took the keys to my Mini, saying she needed to get her practice on the country roads, so we set off to Portland. John transported Uncle Steffan, Carol, Sophia and the twins. Dominic, Mario and Monai were in the back seat of our car. I held my phone at the ready but felt it better to wait on Lloyd's call rather than risk waking him.

I had also taken the decision not to tell the others of my personal plans where it involved Lloyd. I felt that it would only take away from Jack and Jacky's celebrations. Their moment should be theirs, after coming all the way to Jamaica and then missing out on having Dad there to bless their marriage.

When we arrived at the location, Mathew and two of his other children were waiting and were already booked in. Sophia and the twins, who were not expecting to see him there, made such a racket in the waiting area that they were escorted out to the garden. By dinner time, the entire wedding party and a few extra guests were all booked in and ready for the big day. We were later taken to a smaller property only a short distance away from the main hotel building. All ten bedrooms were on the first floor; the dining room, games room and reception were on the ground floor. We were told that the honeymoon suite, which would only be used on the Saturday to Monday nights, was located on the second floor. We were placed two to a room: Jacky and I, Jack and his best man, the mother and father of the bride and the mother and father of the groom, etc. The wedding planner insisted that we have our lunch, then rest for a few hours before gathering for his briefing by six o'clock later that evening. John had stayed on after the journey, so after dinner we went over the emails and bookings before he made his way back to the office to collect a client. Jacky was already in slumberland when I got to our room. Her birth father had requested a meeting with just Sophia, Jack and Jacky. I was interrogated by Rose, who had noticed the ring on my finger during dinner. With my heart pounding, I told her that Lloyd was only making sure I kept my promise to be his friend.

My phone vibrated in my trouser pocket as I entered my room, and I quickly went to the bathroom to answer it, not wanting to disturb Jacky.

"Hi babes!"

"Hello, my petal, would you believe I am still at the bottom of the stairs? I just needed to speak to you before I ventured up."

I laughed. "You are kidding me; it's after ten p.m. What were you up to?" he replied.

"To be honest, I saw the pile of letters, which were delivered yesterday, and your note also. And I should tell you that before I met you, my only passion was my project to transform this property into a first-class clinic. I have been waiting for this approval for more than six months. So I had no choice but to replace my shoes and go back on the road to the post office to collect the package. I have to say I was also extremely hungry, which led me to buy a nice fresh snapper and a slice of pumpkin and yellow yam, so while I looked over the paperwork and instructions which were sent to me, I also made myself a meal. And of course, with the hot sun and a full stomach, sleep took over, and I was slumped in my chair at the dining table for another couple of hours until my phone rang. I must have been dreaming about you because your name was the first on my lips, but it was only Nurse Stewart.

You remember, the nurse I had to take home that morning at the hospital."

I cleared my throat before answering, allowing myself to speak it as I felt.

"Yes, I do remember your X." I said candidly; he laughed.

"She was never my W, so she could never be my X. I had hoped, though, that she would be head nurse when I got this place up and running, but that isn't looking like a smart move anymore."

"Oh, and why is that, Doc.?" I asked.

"Because I am about to make an even smarter move, which would make her no longer suitable for the post. The tone of his voice changed to soft and low. Now, may I have your full attention?"

"Why, of course, I am all ears." I said, feeling a little melancholy.

He cleared his throat and took a deep breath.

"My darling Beth, I have eaten and showered, and I am about to follow these petals to whereverthey may lead me. Will you walk with me?

I giggled, because I know what he did not. I asked.

"What colour towel are you wearing?"

He replied.

"None. And I am now at the top of the stair, opening the door, and standing to attention."

I could not help but sit on the edge of the tub, remembering the picture I had left for him, and not least the vision I was seeing of him at the entrance to his bedroom door. As a fashion designer, the silhouette of the female body was easy for me to replicate on the rumpled sheets using the rose petals as my pencil, carefully outlining the figure with one hand outstretched and appearing to be holding the glass containing the yellow rose. He was silent, so I whispered into the phone.

"Come lay with me, my darling."

I gave him time to walk to the bed from the doorway.

"Lay your head on my breast, hold me close while I kiss your tired eyes to sleep. I smacked my lips twice before saying, Kiss, kiss, and sleep well, my darling."

He replied, "Kiss, kiss, my sweet petal, and bless you."

I held the phone to my ear, not wanting to hang up. Then he said,

"Beth, I can't make love to you holding on to the phone; please hang up."

I hung up and was laughing myself silly when there came a knock on the door and a call for Mum. I left the bathroom to answer the door, quickly placing my finger to my lips to indicate to Monai that she should whisper. I held her hand, leading her out to the balcony before asking her why she was looking so perplexed.

"Mum, you got to help me; my period has started, and I have no protection. Can you please drive to the store?"

"No need, my love, I have at least half a dozen in my case; we can get some more tomorrow. Don't look so worried."

"Thank God, can you believe that this should be happening now? What if I had gone off with the twins and their granddad? I would have been so embarrassed. Mum, can I please stay with you and Aunt Jacky tonight? I am not sure I can deal with the twins just now. They have been acting like six-year-olds since their grandfather joined us."

I gave her my overnight case and told her to go and freshen up.

While Jacky slept, we sat on the balcony and had a mother-daughter bonding. As she snuggled up in my arms, I again thanked God. There were times when I cried myself to sleep, wondering if David would take my children away from me and I would lose sight of them forever. But thanks be to God, and thanks to Uncle Steffan, I now have no such worry. I know that their father loves them as much as I do, but he also has four other children. I know he would not be as devastated to know he may not get the chance to watch over the growth of my two in the way he would have wanted to. He also has the means to travel and see them anytime he wishes. I would never prevent them from having a relationship with their own father.

246

I was so disappointed to know that he didn't care for me enough to look out for my safety, and not once did he try to explain or express the love he showed me when we first met in Paris. When the children went off to boarding school, it was almost as if I no longer existed. He was always too busy, or he had to go away on business. Without realising, I had fallen out of love with him but would not admit it.

I was there, just being a loyal wife because I didn't know better.

Chapter Nine

Following our dinner earlier that evening, we were given our programmes and schedule for the days leading up to the wedding ceremony. The following day, Thursday, Jack and Jacky were to meet with Pastor Fairweather for a counselling session, while I was placed in charge of the remainder of the wedding party to choose their outfits and have them fitted. Jack and Jacky had already purchased their outfits. Jacky had promised to show me her dress later that evening, which would help us to choose colours and style to match and blend in with the bride and groom.

Sleep came as quickly as my head touched the pillow. Still fully dressed, I lay on my side of the bed on top of the bedcovering and not between the sheets. My hand still held my mobile phone under the pillow, which cushioned my head. I felt it vibrate. Lloyd came to mind, and I moved quickly from the bed to the balcony as I pressed the answer button, whispering good morning. On the other end of the line I heard:

"Kiss, kiss, good morning, my petal. I hope you slept as well as I. But if truth be told, I am rested, but I am not sure that I really slept. You were able to keep me up all night, and I have never been more relaxed."

"Thank you." I chuckled.

"It felt good to wake up in your arms, my darling. I hope you know that I am expecting to become accustomed to this." Lloyd, still whispering, continued.

"I really had not given a great deal of thought to romance or thought too much about becoming a husband or father, but last night my mind was on nothing else. I realised that I had loved you from the day your father came to visit me at the hospital and asked that I accompany him to view the house in Savoy Mews. It was a one in a million coincidence that he should have picked the one house in which my life was so wrapped up with. Technically I was the seller. Your father did not understand my reaction and quickly impressed on me that he valued my opinion because his daughter had already fallen in love with the house, but he wanted to be sure it would be a good buy. At which point he pulled out a photo of you. I was floored, in more ways than one. I couldn't take my eyes off you, or should I say the photo. Worse because you were looking right back at me. Your father suspected that I was bewitched and told me to keep the photo, which he had taken only the day before while testing out a new Polaroid camera, given to him by a Chinese tourist. I placed the photo in my breast pocket and felt my heart racing. Your father had always talked about you and your children whenever he came for his monthly appointments. I even said to him at one point that he made you sound so perfect I was falling in love with you without meeting you in person. Of course he kept on insisting that I should visit his home. I didn't want to get involved, knowing you were still married and also had grown children. Things took a turn so fast with him dying. I felt so guilty that I could have tried other medication or even attempted an operation my colleagues and I had been discussing. When I consulted them, they did their best to console me, but I felt so responsible that I should have discussed your father's illness with you before. My emotions were all over the place until the morning of the funeral when you came out on the veranda. I had your photo in the breast pocket of my jacket. You would not believe me, but there was such a connection. I know without a doubt that you had to be my wife. When I asked you to come to my house, I honestly only had intentions of pouring my heart out to you and hoping you would feel the same. I did not for one moment think it would have been so perfect. Beth, I fell in love with you from the day I saw your photo. And now I am so deeply moved that I never want to be without you in my life. I really hope that you are feeling the same because I am asking you now to be my wife."

At that moment tears filled my eyes and I had to exhale. Lloyd cleared his throat and I vision that he was sitting up in the bed, he did not whisper but spoke clear and precise.

Lloyd cleared his throat, and I envisioned that he was sitting up in the bed; he did not whisper but spoke clearly and precisely.

"Elizabeth Creary, will you accept my hand in marriage?"

There was no need to hesitate on my part, but I couldn't help making a joke.

"No, I will not accept your hand; I need all of you, body and soul. Of course I will marry you, Doctor Cain; there is no way I would let you go after Monday night."

We both laughed together before he continued the conversation with words of love and adoration until his doorbell rang.

"Honey, I got to go; I have a lot to get done today. I will call you later tonight after dinner."

"Love you, bye."

I managed to tell him before he hung up. My heart was still pounding, and I felt the smile on my face. My father would sometimes say to us girls, when we made him proud by coming first in class or being awarded for some achievement in school, 'that he felt so good his glad bag buss'.

Meaning he was so overjoyed, his heart was full to bursting. I laughed to myself because I felt that I now knew what love feels like. With David. Back then, we were children exploring and discovering what it was to grow up and discover sex in the comforting arms of a friend and confidant; it never got to love, never got to what I was now experiencing.

My first thought was how the children would react to Lloyd becoming my husband. I returned to our room with the intention of sharing my good news with Jacky.

She was up and unpacking, her back towards me as she shook her wedding dress from the protective plastic case. I promised myself to keep my news a secret until after her wedding.

"Morning, sis, Wow, it's exquisite. I love the shade, and you did say it was different."

"Morning, Beth. I was so tired last night my eyes closed the minute I hit the bed. Wait, is there someone in our bathroom?"

"Yes, Monai, she came on her period yesterday and didn't want to stay with the twins; you know how teenagers get. Come on, fit the dress; it blends so well with your complexion. I love it."

Jacky carefully removed the dress and stepped into it, turning for me to zip her up. It was such a deep red satin brocade without the shine. It hugged her body like a glove from her bust to her knee, where it fluted off to the floor in the front and in a short but effective train to the back. On the front left side, a large gold rose with opened petals over the breast sprang from a green vine which delicately wove its way from her shoulder to drop in ribbon-like strands to her knee. She looked like a movie star on Oscar night.

"What will you do for a veil?

I asked, thinking to myself that it needed that extra touch.

"I don't know. Any ideas? You are the designer."

"Well, a white veil wouldn't work. How about a red nylon or lace drape over your hair? We could go into town after lunch or, better still, call the wedding planners to see what they can come up with."

There was a knock on the door, and Jacky hurriedly slipped out of the dress before I opened the door to one of her co-workers who had arrived late the previous evening and did not get a chance to speak to her. I returned the dress to her suitcase while they went out to the balcony to talk.

Seeing my daughter coming from the bathroom made me think of Lloyd, so I hugged her. "Mum, good morning. I love you too, but you are squashing me."

We laughed together. But I could not tell her the cause of my happiness.

After breakfast, the men all went off together except for Jack, who joined Jacky for a meeting with the pastor. It was previously agreed that Sophia and the twins would walk with Jacky as her entourage. Sophia now suggested that I should take her place, insisting that she had to film the proceedings for their father. Before I had the chance to protest, I was outnumbered, as everyone thought the new plan was the best idea, with Monai as one of the flower girls along with the twins. Despite Mario protesting that he was too big to be a ring bearer, he gave in under kisses of 'pretty please' from his aunts.

So after breakfast, we made our way over to the main office to fit our outfits. Mario insisted that he should be first, as he had no intention of spending his morning sitting around waiting on a bunch of women fussing about dresses. After minutes of shifting the suits on the rack without removing any, he said,

"Mum, I have a great suit at home, and I would really love to wear it."

"Yes, Mario, but as you said, it's at home, and we are here. Besides, it has to match with the colours we are working with."

"But it does; it will match. It's green and has gold trim."

"That is true, Mum," said Monai. "It will match, and it's the best suit in his wardrobe. I know because I picked it out for him in Savile Row."

Rose and I repeated 'Savile Row' with our eyebrows raised.

"That might be so, darling, but your suit is still back at home in St Mary, and we are in Portland." I took out a few of the suits displayed on the rack, but they were either too small or too large and just were not in any way possible to alter to fit him.

"Ok, looks like you win." I looked at my watch. "If we hurry and find our dresses, we can make it to the house and back before dinner, but we have to skip lunch, deal?"

"Yes!" Mario leapt with joy. "I will go change and meet you at the car."

The twins were already dressed in matching white organdie dresses with fussy, puffed sleeves and a big gathered skirt covering their knees and reaching halfway towards their ankles. Rose was attempting to tie a massive green velvet ribbon to the back of one of the dresses, which was folded around the waistline from the front of the dress and held in place by a large red imitation rose.

"Don't we look smashing in these, Aunty Beth?" They both squeaked.

My first impression on seeing them was the memories of my storybooks as a child. Little Bo Peep jumped out at me. They took hold of the small wicker baskets decorated around the edges with white cotton lace and started to skip around, dropping confetti.

"Ok girls, save some for Aunty Jacky's wedding, will you?"

Rose retrieved the baskets while she shooed them to stand still.

"Well, they do look the part," I commented, "but undress quickly, girls; remember your grandad is waiting to take you to the beach."

They were out of the dresses as quick as a flash, leaving them in an untidy heap on the floor. While the assistants replaced them on the rack, Monai stood with her arms folded across her chest, shaking her head disapprovingly from side to side.

"Mum, these dresses are gross; the ones I have tried on made me look like a ten-year-old. I wish I had an outfit at home too; I would never wear these colours."

She tried the last one on the rack, a burgundy dress with cap sleeves and a sweetheart neckline. The bodice was in crushed velvet, but the skirt was layers and layers of organdie frills, which made her appear to be another version of the twins.

"This is the last one, Mum. This neckline suits me, but I really do not like the skirt."

I agreed. I reached for a green shift dress which she had fitted, but for a dress it was short, and at the same time one size too big.

"Mum, that dress was the worst."

I explained that I only wanted to see how long the dress was. The idea in my head worked. The assistant had a pair of scissors and a box of common pins, so I got to work cutting the shift dress from just below the sleeves and attaching it to the waistline of the burgundy top.

When she was fitted again, I pinned the skirt to fit her hips. As it took shape, I got wows of approval from everyone.

"Yes, Mum, love it, but you don't have a machine here. How are you going to sew this?"

"Not me, darling; the fitters will be able to do the alterations for us."

"How about you, Rose? Do you need a dress?"

"No fear, they are not my colours either; besides, I already have a pantsuit. Comfort over style, you know me."

I flicked from one hanger to the other of the half-dozen dresses laid out for me. "Me and you both, sis, I can't deal with all this fuss."

Rose pulled out a white lace cotton shirt dress.

"Hardly suitable for the occasion, but I love it."

The assistant quickly took it from her hand, saying they were the after-dresses for the bride. As she replaced it, another caught my eye. 'Not to worry,' I assured her. "My sister isn't planning on changing from her wedding gown."

The dress I pulled out was a tie-dyed knitted jersey with a simple V neckline with tiny ribbon-like straps dropping to a low-cut back. The dress had no zipper. I pulled it over my head, and it clung to my body; the hemline floated when I moved—long but not sweeping the floor. What made it even more perfect was that it moved from a gold bodice to a gradual burgundy on the hemline.

"Mum, I have the perfect accessories to match this dress, plus it comes with a shawl, so I could fix your hair with it like this."

Monai started to pull my hair from one side of my head to the other. The assistant looked on apprehensively.

"You look great, miss, but are you sure that the bride doesn't need a change of dress?" I reassured her that my sister did not want to change.

"But can you put these two along with the two for my daughter on my bill? We would like to keep them. That's it, Rose; let's get going. "Oh, did you remember the extra fabric we had asked you to take along for us?"

The assistant reached for a clear plastic bag and emptied its contents on a nearby table, with pieces of fabric in assorted shades of green and burgundy. A very thin nylon square caught my attention — a mixture of dark red and green; the edges were already sealed with neat scallops all around.

"This will be perfect; please be sure to bring it along tomorrow with the dresses, and thanks for your help."

On the way to the car park, we had to pass the lunch area, so the kids grabbed apples and soft drinks for the journey. With clear roads and brilliant sunshine, the drive was pleasant and enjoyable with Rose behind the wheel. When we arrived at the house, the yard was deserted, but the grounds were covered in dry leaves blown from the many fruit trees: mangoes and cherries were scattered all over the ground, while ripe ones begged to be picked. The house phone rang out a few times before the answering machine picked up.

"Rose, please remind me to turn down the ringtone on the phone before we leave. I now see why Dad always thought that it would attract the wrong people at nights. Especially when the yard shows signs of no one at home."

I retrieved the messages from the phone and was grateful that we had made the trip. One of Dad's old customers, who did not get email or have one of the new cell phones to receive text messages, wanted to book for the coming month. Mario entered the sitting room as I completed the return call.

He looked stunning and grown up in his full suit of lime green. The hem and neckline of his tunic were embroidered in burgundy and gold threads.

"You were right, son; it will blend in with your aunt's wedding colours, and it's perfect." Mario's face lit up with satisfaction.

"Ok, change and come help me open Dad's trunk."

Rose and Monai were busy in the kitchen washing mangoes, cherries, and June plums to eat on the return journey.

"Ready when you are, girls. Did you find the things you came for, Monai? If not, I can have this set which Dad gave to me for my birthday."

"You can take it along with you, Mum, if you wish. I know my set is perfect, but I am not going to show you; it's a surprise."

"I trust you for style, my darling. I have seen your designs, but I think I will walk with this anyway. Make sure you put all the stuff in the car and take along some paper towels and a bottle of water to wash your hands."

I could not leave without raking up some of the leaves, knowing that John would be on the road full-time until after the wedding on Saturday. We had just passed the turn-off for Golden Eye when the rain came out of nowhere, bringing the drive to a crawl. Another half hour and it became a full downpour, with flooded roads and debris all over the roadway. Rose lost her confidence when we were told to take a detour up a very slippery slope above the main road. A group of young men were assisting a fellow motorist who was stuck in the deep pool of water which lay menacingly ahead of us. After a few other unplanned detours, we were again driving in sunshine for the last leg of our journey. The fruit we had packed was still in the bag, untouched, so intense had the return journey been.

The others were settling down for their evening meals on our return. Carol waved for me to join her table as we entered.

"Where have you been? Lloyd has been trying to get you, and so have I; your phone been going to voicemail."

I reached for my phone and saw all the missed calls and messages from Lloyd and the others. I dialled Lloyd's number.

"So sorry, my love; you would not believe the intensity of the rain and the state of the roads coming back through St Mary."

I went on to explain to him why we had taken the journey up to the house in the first place, but I did not fully admit how concerned I had become after taking a detour into unknown territory.

"I thought that I would have had to call up a search party," he said jokingly. But pet, I have good and bad news. The bad news is that I will not make it down for the yacht party. The Budd's has asked me for a drive, so we will be leaving early on Saturday morning because they were not too keen on staying in a hotel overnight. And the good news is unbelievable. As luck would have it, Nurse Stewart called in at the hospital yesterday, accompany by three Cuban doctors. She was on the job, of course, acting as chaperone to them for three weeks while they await their visa to Connecticut for a two-year course. In conversation I mention that I would welcome them taking over my duties for a weekend to allow me to attend the wedding. That ended with them accepting the offer and agreeing to do my hospital duties, each of them working alternately over the two weeks if I allowed them free food and accommodation. No way could I have refused such an offer.

Of course I had to do some quick phone calls to get approval from Kingston. But thank God for emails; their credentials were vetted and approved. So my darling, I will be all yours for the next two weeks. Honestly, my pet, I could not believe my good fortune. But I have to go because I still have a lot to put in place by tomorrow. Sleep well, pet.

I held the phone to my ear, still trying to digest what was said. But I was distracted by the cheers from a group who appeared to be listening intently to my children and Rose, who were dramatising the ordeals of our drive through St Mary. Carol pulled me away from the table to whisper that Matthew had a meeting with Jack and Jacky while we were on the road, where he apologised and begged forgiveness for the way he had treated her over the years and said he had made a promise to himself and her father to put things right before her wedding.

"I must say we were all in tears. Got to give him credit for a great speech. Short story is that he will be walking her down the aisle on Saturday."

"I am so happy for her. I know she had asked Dad and also made arrangements before he died that he should be her 'give-away' father. And I know that Dad had a lot to do with Matthew coming to his senses."

Carol realised my sudden discomfort and gave me a hug.

"Something wrong, Beth?"

"No, not really. I was looking forward to the party at the marina, but Lloyd isn't able to come down for it. But he will be spending some time after the wedding, so I guess I should be looking forward to having him to myself."

I realised how gloomy I sounded and shook my body back to reality.

The manager came in to do her nightly announcement and short stint of entertainment for the evening before informing us that she had to bring the time of the wedding forward from four to two p.m., the reason being that they were double-booked. But with our co-operation we would all be guaranteed the hotel's 100 per cent, which we all deserved. The good thing was that only John and the office staff were travelling down on the Saturday. No need to call him, because they had planned to make a day of it by setting out early.

Also, Lloyd and the Budd family were expected by eleven, in time for lunch. But I thought that I should post a message to Lloyd's phone anyway.

I was still being nagged by my disappointment, so after a few drinks with Steffan and Carol after dinner, I went up for an early night and was still awake when Jacky and Monai returned to the room but pretended to be sound asleep until they settled down and were themselves asleep before I went out to the balcony.

The thought of Nurse Stewart was still on my mind, remembering her now on the day when we first met at the hospital. 'I was asking myself, had she returned to claim her man?' Were they together now? I really could not understand why I was so perturbed by just the mention of her name.

My phone rang. I had no reason to think it would be Lloyd, telling myself that he would be too wrapped up with his nurse to call me back at that hour.

So I answered in my office voice, expecting it to be a booking from some overseas client. "This is Elizabeth. How may I assist you?"

The voice was low on the other end of the line. I pulled my hair back and pressed the phone closer to my ear.

"I miss you so much. I am not able to sleep, and I turned on the lights and found one of your petals in the pillowcase. It is looking as lonely as I am feeling. Can I get a hug, please? I want your arms around me. To smell the fragrance in your hair, to feel the silky smooth texture of your body. The smooth velvet of your lips. Sweet pet, will you kiss me, please?"

I was choked up. The warm tears were blinding my eyes and washing my face as I replied, "I love you so much; please never ever let me go."

He realised then that I was crying, but he didn't ask why. He reassured me of his loyalty and love. He spent a long time telling me about his life at college in the U.S.

"Darling, I am getting a little sleepy, and I am sorry to be keeping you up also, so let's get some sleep. I will call you after I wind up proceedings at the hospital tomorrow. Kiss, kiss, sleep well."

Friday morning was the rehearsal of the wedding march, after which we were to have our hair and nails done before the party on the marina. The children did their walk all of six times. I did my walk just once, and so did Jacky and Matthew, before Rose, acting as the preacher, made Jack and Jacky take their vows, after which they would continue their walk hand in hand up the stairway. At the top of which they would kiss, while white doves would be sent flying above their heads. They would continue walking, only this time, the stairway would descend on the opposite side down to the sea wall.

They would be hidden from view while they signed their certificates and had some time on their own before returning to the big tent, by which time it would have been rearranged into a dining hall for the reception.

Rose started a discussion on the preference of the doves or butterflies being used at the top of the stair. Also, the music and some of the vows were changed. Rose reprimanded me for not paying attention. I told her that I was not the one getting married. She in turn insisted I should know because Jacky may forget, and it was up to me to assist her. The children were in fits of giggles because of the way she was practically preaching to me.

I related this to Lloyd when he called later that day, and he also found it quite amusing.

I went on to inform him, "And she also insisted on going over every detail of our plans for the following week."

Lloyd also wanted clarification, so I explained.

"Well, we should all be leaving here by midday on Monday. The hotel bus will take us to Frenchman's Cove for our family bonding. I will be leaving with Steffan, Carol and Dominic to MoBay about six a.m. on Wednesday morning. They will be the first to leave. Their flight is six-thirty p.m."

"I am planning to stay on in Mobay with Mario and Monai for a couple of days until the others join us on Friday. We can all have our last evening meal and chat. Then Mathew and his entourage will leave after dinner. The rest of us will all make our way back to the airport the following morning. Jacky and Jack's flight is for midday Saturday. So those of us who are left will then enjoy lunch before Sophia and the twins' flight back to London leaves at six p.m., after which Rose, Mario, Monai and I — oh, and you, now I know you will be staying — are booked for a couple of days' stay in Negril.

Of course, now you will be on your holiday; maybe we should consider that drive around the island that I had always wanted before getting back into the work routine. Rose and I have a lot of bookings to sort out for next month. You will have your new building to pay attention to. And somewhere in between, the children will be planning for work or university; not to mention that we have to plan our move to Savoy Mews.

So there, that's about it — a lot more than a mouthful. But what I always appreciate with Rose is that she agrees with me about planning ahead. It is so much easier to wake up knowing where you're going and being able to plan what to wear."

"I could not agree with you more, my pet," said Lloyd.

"It also makes it a lot easier to deal with the little emergencies that will crop up, but I have to love you and leave you to deal with one of those little unplanned events right now. I will call you when we get to Port Antonio in the morning. Kiss, kiss, love you, my pet."

I plugged in my phone to recharge after switching it off. I was smiling inwardly, feeling the warmth of being loved. I promised myself there and then never to doubt Lloyd's love for me ever again. When I woke the following morning around five, it was to Jacky switching the bathroom light on and off. Each time she did this, the switch clicked loudly.

"Morning, sis. Are you alright? Don't tell me you are getting nervous; it's a bit late, don't you think?"

I reached up and pulled her down to the bed, rubbing my hand playfully in her hair.

"No, not nervous, Beth, just a little uneasy. You could say I had a nightmare of some sort."

I hugged her after sitting up in the bed, setting up the pillows against the headboard to brace my back.

"What sort of nightmare?" I asked.

She sighed deeply. "I was dreaming of getting to my wedding, in a big white dress, and my ex-husband walking towards me. Each time I turn to wonder why he was there, the scene changes to us being on the boat or him in hospital or his funeral. What do you think it means, Beth?"

"I think that you are subconsciously saying goodbye. Sounds to me like you are just remembering the past in order to say goodbye to Nick."

Jacky laughed. "My wise old sister! You always were the practical one. Come to think of it, my dream wasn't fearful, just a very mixed-up look back on my life. Which I had not done before. After Nick's funeral I just dusted myself off and forgot. I really had not told Jack very much, just that my first husband got pneumonia and died after undergoing surgery for cancer.

And he told me that his first wife died following a car accident while giving birth to their son as a result of a premature birth. Neither of us gave much detail about our previous lives. Except to say that we were never in love with our first partners but just went with the flow and weathered the storms whenever we were faced with them. So I guess it's just as you say; my dream is just me making peace with the past."

Before I had a chance to respond to Jacky, Rose was knocking and calling loudly at the door.

"Come on, sleepyheads, gym, massage and beauty treatments before breakfast on the double."

Jacky tossed one of the pillows at her as she entered, and before long we were ten-year-olds again.

"Mum, I hope you realise that I won't have any sisters to play with on my wedding day." Monai remarked as she joined in the pillow fight.

"Where did that come from?" I asked her, surprised, while trying to catch my breath.

"Just saying, it would be nice to play silly like you guys. Is it true that Aunty Jacky has to have something borrowed and something blue to wear today?

"Well, I have your blue right here."

said Rose, who was trying to get her head from under Jacky's pillow, holding up a shopping bag, which was still trapped around her wrist. I undid the plastic strings from her wrist and emptied the contents of the bag on the bed. Two sets of blue lacy bras and panties scattered on the rumpled sheets.

"One set is for you, Beth, and please don't say it. Just humour me and wear it, please. The bras are strapless so will work with your dresses, so no excuses."

I had to admit that they did look good and a pleasing shade of powder blue, so I accepted.

"So what is borrowed?" asked Monai.

"Well, Beth, you are borrowing my sandals, which match perfectly with your dress, and Jacky is using your pearl earrings and necklace. And, I dare to say, you are both old! So let's get going."

Without hesitation we all stood up in single file behind her as she marched us out the door dressed in our towel robes. Rose had a way about her which made everything she said become signed and sealed.

Morning exercise and massages over, we made our way to the dining hall for refreshments. Then I went to our room. After a long hot shower and a shorter than usual call from Lloyd, he let me know he was parked outside the Budd's, so he was safely on his way. We had a louder than normal 'good morning' welcome from the manager and the wedding planner as we sat down to breakfast. We were told to eat to sustain us through lunch, because it wouldn't be possible to serve lunch and get to the wedding service by two p.m. So only coffee or water would be available at the tent while we got dressed for the wedding.

Sophia started to click on her camera, prancing around like one of the professional cameramen seen on TV, while we all posed and did all sorts of funny faces. A loud clap and shouts went up when Prudence entered the dining hall. Sophia remarked sarcastically, but in good fun:

"Thanks for the vote of confidence, guys."

Prudence was dressed in a light grey linen trouser suit with red accessories, her hair cut short and styled with neat waves reminding me of the roaring twenties. Her husband followed her in, carrying all her photo equipment, some strapped cross over both shoulders and with both hands full of some other paraphernalia.

After hugs and kisses, she told us that Jenny, Pauline, and Patricia were booking in at a hotel in Port Antonio and should be on time for the wedding. The morning went by quickly, and everyone was surprised when Rose clapped her hands loudly to inform us that it was time to proceed to the big tent to be dressed. Jack, Matthew, Mario and a few others had remained on the yacht and were leaving from the marina to the wedding. While Monai and I assisted each other to dress, Rose took care of the twins, and Sophia was able to assist Jacky, while Prudence, without us even noticing, was clicking away, assisted by her husband.

"Mum, I quite like this 'jerry curl' hairdo. I didn't realise that my hair was so long. I have to remember not to keep touching it though; it's really wet. Anyway, Mum, I need to fix your hair; please sit for a minute."

Monai twisted the middle section of my locks on the long scarf and brought it under my hair from the back, then made a large knot in the centre of my forehead, then used a thick strand of my hair with the two ends of the scarf to make a large plait falling back like a ponytail down the centre of my head. The scarf flowed off where my hair ended, to float in the wind. It was a simple enough design, but with the golden yellow framing my face, it gave an elegance to my profile.

She brought out the box containing the set of jewellery we had gone back to the house to collect and insisted that I would not see it until now, as she slipped on a thick gold bangle on my right hand, with a chunk of gold as large as an unshelled peanut sitting in the middle as a clasp.

'When you see Nigerian gold, there is never a question, because even if you did not know gold before, one look and the word "GOLD" would be on your lips.'

The earrings she designed consisted of three peanut-shaped gold nuggets connected to each other by a pea-shaped crystal which picked up all the colours around it. Another bracelet went around the bicep section of my left hand in a spiral design. Then the necklace was formed into a choker with three drops of the nuggets at the front, the middle section dropping to rest at the top of my cleavage.

"Look in the mirror now, Mum."

She spun the chair around so I was face-to-face with an image in the mirror, which took my breath away.

"Hold it there, Beth; that's fantastic."

Prudence clicked, and I was still looking back at the mirror, dumbfounded.

"Darling, thank you so much; this is exquisite. I love it absolutely."

I turned to hug and kiss her. The wedding planner called from the door of the tent.

"Fifteen minutes, ladies; the music is about to start."

Jacky was already in her gown, and Rose was fixing her head scarf. One end of the V shape fell over her face, stopping below her chin, where the other section draped around her shoulder to hang as a train down the back of her dress. Prudence was clicking away while everyone, even the twins, was complimenting Jacky on how great she looked. Monai turned her back towards me.

"Zip me up, Mum, and please can you pin up my hair at the back? It will prevent me from touching it every five seconds."

She handed me a comb clip, and as my daughter turned around to face me, she was transformed from a teenage girl to a twenty-two-year-old woman. To hide the tears, I quickly pulled my dress over my head, hoping I did not smudge my makeup.

"Okay everyone, ready?"

Sophia shouted. "Prudence, wait, just one last photo, please. I simply can't get over how divine my sisters are looking. Believe me, ladies, you are all giving me goose pimples. I will be showing you off at my hospital for the rest of the year."

Sophia went around the room hugging and kissing everyone, posing for photos. Rose ushered out the twins to start the ceremony. Then it was Monai's turn. I tried to get to the door just to watch her walking.

"No, you will see the recording; you don't want everyone to see you peeking out."

Rose restrained me from getting to the opening of the door. I took a deep breath and waited.

"Ok, sis. Your turn. And you look a million dollars. I love you. Oh, if Dad could see you now."

She was ready with the handkerchief for my tears while she hugged and kissed me before gently pushing me through the drapes.

I stopped instantly in my tracks, refocusing my eyes, wondering why I would be face to face with Uncle Steffan. Though I know he always showed preference for western clothes, he was immaculately dressed in a white dashiki long shirt with matching trousers and headdress. He placed his index finger to his lips, blowing me a kiss as well while whispering.

271

"It's ok; your sisters did some changes for you."

I turned to question Rose, but she quickly closed the drapes over her face.

"Just go with the flow," whispered Steffan.

I was about to place my arm around his elbow when he bent as if bowing and handed me his hand, bent with an upturned palm.

"My queen, please allow me."

I giggled and wondered what next. Then the music changed and we started the walk. I was looking through the crowd on either side to find Lloyd's face. We were almost at the end of the walk, so I turned my head to focus ahead. My heart jumped in my chest to be face-to-face with him as he held his hand out towards us. Steffan removed my hand from his, kissed me, and placed my still extended arm into Lloyd's.

I was lost, unable to think straight, when Lloyd took my hand and led me towards the altar. My mind was now in overdrive — this could not be happening for the second time. I had not told Lloyd anything about my first wedding. When it happened, I was a giggling schoolgirl; I thought very little about love. But now, there were so many different feelings going through my mind and body. It's uncanny to believe I am doing this for the second time. Yet my first was just like a dress rehearsal. I was still more confused when we walked up the stairs, and he placed me to stand on the step above Monai, then took his place on the other side, facing me as he stood above Mario.

I could not imagine how he managed to get such a perfect-fitting cream linen suit, not to mention that his vest and handkerchief matched the scarf adorning my hair. He and Mario shook hands and looked over at me with the sweetest of smiles. I was blinded by tears. Monai reached up and patted my eyes dry in time for me to see Jacky taking her father's hand.

The music changed, everyone stood up, and she floated down the walkway towards Jack. As he took her hand and they came up the stairs, she blew me a kiss, and even under the veil, I saw her giving me a wink. They stopped on the steps above me and turned to face the congregation. I was whispering to her to turn around, thinking, 'Oh no, Rose was going to blame me for things going wrong.' Pastor Fairweather stood at the bottom of the steps, Bible in hand. First of all, he was not the person slated to do the service, so I was thinking, 'What else was going to go wrong?'

The music stopped, and he cleared his throat a lot louder than expected, made the sign of the cross, then turned to face the crowd who were seated in a semi-circle around the stairway. The bridal group walked through a passage in the middle, so the pastor was not blocking the view of anyone. He held up both hands to the heavens and pronounced, "Let us pray." At the end of the prayer, he again turned to face us on the stairway.

"Ladies and gentlemen, I hope that you all will agree with me that this is a most exquisite setting. Mr Creary must be the proudest father, and I know that he is here with his daughters today. And I would not have missed this for the world. I am also feeling most privileged to be given the opportunity of conducting this service. These four individuals have all known a previous love; they were not successful in their first marriage, but God needed to allow them that first experience in order to make this, the perfect union. But the law requests that if anyone has a reason why any of these persons here should not fulfil their desire to be together, please come forth and speak your peace."

There was a hush under the tent; it was so quiet I could hear my heartbeat. I dared not move because I was wondering if I had heard correctly. But Pastor Fairweather's voice interrupted my thoughts.

"Now, Jacky Brown and Jack Jackson, you have planned this meeting of your friends and family to bear witness that you both have a burning love that brought you together, and you wish to share with them your pledge to yourselves and to us of how you both feel. Can we hear what you wish to say to each other and to all of us present here?"

Pastor Fairweather had practised the words, which were carefully written by Jacky, myself and Rose, because Jacky had insisted that she did not want the usual wedding talk. I avoided looking in the direction of Lloyd as I looked up towards Jack and Jacky. They were holding each other's hands as they pledged their love to each other. Then, as they ended and were about to kiss, the pastor called out. "Seal it with the rings before that kiss, please."

This brought giggles and laughter from everyone. One of the twins walked towards them, holding up her basket for Jack to take the rings. Then the kiss. Cameras came out flashing, while claps and shouts of 'woo' went up. This went on for some time, then everyone was again seated.

At this point I expected the couple to turn and continue up the stairways, but the pastor resumed his position.

274

"And now, Elizabeth Creary and Lloyd Patrick Cain: you two have both accepted to be caretakers of each other's lives from this day forward. Would you like to share with us and each other your pledges?"

Monai reached up to blot the tears from my eyes. Mario stepped across to hug me before Lloyd took hold of my hands in his. Even with my heels on, I had to look up. Lloyd's face was all bliss as he said.

"My darling petal, my Beth, you have held me captive in sweet love from the moment we meet, but even now on this day, I wish to ask. If you love me as I do you, will you allow me to walk alongside you through this journey to the end of our life here on earth?"

Monai came with her hanky before I found my voice to answer.

"My dearest Lloyd, I too have loved you from our first meeting, and I promise to walk with you as long as you never ever let go of my hand."

It would have been natural to kiss, but again the pastor had to put a stop to it by calling for the rings. The other twin ran up the stairs to present her basket to Lloyd. The ring was white gold, edged with yellow gold. It was half an inch in width, and in the centre was a clasped hand. Lloyd pulled it apart, because it was actually two rings in one; each had one hand, but together the hands came together. Four heads met as the kids and Lloyd smothered me with kisses. Lights flashed, and shouts of 'Look this way, smile, say cheese' went on for some time.

Lloyd explained to me later in the week that he did not find time to buy me a wedding ring and was racking his brain about what he could use temporarily, hoping that he might find something suitable when he got to the hotel. But while packing he found the box with the ring still unopened, which he saw while buying a new watch in Boston. The ring caught his eye, and the assistant told him it was one of a kind. He bought it even though he had no need for it. He felt so attracted to it.

Again the pastor took to the mic.

"Ladies and gentlemen, it would be remiss of me not to close this section of the function appropriately, so allow me please to congratulate Mr and Mrs Jackson and allow them to sign and seal their documents.

And to Mr and Mrs Cain, who are now my adopted son and daughter, double congratulations, and son, one glance to your side and you will always see that beautiful face smiling back at you. So never ever get so wrapped up in the struggles of life that you have to turn to find your wife; keep her always at a glance."

Cheers and applause of approval came from the audience. Jack and Jacky turned to complete their walk to the top of the stairway after we congratulated, hugged, and kissed each other. Pru was in the mix snapping away.

"Beth, just hold on until Jacky gets to the top and the doves are released.

We want a clean shot for the video."

I thought to myself that it would be the least I could do so as not to take over my sister's wedding entirely, even when she reassured me that it was her idea. Lloyd had asked her the colour of the outfit I would be wearing so he could wear a suit to match it. They continued the conversation, and one thing led to another. As they say, the rest is history. We watched as Jack and Jacky turned at the top of the stairway; the doves flew up and white streamers came down. It was magic.

"Your turn, Mum," Monai giggled. And Dad."

So Lloyd and I started our journey to the top. When we turned, I had only expected some streamers; instead, we were showered with rose petals and butterflies. Lloyd whispered, 'Your petals will always give me butterflies.' Our bodies locked in a kiss while the cameras flashed.

The rest of the evening was just a daydream, and I was more than happy that my sisters, including Jacky, were as happy as I felt. The speeches were few but impactful. Then we shared the cutting of the cake and exchanged partners after our first dance. Shortly after that, Jack and Jacky disappeared.

Lloyd whispered that we should do the same, but it seemed that the requests for photos were unending. But about midnight, when we got a chance to dance a slow waltz, he danced me over to the back entrance of the tent, and we slipped out to the cool night air. He had already arranged for us to stay at Frenchman's Cove until the others joined us on the Monday evening for our family get-together.

The remainder of the holiday went as planned, as did the departures. Lloyd agreed that we would use the opportunity to explore the island together as a family. So we left our cars at the rental lot in exchange for a twenty-seater bus.

I should add that Winston, who was present at the wedding with his father, had become an honorary family member, becoming a big brother to Mario. They shared a lot in common, and of course there was also a strong connection that he shared with Rose.

Albeit a brother-and-sister friendship, he fitted into the family like a glove.

We took turns driving and stopped at random locations along the way. From Montego Bay we made our way to Lucea, Negril, and Savanna-la-Mar, and into Black River, spending some time boating on the river before turning off to visit Lover's Leap, taking the road along the south coast of the island. Mandeville was the next stop, then May Pen. From Spanish Town we went on to St Thomas; all had their minds on visiting the mineral bath in Bath, then on to Portland. We could not have passed Boston without stopping, all on board being pork lovers. The day was well spent cooling off at Reach Falls. So we rested that night at a beach house in the area before moving on.

We had planned to return from there to Ocho Rios, but conversations between the men, who felt we should visit the University of the West Indies and CAST, which was another college in Kingston…"

All for the benefit of Mario. It was Friday, so we still had time on our hands. Lloyd had never visited Castleton Gardens, so most of the morning was spent there. The junction road took us through Stony Hill to Papine. We collected as many informational leaflets as possible at the college and university before stopping at the Hope Gardens restaurant for lunch. We had driven past Port Royal a few days before, so after stopping at Heroes Park, we drove out to Port Royal and had to be rushed out because it was well past closing time. Lloyd would not leave without getting a plate of the fish meal that Port Royal was famous for. With nightfall setting in, we called ahead to Montego Bay to book rooms for the night. When we drove through Ocho Rios and Falmouth, this time returning via the north coast, only Lloyd and myself were awake to watch the road as we made our way to rest for the last night of our round-island trip.

We all slept late into Sunday morning, missing breakfast and vacating the rooms later than we intended. After collecting our cars, everyone was ready for lunch. We found a roadside café in Duncan's and had an enjoyable lunch before heading home. I and Lloyd were in his Jaguar, Winston and Mario were following in the jeep, and Rose and Monai led in my Mini. Over lunch, the children decided that they wanted to stay at the old house until things were settled. So our decision was that I would stay at Lloyd's house, and we would meet up at Savoy Mews on the weekends until it was ready for us to move in. We drove to the old house and made sure they were settled, as well as getting a change of wardrobe for myself.

Mario insisted that Winston share the back room with him after being told a few days before that he did not have a bed for himself at his father's house and he was very much in the way of his stepmother, even with his best efforts. So I called Mr Wright, and he agreed that he had no problem with the arrangements. We did this although Winston was fully grown and his own man, but Lloyd felt it was the right thing to do.

Chapter Ten

Fast forward three years, and plans for the coming Easter when Monai will be planning her twenty-first birthday. She had requested of my sisters, her aunts, to return to Jamaica at that time to celebrate with her, and everyone also thought that it would be a fitting time for a family reunion.

Monai has become, in such a short time, a woman to be reckoned with. She spent a year in Kingston, attending the Arts College, boarding with Mario at the home of a sister of the matron from Lloyd's ward in the hospital, whose widowed sister lived on her own in an area close to both their colleges. Mario also started a three-year course in engineering and remained in town to complete his course of study. Monai designs her own fabric paintings and tie-dyes. As soon as she got the opportunity, she rented a shop in our plaza and employed two young ladies: one to assist her in sewing her designs, the other to be a personal assistant and manager at the boutique while she made her sales between the resorts that would accommodate her work. All her designs were a full package: necklace, earrings, handbags, and hats to go with the appropriate dress or simple trouser suit. She would source the shoes as she went along. But as a businesswoman, she could very much hold her own.

Mario was doing so much more than the course he was presently studying. He made it home to go fishing on Winston's boat, not always on the weekends. He called every day, but we hardly ever saw him face to face. Yet we never had to wonder where he was or what he was up to. For his twenty-first birthday the year before, he travelled to France with Winston for two weeks to meet up with his father and Uncle Stefan. He had so much planned for his future that we could only wish him well, knowing that whatever the final decision, he would do well at it.

Winston now works alongside Rose at Pauli-May as the main driver of the van. He was able to step in when John left to join his daughter and grandchildren in Washington. She had filed for him, and he was happy for the opportunity to be with his family.

Rose has fully established her mark on the company and on the staff and customers. And rather than get the car of her dreams, she instead added another dimension to the company and sent back to England for a black taxi cab, which is used to transport couples on their honeymoon, the cab being private and spacious. And between herself and Winston, they drive Dad's jeep when needed. So my Mini was given to Mario.

Ms Mac, along with her husband, between them managed the complex: she cooked for everyone, and her husband took care of the parking lot and manageable small repairs to the shops.

Gertrude now runs her own grocer's shop from her front yard. Her married daughter took over her day's work duties, working for two days at the old house and two days at Savoy Mews.

Mr Wright no longer runs the garage because he lost the use of his eyesight and felt it best to sell out and retire. Two of his best workers were recommended to join Pauli-May as driver/mechanics."

Another disappointment affected the Budd family. Mrs Budd suffered a massive heart attack, but thanks to the quick action of Lloyd and one of his Cuban doctors, they were able to fly her to Cuba to perform a triple bypass. Mr Budd had to stay with her in Cuba while she completed her treatment. They returned after three months, but Mr Budd was never the same. They had no children between them, but Mrs Budd had a daughter before marriage. She came down to visit her mother from Canada, and two months ago, we had a going-away party for them when they migrated to Canada. It was still so sad to see them go. As promised, Mr Budd calls me every week to tell me how to take care of the gardens. There was no mention of selling their house, and I felt it was too soon to ask.

We visited the church as a family whenever it was possible, and more often than not Pastor Fairweather would stop by on a Sunday after morning service for lunch and a good chat.

Lloyd had planned for how his clinic would look and operate over the years while he was working at the hospital. Like Dad, he was able to organise the use of his funds to the maximum. His house was bought with his own money from savings, but in the planning and operation of the clinic, those funds came from the money he inherited. He intended to rent the portion of the house which would be the clinic as a business. Albeit to a company of which he would be the owner. After showing me the plans and explaining his dream, he also told me a little more about his life in the States. When his adopted mother became sick at the very time she had arranged to have him returned to Jamaica, he was then twenty years old. He knew she was sick but took no interest in knowing the details. She had a personal doctor who she would visit from time to time, so he was called after she was admitted to the hospital. Her doctor, who had been working at the same hospital, was originally from Poland but was also of mixed race. He had always taken an interest in Lloyd and always spoke to him with a lot of compassion. He explained to Lloyd that he would have to be strong and be ready to nurse his adopted mother for the remainder of the time, because she would be getting weaker as her sickness worsened and her body deteriorated, but if Lloyd was not up to it and wanted to return to Jamaica, then he (the doctor) would arrange for her to be in a home and receive special care. Lloyd stayed, and the doctor was instrumental in the outcome of his welfare and his future."

Because his adopted mother was in denial of her illness and felt she would soon be on her feet and back to normal, she requested a second opinion and then agreed to undergo an operation which her own doctor felt was unnecessary. But he told her if she insisted, then she should make him executor of her estate so he could see to her welfare until she was out of danger. This proved to be the source of Lloyd's fortunes. After his adopted mother passed, the doctor presented Lloyd with an acceptance letter to a university where he would be studying medicine, all his fees paid up for the five years.

He was comfortable with having the doctor as a mentor and a friend and accepted all the instruction and advice he was given. After two years, he also earned a scholarship for the remainder of his studies. At his graduation the doctor was in attendance and invited him to have dinner at his home, where he further explained that all of his adopted mother's remaining estate would be handed over to Lloyd, which was the doctor's intention all along. Lloyd completed his internship and worked for a number of years. He was called to the bedside of his old and dying friend, and it was during that time that he made up his mind to return to Jamaica.

The first change he made after our marriage was to order an SUV for me and, for himself, a custom-made van almost similar to an ambulance. It was fitted out with the children, whom he had planned to be his major clients, in mind, and with all he thought was necessary to collect and take them to the clinic or to take them along to the hospital in Kingston if necessary. The Jaguar he kept for our romantic getaways.

The building and renovations took just over three months, and to get the rooms inside organised with the furniture and fixtures, and the two doctors and four nurses in place, took a further couple of months, so it was six months before the grand opening. He had a manager for the clinic in the form of his trusted matron, along with three receptionists who worked flexi-hours in order to be present seven days. Lloyd made provisions and secured sufficient funds to pay staff, overheads, and any other small emergencies which might occur during the first year, at which time he expected to at least break even as a business.

He took a further week off work to fly to the U.S. to secure the most up-to-date equipment and hospital beds for the overnight rooms, toys and garden furniture, bed linen, and just about all that was needed to make the dream a reality.

I worked between Lloyd's house, the old home and Savoy Mews until we were able to move in as a family, or at least part family: Lloyd, myself, and Monai. While Mario remained in Kingston, and Winston and Rose, who were becoming closer by the day, remained at the old home. We were looking forward to our second Christmas at Savoy Mews and the birth of our twins, Lizzy and Rick, to the absolute delight of their father and adopted grandfather, Pastor Fairweather. I still had the energy to report to the office for a few hours each day and managed the paperwork while Rose and Winston met and greeted and transported our guests around the island.

Sophia sent a phone text confirming her arrival date along with her new husband, who happened to be an Anglican minister. They were married after a six-month courtship, after which she moved into the church cottage and took on the teaching of the Sunday school as if she had been doing it her whole life.

The twins were in college and insisted that they be allowed to continue living with their granddad. From all reports the Rev. and his wife could not be more in love with each other and with the Lord.

Prudence and her husband moved into her mother's home in London. She was offered full-time employment at the B.B.C. The house was empty, so she took on renovating and redecorating. She kept in touch but would not be able to attend the birthday party.

Not attending also would be Patricia, Pauline, and Jenny. After my wedding, they made it known that they would be migrating to the south of France. We had all wished each other well and, to date, have not had a letter or call from them.

I was about to call Jackie when Lloyd called my mobile to say he was on his way to collect Carol, Stefan, Dominic, and his two brothers who were born in Singapore. The eldest was almost three years old, and the other was the same age as my twins.

The gate to the garden flew open, and Jacky's two girls came through at speed, the younger chasing the older through the garden. Two months prior I was sitting in a similar fashion on the veranda in Savoy Mews when a large trailer truck drove into the road and parked. Before I could wonder what was going on, a red SUV drove up and parked at our front gate. My twins were asleep, Lloyd was working at the clinic and Monai was cooking up one of her specialities in the kitchen. I looked on with interest. The Budd family had not mentioned having any visitors regarding a sale of their house. We had spoken only two days before, and he said nothing about selling his house. The door of the SUV opened, and two small white girls were let down from the seat to the pavement. I got up at that point to walk out to the gate, feeling sure that the drivers had lost their way. As I got closer, the two little ones waved and started to walk towards the gate. Then the driver's door opened and a woman stepped out with a haircut which reminded me of young Jacky. I started running before I was even sure. Further down the road, the driver of the trailer also jumped from the cab, taking off his cap and letting out a loud "Jamaica, we are home."

After the greeting, tears, hugs, and kisses, Jacky started their story. She gave birth to her first daughter only two months after returning to Australia. She had no idea she was pregnant during the time she was in Jamaica. Luckily they were in the town, shopping for their house, when she started feeling pains and decided to check in with a doctor on the High Street. Twenty minutes later she was rushed to the hospital. Her daughter came at eight months and weighed just six pounds but was perfectly fine. But she had minor complications, so Jacky had to remain in the hospital for two months. From then, all the plans they had for starting the business went downhill. Jack rented a house to be near the hospital, which was just as well because heavy rains started in the location of their property, and they were unable to gain access because the road became impassable with floods and landslides. After six months the roads and bridges were repaired, and they returned to salvage and set up their company, but the water continued to rise until it surrounded their house. Jacky was again pregnant, and the situation did not look favourable. They bought a smaller house in the town and moved. Jack started to do short excursion trips with their private plane, but he had heavy competition and wasn't comfortable that the business would go as they planned. So they started to sell off the equipment, having a garage sale each month. Their plan B was to return to regular flying, but when they were reminded that Monai's party was coming up and further news about Mr and Mrs Budd, they called Mr Budd to offer some comfort. Then, after enquiring about their house, a plan came into being. They both decided that Jamaica was to be their future home. From then everything fell into place.

Monai was sentimental about just having a close family gathering. So her plan for her birthday was to have three separate parties, starting in the morning for the workers at the plaza, with Ms Mac fixing a box lunch with birthday cake and a drink of their choice. The second was a luncheon for the hotel staff who arranged for her to sell her products and a few other selected persons. Then the third, and her chosen party, would take place after six p.m. at Savoy Mews. The only non-related members of our family were our pastor, Winston, and Mario's girlfriend. Lloyd's birthday gift to her was an overnight at her favourite hotel, the Half Moon in Montego Bay. The parties were held on Friday. Two coaster buses came to collect the family midday on Saturday for the journey to Montego Bay, where we had dinner and danced. Then came her biggest surprise. Steffan had spoken to Lloyd and me about her father's arrival and wanted to know how we would arrange for it to happen. So at eight o'clock the family gathered to cut her cake and offer her their presents. Mario was the first to spot David, and because of his reaction, Monai turned around to face her father.

The children stayed on for a week to spend time with their father while the rest of the family returned to Savoy Mews. Sophia and her husband, Steffan, Carol, and their boys would later leave. Then Savoy Mews was left only to produce more love and sweet memories.

Now that was a birthday to remember if there ever was one. It's going to be hard to top that.

Time

Now that you are on your own.

What will you do? To whom will you turn?

In the dark, as you sit all alone

A silent tear drops unseen.

With memories of the past still fresh on your mind

Your hands unfold and then entwined

Will you give up and walk ahead blind

Or will you go on knowing that

Joy will be yours in time?

By: Gloria Russell